C000081899

ULTIMATE BURLESQUE

A collection of thirty erotic stories

Edited by Alyson Fixter and Emily Dubberley

Published by Accent Press Ltd – 2008
ISBN 9781906373634

Copyright © Accent Press Ltd 2008

All rights reserved. No part of this book may be reproduced,
stored in a retrieval system, or transmitted in any form or by any
means, electronic, electrostatic, magnetic tape, mechanical,
photocopying, recording or otherwise, without the written
permission of the publishers: Accent Press Ltd, PO Box 26,
Treharris, CF46 9AG

Printed and bound in the UK by
Creative Design and Print

Cover Design: Sam Eddison / *www.zoointeractive.com*

For Jean Dubberley, whose bravery and strength through her cancer was the inspiration behind this book; and to anyone who's been touched by cancer, and the charities that help them.

Twelve new titles to please and tease!

Bad Girl

Seriously Sexy One

Naughty Spanking One

Tease Me

Down & Dirty One

Seriously Sexy Two

Juicy Erotica

Satisfy Me

Naughty Spanking Two

Seriously Sexy Three

Down & Dirty Two

Seduce Me

For more information please visit
www.xcitebooks.com

Contents

Introduction
by Chris Manby

Thank you for buying *Ultimate Burlesque*. You're clearly a person of great taste. This delicious little book of erotic stories is part of a wider initiative called *Burlesque Against Breast Cancer* (www.burlesqueabc.com), which was created to raise money for Macmillan Cancer Support.

Burlesque is a style of entertainment renowned for its wit and saucy edge. Originating in the Victorian era, it encompasses comedy, music and, of course, striptease. Its recent revival has given a much-needed shot of glamour to the world's stages and reminded us with its new stars that sexy women come in all shapes and sizes. That's what makes burlesque the perfect way to help support the fight against breast cancer.

I lost my cousin Clare to breast cancer when she was just 35. In our conversations as she neared the end of her brave fight she reminded me how important it is to enjoy life to its fullest. Don't worry about having an extra inch on your bottom. Just stick on your high heels and wiggle it! That's why I've jumped at the chance to be involved with Burlesque Against Breast Cancer.

In buying this book you're showing your support for a fantastic bunch of people doing a very difficult, but worthwhile, job. Macmillan provides practical, medical, emotional and financial support, as well as pushing for better cancer care. So enjoy the warm glow that comes from knowing you're helping them achieve all that. For another sort of glow, maybe you could act out some of the stories …

Chris Manby, 31 July 2008

Inner Diva
by Jo Rees

I could never tell her this, but I can tell you. You see, my feelings about her were always completely secret. They still are. But the essence of them, of what she did for me, has fuelled me all this time. I'll tell you it all from the beginning, so you understand.

As far back as I can remember I've been enamoured with the theatre, in the way that countless girls before me have been. Bette Davies in *All About Eve* was particularly inspirational. You see, in my wildest fantasies I imagined myself as a diva, uttering a *bon mot* to a devastatingly handsome man as I draped myself over a banister in a long, sexy evening gown, cigarette in one hand, dry martini in the other. In other words, just about as far away from the real me as it was possible to get. I was shy and skinny, ashamed of my freckly legs and flat chest. I dressed like a boy, in jeans and shirts, and I never wore make-up.

But, just like those old movies, the theatre was timeless, un-beholden to the fashions that I got so wrong at school. The theatre let me be me; as soon as I walked through those swing doors my normal reality was completely forgotten.

Star-struck as I was, I quickly realised I was terrible at acting, but that didn't put me off. I worked wherever I could. Right from when I was fifteen. I'd work in the bar, in the green room, dusting off props and painting scenery. I learnt how to work a lighting grid and filled in as the prompt for the countless semi-professional troupes that came to our provincial theatre.

I loved them all. I knew most of the Noël Coward plays by heart and all the usual musicals. As time went on I got to help out with hair and make-up and the costumes too. I hung out with the cast, ingratiating myself with all the little favours I did these greater mortals. I could magic up take-away pizza when it was most needed, and I could find a bar open at 11.30pm when the town was asleep, where we could drink red wine until the early hours. Anything to keep the camaraderie alive, to keep the spell going.

More often than not I had a one night stand on the last night of a run, with one of the actors who I'd taken a shine to. Even at the time I'd wonder whether they were doing it out of sympathy or just because even when the groupies had gone home I was still there, still willing. But the encounters left me strangely empty. The reality never matched up to the fantasy. When the run was over, they were, after all, just out of work actors. I knew I was destined for something bigger, something greater. I just didn't know what.

Then Lionel Bartlett took over as the theatre manager and I was employed permanently, thanks to the council grant that had been issued to Lionel to put our theatre on the map. There was a big overhaul and the naff theatre lounge with its gold bar and mottled framed posters replaced with a cool glass spacious one that sold posh champagne and ciabatta sandwiches.

Lionel, or Mr B, as I called him, had come from the West End, but why he'd come back to our town I never fathomed. He said that he wanted to bring something back to his roots, having spent some of his childhood nearby. But I heard that there'd been some sort of disgrace and he'd left his old job in a hurry. He never admitted he was gay, but I'm sure he was. He certainly never made a pass at me although, to be honest, I wouldn't have minded so much if he had. We became friends as much as colleagues. He asked me to go on various scouting missions with him, spying on the other theatres and working out which acts would be popular at our theatre.

The first time I saw Kathy Au Lait perform, I immediately felt like Calamity Jane seeing Katie in Chicago. She was from another world. I was hopelessly smitten.

Mr B was sceptical about a burlesque performer. He told me that the *Daily Record* had found her striptease show disgraceful and it would never wash with our regulars.

But for once I didn't care. Even from a distance, watching Kathy Au Lait in the darkness of the stalls, I was struck by her stage presence. She had dark, sparkling eyes and wavy black hair. She was voluptuous, beautifully curvaceous in the way that I could never and would never be. The way she strutted around the stage wiggling the feathered bustle on her bum made something inside me ache. Here was my Diva. I had to get close.

I begged Mr B to get her to come to our theatre. My head was buzzing with marketing plans. How I'd call everyone in my autograph book to get them to come and see the show. Kathy Au Lait was sensational. We had to have her.

On the day she transferred to our theatre, Mr B offered her my services. My stomach was churning with nerves as she looked me up and down with cool disdain. 'Call me Kat,' she said. I expected her to have a French or German accent, but she sounded quite English and proper. I wanted to drop on the floor and kiss her polished toes.

It was clear from the start that she was ambitious and totally professional about her art. Despite her plump curves, she was supple as a gymnast. In the week of rehearsals that Mr B had pencilled in, she turned up only once, limbering up on stage in dancers' tracksuit pants, folded over at the waist, and a T-shirt knotted just above her stomach. She gave a flawless performance, then plucked her designer handbag from the chair and flounced past Mr B and me to zoom away in her convertible Mercedes outside. We were both besotted.

When the show opened, I was too nervous to watch her performance, busying myself in her dressing room, magnetised by her costumes and her pots of make-up. I knew that I was

3

behaving like an infatuated schoolgirl, but I couldn't help it.

Off stage, in her dressing room, she was cool and distant. She was such an enigma, I found myself dreaming about her. I would dream about the way she wore her robe while sucking on a cigarette. I would fantasise about it falling open so that I could catch a glimpse of the curve of her creamy breasts. I would wake sweating.

Then, on the second night, she seemed to have made a decision about me. She called me over to help.

'Do these, will you?' she asked, handing me a pair of nipple tassels and a small, nail-varnish sized pot of glue. 'They stay on better, if someone else does them.'

She let her gown fall open. She was naked. Her pussy was waxed to a thin line of black hair, but all I could really concentrate on was her beautiful breasts, right there. Right in front of me.

'Paint the glue on first,' she instructed. 'Right on the nipple. Then press them on.'

I'd never had a lesbian urge before, but now I craved her. I wanted to cup the smooth, creamy flesh in my hands and feel the weight of those curves. I wanted to nuzzle my face in between them, squeeze them onto my cheeks. I wanted to be lost in their warmth.

I wondered whether she knew how much I secretly desired her. She looked straight ahead. Cool and collected. Bigger than her body. Transcending it. More powerful.

But I wasn't. I was a slave before it. I wondered if she could hear my beating heart as I unscrewed the top of the glue pot. My hands were trembling as I wiped off the dripping liquid from the brush and then reached out to her and brushed the liquid over her nipple. Gently. Slowly.

I saw her skin pucker, her nipples harden at the coldness of the liquid, but she didn't comment. I felt my own nipples harden in unison. Aching. Screaming out to be touched. I wanted to rip open my shirt, glue my nipples onto hers. It was almost unbearable.

Then I pressed the nipple tassels onto the glue. She put her hand over mine and pressed down with me. It was so intimate. I felt my pussy become wet. Wetter than it had been after my dreams. I don't think I'd ever done something so sensual, so erotic.

'There,' she said. 'Good job.'

She smiled at me. It was friendly and all at once I felt the magnitude of my secret. But I wasn't ashamed, only grateful she'd given me so much to stoke the fire of my desire.

I was in a trance afterwards. I could only think about her nipples, the way she smelt. I counted the minutes until I could do it again. The next time, I thought, I would accidentally risk touching her skin. I felt sure she wouldn't mind. Would it feel as soft and warm as it looked?

But the next night I was in for a shock. I didn't even know Kat had a manager, until I found Tony Cramer sitting on her dressing table using his mobile. He was wearing jeans and a checked shirt, unbuttoned to reveal his tanned chest. He had a short beard and a dark, mussed-up hairdo. He looked at me as he finished his call, his wolf-like light blue eyes boring into me, assessing me. Then he finished his call with a simple, 'Ciao'. I flushed deeply as the silence between us grew.

I immediately felt jealous and furious he'd interrupted the intimacy I'd started to share with Kat, but there was no doubt he was attractive. And Kat thought so too. I watched her hug him, light up for him. I shrank back, watching. Were they together? A couple? It was hard to tell. But I felt him watching me watching them.

That night I dreamt of Kat again, but I was Kat and Tony wanted me. I pictured him naked with his hands on his hips, his hard cock glistening. I woke up confused. It was bad enough dreaming about Kat, but dreaming about them both felt way more intimate.

On the fourth night, Tony turned up during the interval. Kat had sent me off for drinks. When I came back, I heard giggling from behind the dressing room door. It was open just the tiniest of chinks. Still holding the tray, I put my eye up to the gap. I could see the mirror.

In its reflection, I saw Kat was half-naked beneath her open sarong. I could see her breasts. I couldn't take my eyes from her breasts. My breasts.

She loved them. I saw that now for the first time, as she cupped them in her hands, showing them to Tony.

So they were together …

I felt my own nipples grow hard. Aching to be sucked. I shifted in my jeans, feeling myself becoming wet. Mesmerised, I watched her reach out to squeeze the bulge in Tony's jeans. Then, looking at him, she nodded, biting her lip, daring him. I watched him take out his hard cock. She smiled at it appreciatively. It was long and smooth, just as I'd dreamed it would be. She licked her fingertip and ran it around the end of his cock, then used the moisture to circle her own nipple.

I gasped, stunned by my longing. I wanted nothing more than to burst in, to beg Tony to take me. I wanted to lean over the dressing table while he fucked me and I wanted to suck her nipples hard at the same time.

I'll never know if I made a noise, but suddenly they were both startled. Tony quickly slipped his cock back in his jeans and Kathy lifted her gown back over her shoulders.

I didn't know what to do. So I pushed open the door with the tray of drinks. I don't know if they noticed my blushing. I could hardly walk. It was agony, the longing between my legs.

I put the tray down on the dressing table.

'Here. These are for you. It's that time again,' Kat said, holding out the nipple tassels.

She opened her gown, so it was obviously cool with her that Tony was there to watch. Or maybe she thought it was just a professional thing she did in front of him. But I felt caught. Implicated. Was she letting me know that there was something sexual between her and Tony? Or letting Tony know there was something sexual between her and me? Did she know I'd been watching? Did it give her a thrill to know that Tony's cock juice was drying around her nipple? Did she think I didn't know?

I realised then that I liked being a voyeur. In the spotlight now, I felt terrified, but exhilarated too. This was our own theatre. Right here. This complex, fantastical threesome. The tension was unbearable.

I felt Tony watching me as I unscrewed the little nail-varnish sized pot of glue. I could feel her heat. Smell her. I knew she was watching Tony. And I knew he was watching me.

I painted on the glue and pressed the nipple tassels into place and stood back. She looked very beautiful. I wanted so much to touch her. I felt my legs heavy with blood, my head giddy.

'How does it feel?' I asked. I said it out loud. I meant only to think it.

'You want to try a pair?' Tony asked me. His voice was soft. Amused. 'You should.'

There was a beat. I looked between Kat and Tony and saw their offer. But I was a moth that had flown into their brightness. 'Maybe. Not now. The curtains …' I mumbled.

I hated myself then. Right at that moment. I'd been asked to open the door to a fantasy and I'd refused. I was a trapped bird in the cage of my own conventionality. People like Tony and Kat would always be on the other side.

Kat got dressed and I helped her on with her clothes, but I felt crushed. I wanted to say something, to bring back the moment, but I knew it was lost.

'We'll watch from the wings,' Tony said, as she went back on stage.

I stood next to him as we both watched Kat start the second half of her show.

Her nipples. The brush stroking her nipples. It was all I could think of as I watched her. I felt defeated. Jangled with sexual tension I didn't know how to disperse.

'I like watching her like this. She's got a great ass,' Tony whispered. 'You like watching her too, don't you?'

His tone said it all. I looked up at him. I saw in his face … amusement, sympathy? He'd rumbled me. All at once I saw that he knew everything.

But before I had the chance to say anything, I felt him slide his arm around me.

Then his hand slipped under my shirt and down the back of my jeans and down the back of my pants.

'She makes you wet too, doesn't she?' he whispered.

I felt his finger sliding inside me. I didn't have to answer. He could feel for himself.

'It's OK,' he said. 'I know.'

I didn't protest. I knew it was wrong. But everything I'd felt earlier suddenly came rushing back.

'Come,' he said.

He took his hand out of my jeans and led me to the worn sofa that was outside the green room door. It had a broken leg and was propped up, its back to the stage. We used it to fling costumes on.

Now Tony unhooked my jeans, quickly yanking them down with my knickers. I gasped. It was unthinkable that he should do this here. In the wings. What if someone came? What if Mr B passed by?

But the thrill was greater, my desire and need too strong. He held my hand, guiding me to kneel on the sofa.

'Watch her,' he whispered. 'This is the best part of the show.'

Then Tony knelt down behind me, bending me over the sofa back. His face was right under my hot pussy. I felt as if I might melt onto it.

He eased my legs apart. 'Watch her,' he whispered again.

I watched as Kat unhooked her basque. Suddenly Tony darted his tongue right into me. I heard the noise my wet juices made, clicking over his lapping tongue. Then his chin pressed into me as his tongue licked at my clit, then sucked it, hard. I could feel my legs shaking. I clung onto the back of the sofa, gripping the worn velvet. And then Kat's basque was off and there were her breasts, full and free. The audience applauded as she wriggled her shoulder and the tassels swung around. Then she bent over and I saw just a glimpse of her pussy.

And I came. Right then and there in Tony's mouth as he sucked at my engorged clit. Quickly and furiously, I felt the pleasure crash right over me. My knees buckled. I gasped.

As the audience applauded for Kathy Au Lait, I felt the applause was all mine. I felt like a firework, showering out hot sparks of energy.

I didn't feel shame, you see; I felt gratitude. I felt initiated into a world where a sexual favour, like the one Tony had bestowed on me, was the kindest gift a person could give.

We didn't discuss it. It was beyond words. Instead, we both acted as if nothing had happened. I don't know if he ever told Kat. Two days later, the show closed and I never saw her again.

But in her wake I felt as if I'd been reborn. Something real had happened. And at last it had happened to me. I couldn't put it into words, the thing I'd learnt, but I knew that my inner Diva was set free. That's the thing about the theatre, you see. It's open to anyone who has the guts to perform. So I did. I learnt a routine. I found the most outrageous props I could and I set about titillating my audiences. Making them feel the camaraderie, keeping them in the bubble of tension I'd learnt all about from Kathy Au Lait.

And that's the story. Except for this very last bit. Because, in all the years I've been working, our paths never crossed again. But last week Kat's agent called. He said that Kat wanted to pass on that she was pleased to see my career doing so well. The erotic theatre club I set up with Mr B is now so famous, after all. She wants to meet to discuss doing a double act together!

Tony Cramer, her manager, suggested it, apparently. So I'm meeting them both after my show tonight.

I'll let you know what happens ...

Watching
by MonMouth

It began with the two of them standing facing me, smiling wickedly. Then his hands slid down her body, cupping her breasts, stroking down her stomach and clasping her hips. He began to unbutton her blouse.

'No,' I said. 'Pull her skirt up.' It was pretty short, so hubby didn't have far to pull, revealing the flimsy excuse for underwear underneath. He pushed the knickers aside and spread her pussy open with the other, giving me a good look at the glistening wetness. Leaning back into his embrace, she cocked her hips at me, her legs apart.

'He's got you on display. You like being shown off like that?'

Eyes shut, smiling, she purred, 'Yes ...'

But this isn't really how it began. Not even close.

It began in the shy, quiet manner of a thousand illicit fantasies, churning away in the minds of Chloe and Sam. Sometimes, she told me in one of her emails, she liked to bend over the back of the sofa and tell him to do whatever he wanted to her, imagining that on the other side, just behind his back, was a silent audience of wide-eyed men. In her mind the back wall of their house opened up into a darkened auditorium. She imagined herself as the climax of a variety show. Before her, there would have been dancers, singers, magicians, each act showing progressively more flesh. And now the spectators would be anxiously waiting for Ms Chloe and her shameless spectacle of debauchery. The audience would be arranged in a semi-circle, on a row of theatre benches, upholstered in old-fashioned burgundy fabric, the worn springs of the cushions squeaking beneath the men as they shifted uneasily in their seats, angling for a better view of her upthrust buttocks and Sam's cock sliding in and out of her.

Chloe kept this to herself, but finally she mentioned it to Sam when she came home, tipsy and horny, from a night out with some girlfriends. Sam wasn't in the mood, lounging around watching trashy bloke-TV in Chloe's absence. But when she sat down and told him about the show, he caught on fast. It wasn't long before Sam had her bent over the back of the sofa, taking it slowly, pushing her skirt up over her hips, removing her wet knickers. Then he pulled her buttocks apart, spreading her open with his hands.

'They're all looking at you,' he said, matter-of-factly.

The words hit Chloe like an electric shock. She immediately reached down, sank two fingers inside her pussy and came almost instantly, moaning into the cushions while Sam watched, his hands still splaying her bottom for their imagined audience.

Or maybe this was part of the fantasy. I only know what they told me, because I didn't get involved until much later, through the comfortable anonymity of email. They had read my blog, and we corresponded a bit over a few months, mostly about their experiments in kink. I liked them because they wrote funny emails about hiding lengths of rope in their bedroom and how the lube bottle got left on a living room side-table when the parents visited.

Naturally, when I found out that I'd be spending a weekend in a city close to their village, I let them know. Why not? I might get a pint out of it, at least.

The email went silent for a few days. Then one morning there was a long one in my inbox, starting with the sentence: 'We have a proposition for you, but if you'd much rather just have a civilised drink with us we would understand

11

completely.'

That's how the transition from fantasy to reality began, with a proposition and directions to their local pub. It proved tricky to find, but when I arrived half an hour late they greeted me like the prodigal pervert and brought me a drink. We toasted my navigational skills, chatted and got comfortable in each others' presence.

After a while, Sam said something about the two of them not being as adventurous as they would like to be.

Chloe put her drink down. 'Yeah. We're so normal, sometimes it makes me want to tear my clothes off and run down the street screaming.'

'Maybe we can come up with a compromise?' I suggested. 'You keep your clothes on until we get home, and then you can scream all you want.'

We didn't stay long at the pub after that. We all had one thing on our minds, and the conversation hovered quietly around sex, fantasies and the forbidden excitement of what we were about to do.

And that's how I found myself getting comfortable on their red leather sofa, smiling lustily at Sam as he pulled the hem of his wife's skirt up the pale curve of her thighs.

'I feel like you both want to eat me,' she giggled. We were sober, but I think we all felt a bit tipsy from nerves.

'If you ask nicely, maybe someone will eat you ...' I smiled and patted the cushion next to me. Chloe detached herself from Sam and sat down.

'Move over there for a better view,' she suggested, and I pulled up a chair. She stroked herself, leaning back on the red leather sofa, legs spread to give us a good view of her fingers.

'This ...' she said, sinking two fingers inside herself, 'is even better than I imagined.' When she stood up we saw the glistening wet patch.

'We can't have that,' I told hubby. 'Lick it clean, please.' He bent over. She stood next to him, watching him clean her juices off the shiny red leather, fingering herself. I was sitting

12

close enough to smell the rich scent of her arousal, inches away from my face. Then she turned to give me a good look at her pussy, already plumped up and juicy from her masturbation.

There would be no touching. No participation. This was the agreement. I was only there as a highly-aroused pair of eyes, my role to watch them, talk to them, and make suggestions. So I sat still, watching her remove her clothes, item by item, while Sam sat on the sofa, stroking his hard cock, waiting for her to complete the slow striptease.

'Are you nervous?' I asked Chloe when she straddled him, facing me. She bit her lip, smiling.

'Yes ... but in a good way.' When she spread her legs and slid down on his cock, I saw only lust in her eyes. Chloe rode her husband slowly at first, the glistening lips of her pussy bulging around his shaft when she took him in all the way, then raised herself up, riding the length of his cock, smiling at me.

After a while Chloe seemed about to come. But just as her breath quickened and she whispered, 'Yes, that's it ...' Sam pulled out. Chloe's eyes widened with frustration and she began to object.

'Sweetheart, I don't want to hear it,' Sam said pleasantly.

'But ...'

'One more word,' he interrupted, 'and you know what happens.'

'It's just ...' she began, but fell silent when he got up and reached for a black sports bag that had been sitting unnoticed next to the sofa.

Sam unzipped it and pulled out a white ball gag. 'Come here. Let's show our audience just how much of a slut you are.' Chloe opened wide to accommodate the gag, and Sam fastened it around the back of her head. He bent her gently over the sofa so that she was kneeling on the cushions, facing away from me. Then he tied her hands behind her back with a length of red cotton rope.

'Can you get the camera out of the bag, please?' he asked

very politely while he was securing the knot between his wife's wrists. I obliged, switched it on and moved to get a better look at Chloe's face. The white ball gag had a smudge of red lipstick on the front. Bent over the back of the sofa, hands tied behind her back, Chloe looked almost sleepy, her eyes unfocused. I noticed that the glistening middle fingers of Sam's right hand were buried in her pussy. He was bent down behind her, kissing his way down the small of her back. I snapped a picture just before Sam pushed his tongue into her ass. She squirmed, helpless with pleasure. Sam spread her open, showing me the shining wetness of her pussy and arsehole. I could see the buzz of arousal vibrating through Chloe's body. When Sam sank his cock into her from behind she wiggled so much that he had to hold her down. The sound of his cock pounding in and out of her very wet pussy mingled with the synthetic snapping of their digital camera and her man purring, 'Yes, yesss, such a good girl'. Chloe's moans were muffled by the ball gag filling her mouth.

Compared with the intensity of the build-up and their fucking, they seemed almost subdued when they came, Chloe first, then Sam, fucking her hard. I caught an amazing, blurry image of his cock as he withdrew, the milky white cum covering it, dripping from the lips of her pussy.

Then he casually stepped to the other side of the sofa, removed the ball gag, and had Chloe lick his cock clean before he got around to untying her wrists. The evening's performance had come to an end.

We did this a couple of times, me watching, instructing, photographing, enjoying their pleasure in the display. But no touching. Just observing as closely as I could without directly participating in the sweaty, intense fucking.

'Having an audience brings out his aggressive side,' Chloe confided in an email a few days later. I could imagine the satisfied smile on her face when she typed the words.

The second time we met was more hurried and improvised. I

was in their city on short notice, but when I emailed ahead I got an almost immediate response. I don't know, but I imagine a furtive lunchtime phone call, the two of them whispering into their mobile phones somewhere out of earshot of colleagues.

This time we started in their dining room, Chloe's skirt pulled up around her hips. She sat on the edge of the table and leaned back, inviting him between her legs, two fingers teasing her labia. Sam took her in his mouth with a growl, his mouth settling over her sex, pushing her fingers away. They stumbled from table to chair to sofa, bending, sitting, stretching their bodies to put on the show they wanted. I noticed with pleasure that she'd gone to the trouble of making sure that the seams of her stockings were straight when she'd put on her black, lacy lingerie.

Her orgasms were intense, but very quiet. There seemed to be a playful expressiveness about her this time around. She relished the exhibitionism of what we were doing: She dressed up for me and Sam, and I appreciated the care she took in making sure that my line of sight was always as direct as possible, that her body, her arousal and her pleasure were always on display. Chloe was learning to love the attention for its own sake, not just as a means of fulfilling her own fantasy.

In their bedroom, Sam came in her mouth. Standing in front of her, he grabbed her hair with both hands, holding it bunched in his fists, and pushed her down. She knelt in front of him, eyes closed in the deep pleasure of being ruthlessly used, and he seemed to have no restraint left. Fucking her mouth in long, deep strokes that she struggled to accommodate, he let out a loud, deep roar of primal satisfaction. His cum, mixed with spit, dribbled down her chin when she pulled back and caught her breath.

Falling to his knees, facing her, he kissed her before she had time to open her eyes, lovingly stroking the curly mess of her hair.

'You looked funny just then,' she told me afterwards. 'The way your mouth hung open was terribly cute.'

The same can probably be said about the rest of the audience. Behind me, while I watched Chloe and Sam, I could almost hear the quiet rustling and the creaking seats of the imaginary spectators, each and every one of them eagerly straining for a better view.

Like Those Girls
by Alison Tyler

'Forty bucks.'

'An hour?'

'To do the job right, it'll take you longer than an hour.' Ms Lawson looked me up and down as she said this, almost as if she were trying to figure out how much I weighed. I would have told her if she'd asked. 112. But she didn't ask, so I held my tongue.

It was easy to stay silent. The way she was offering me the money made me feel dirty, as if we were talking about sex instead of rooms.

'The last girl got it down to two, and she worked here nearly four years. Granted, she was a bit meatier than you are.' She spoke the words as if serving up a challenge, telling me that I ought to be able to do as well as the previous maid, even a scrawny thing like me. I tilted my head back, paying attention to the fierce green eyes, the grey-streaked, wheat-coloured hair. Two hours would be 20 bucks an hour.

My mother had heard about the job through a friend. 'You'd be perfect,' she'd said smugly over one of her casserole suppers that she'd devoured while I'd picked, avoiding all the peas, the pearl onions, the slivers of shiny white fish. 'That is, if you weren't such a sloth.'

The word had tripped something inside of me, which is why I found myself showing up at the B&B, dressed in what I thought were maid-like clothes: grey slacks with only a hint of lint on the shins, a barely wrinkled white shirt, my black hair tied securely back with a blue ribbon.

I lived in my parents' basement, sharing the dark room with the laundry machine, the dryer and a few families of spiders. There was nothing on my walls but a faded felt dartboard and I never thought to bring a vacuum down the steep stairs. But here I was, presenting myself as a maid, hoping to be accepted as one.

'You'll want to wear something less formal,' Ms Lawson told me sceptically after I had accepted the terms, which were simple: 40 dollars for however long the job took me. 'Jeans and a T-shirt's fine for this type of work. Gets hot. Especially in the attic. You have nobody to impress but the dust bunnies.'

The B&B wasn't what I'd thought of when I'd envisioned bed and breakfasts. I always imagined kitschy little places filled with chintz and antiques. A lot like my home, crammed full of things I wasn't supposed to touch. But this B&B catered to longer-staying guests who decked out the bare rooms with their own assorted collections. Ms Lawson lived downstairs with her mean-faced cat. The upstairs was for the tenants – three rooms to let, not counting the space beneath the peaked roof.

The attic, Ms Lawson said, was for artists. She said the word as if it left a bad taste in her mouth. I wondered if she'd ever had a husband. Whether she was a spinster, widow, or divorcee. Whatever she was, she was bitter.

Ms Lawson's B&B offered once-a-week bedding changes, a shared bathroom, and kitchen privileges. My job was to strip and remake all the beds, clean the bathrooms, dust and vacuum.

'Damn good pay for mindless work.' That's what Ms Lawson said, but it proved more difficult than I'd thought. First time, took me nearly five hours. Thankfully, I didn't have to interact with anyone, aside from the owner. That made the job worth more than the money in hand. I was too reticent to work retail, too paranoid to work in an office, and too stoned most of the time to do much, other than sit in the back of the classes at the local junior college and imagine my professors taking off their clothes.

But here was my chance to shine.

My goal was to be the model maid, moving heavy furniture to vacuum and dusting every last inch, including the skirting boards. I made the beds so neatly that I felt it would be a shame to slide under the covers, if not a downright sin. Yet a part of me wanted to slip under those sheets once they were pulled tight.

The work was mindless, as Ms Lawson had promised, but taxing. I sweated through my thin cotton top as I scoured the shared bathroom, even washing the tiny panes in the stained-glass windows, then polishing the mirrors in careful circles to avoid telltale streaks. I worked through the rooms methodically, and by the time I reached the handle to pull down the stairs to the attic, even my hair was wet.

When I reached the top step to the room beneath the peaked roof, a chill ran through me. Oh, to live in a room like this. With the gleaming brass bed in the centre and a carpet that had faded to the colour of spilled wine. This room was taken by a painter, and aside from the bed and an easel, the space was empty of furniture. Canvases with their backs to me lined the walls. I didn't move the paintings, didn't dare touch them, but I stared at the finished picture on the easel – the nude with her head down, long blue-black hair hiding most of her face.

No, she wasn't nude. I looked again. She had circles covering her nipples. Pasties? Was that what they were called? Sparkling ruby-red with tassels that draped down. Her stomach was concave, and she had on black net stockings. In the background were candy-pink fans made of feathers, so real-looking I felt that if I ran my fingers over their tips, I would feel each individual bit of fluff.

I'd never been one to go to museums, was only taking an art history class at school for an easy credit. But I stayed in the back of the room and stared at the blur that the paintings became when my brain was fully fried on weed. The picture on the easel captivated me. I wished the model would look my way. I wished I could see her eyes. Were they blue? Grey? I could see her lips. Full, rouged red. A colour my mother would have frowned at – that type of lipstick was for 'those girls,' my mom always said. She chose a salmon-cream for herself. But I stared at those lips and wanted to kiss them.

Carefully, I emptied the wire trash basket by the side of the bed, looking at torn receipts, a ticket stub, an empty packet of cigarettes. I hadn't paid attention to the garbage in the other rooms. Why did I have to fight the desire to take this trash home with me?

When I was done on that first day, all of the rooms were much cleaner than my own room at home, and the picture of the nearly-naked woman clung to my thoughts. Was she a dancer? A stripper? But Ms Lawson didn't seem to notice how hard I'd worked or how flushed my cheeks were. She gave me two crisp 20 dollar bills without more than a cursory check.

'You put on clean sheets?' I nodded, wondering if she expected me to curtsy. 'Find anything odd?'

'Odd?' Like the bong in my bedroom at home? Like the vibrator under my mattress? Had she thought I'd go through her tenants' trash, or worse, could she possibly have guessed that I actually had?

'How about in the attic?' The question was weighted, seemingly filled with mistrust for her tenant.

'No, nothing,' I told her, adding, 'Ma'am' as an afterthought.

'See you next week,' she said, shutting the door behind me.

For the next six days, I replayed every moment I'd spent at Lawson's B&B. I remembered what each room had looked like at the start of my work and how neat the places were when I was finished. This thought swelled me up with a crazy form of pride. I was a maid, but I was a damn good maid.

Late at night, I fantasised about the canvas on the easel. I thought about the woman while I spread my thighs on my rumpled duvet and edged my vibrator around my clit. Sweet humming accompanied the circles that I liked best. Counterclockwise rotations around and around. I never pressed the vibrator inside myself. I'd never been fucked – not even by a toy.

Why had the girl been dressed like that? When she moved her body, did those tassels sway? And how did she use the feathered fans?

Usually, when I masturbated, I spent most of my time with my ears straining for sounds, listening for the door at the top of the stairs to open, alerting me to the fact that my mother was coming down the stairs with a basket of laundry. I'd always have time to thrust my vibrator under my mattress and throw a schoolbook up on my pillow, pretending to be studying. But now, my thoughts were consumed by the picture I'd seen in the attic. By the girl whose face I couldn't catch through her haze of hair. By the vision of what life would be like to be painted like that.

I didn't want to fuck her. Don't get me wrong. I wanted to be her. I wanted to sit on a chair, with my hair in my eyes, and be painted by a stranger. I wanted to strip in front of someone I didn't know, in front of an artist – and I said that word to myself in an entirely different way than Ms Lawson said the word. I wanted to be made into art.

As I came, I realised that I was looking forward to cleaning. In my whole life, I'd never got any sort of satisfaction out of dusting, or washing, or folding, or vacuuming. Maybe because I'd had to do all of those chores under the hawk-like gaze of my mother, who always made sure I didn't simply dust around her tchotchkes but lift each one and dust beneath.

Ms Lawson didn't watch me work. And the rooms I cleaned were inhabited by strangers. Is this why a dangerous sensation crept over me as I cleaned? That illicit feeling I sometimes got when I went to art history class really high. Watching from the rear of the room, almost as if I were viewing from behind a two-way mirror. Not part of the class, but a secret observer.

On my second week as a maid, I did nearly as good a job as

I had the first time, but I snooped a little more while daydreaming about the room I was saving for the end. My mother would have been shocked to spy the gleaming mirrors. The careful fan pattern I had figured out how to make while vacuuming the carpet, backing out of the room slowly at the end so my own footprints were invisible in the thick, blue shag. And then finally, it was time.

I felt as if the attic was waiting for me.

The air was so still and warm and welcoming. I tiptoed into the space and held my breath for a moment, before finally breathing in deep. I could smell him. I was sure. The scent of him; the left-behind essence of a man who could paint a woman like that.

But when I walked to glance at the easel, the nude I expected to see was gone. I had recreated her image in my head all week long. I had come to visions of her, to the thought of taking her place on the stool, to holding so still while a man I didn't know captured my form. Now, on the easel stood a half-finished picture, face half-hidden by a raised hand holding a fan. All that could be seen were her lips drawn down in a frown.

Why was she sad?

Like the first, she had on pasties and boy-style knickers. The thigh-high stockings were a more tightly woven net, and she was wearing short, shiny black gloves. Behind her was a spider web of rope, and her body pressed against the centre, as if she were a black widow, awaiting her prey.

I stared at the picture on the easel as I dusted. Then I sat down on the bed and imagined someone painting me. If I were going to be a model for an artist, if I were going to be made to look so pretty on canvas, wouldn't I smile? I thought of taking off my clothes. I thought of coming on the artist's bed, of touching myself through my panties, of touching myself with his brushes, but I couldn't make myself do it.

'Took you long enough,' Ms Lawson said when I'd finished. 'I'm not paying you by the hour, you know.'

'I know.'

I wondered if she knew what I was doing. Her eyes were narrowed. I wondered if maybe she'd guessed?

A model maid is someone you never know was there.

But I left my plain white panties under his mattress.

The week passed in tiny increments of time and smoke. I lay in my bed, feet up on the plaster wall, and I closed my eyes as I inhaled the best pot I could find on campus. The smoke swirled around me, weaving a silver cloak around my naked body. I let myself float away as I tried to imagine what confidence a girl would need to pose in front of an artist. I didn't have any confidence. I had long dark hair and light blue eyes and a sharp chin. My body was thin and taut, but the swirling smoke gave me curves.

One night, too high to talk myself out of it, I pulled a mirror from the rear of the garage and carried it down to my room. I took off my clothes, then sat on my bed and pretended to be the model, struck the same pose she'd held for the painter.

Chin tilted down. Just so. My hair forward, hiding one eye.

But there was something wrong. Those girls hadn't been nude. What they'd worn had made them sexier, I thought, than if they'd been all the way naked. I tore through my tiny collection of underwear with no success – had I really thought I might find pasties there? I needed stockings. I needed pretty lingerie. I needed gloves.

Using the one lipstick I had in the back of my drawer, I rouged my nipples. Using an eyeliner I'd never worn, I drew a seam down the backs of my thighs all the way to my ankles. Then I looked in the mirror again, and I could see the change. Starting slowly. The way that pot starts slowly, the effects gradually building. I could see, until I collapsed back on my bed with my vibrator and ran the toy up and around, up and around, until my whole body fluttered with a pleasure I'd only experienced all by myself in a dingy basement room.

Would he find my panties?

What would he think if he did?

The next week, the rooms went by in a blur. I tried to work faster without sacrificing quality. But I finally understood that Ms Lawson didn't seem to care about quality. So I became cleverer. How much could I get away with? I ran the vacuum while peering around the rooms, paying more attention to the titles on the shelves than the dusting of the shelves themselves. Until, finally, to the attic. To the artist.

To my artist.

Up here were full ashtrays to empty. The man smoked cigarettes I'd never seen before. Foreign packages with gold foil interiors. I dug the empty boxes from the trash to take home with me. I looked at the new painting, another half-finished one, this only showing a girl's legs, in high heels, stockings, motion to the picture as if she were dancing. But I knew that she hadn't been. She'd been bumping and grinding to some throbbing beat. I'd done enough fantasising to work out that these must be models from some burlesque show.

These girls were 'those girls'; the ones my mother always talked about in that snipped, pinched way of hers.

I felt as if I should have been the one to pay Ms Lawson, to give her two neat twenties for the opportunity to spend time in her attic room. Instead, I took the money she gave me, and slunk home as quickly as I could. I was hardly in my room for a second before I had my clothes off, my vibrator in hand.

Oh, that was fine.

The way the motor rumbled. The way the whirring seemed to speak magic words inside of me. I'd always gotten off easily, especially when stoned, but now when I came, I thought of him. I thought of him lighting a cigarette for me, of blowing smoke on me. I thought of him taking the vibrator out of my hand and fucking me with the shiny synthetic toy. And then I thought of him tossing my vibrator away and fucking me himself. What would it feel like to have a man in my bed? What would it feel like to have a man between my legs?

On the fourth week, I found his passport in the bottom of his underwear drawer. I stared at the face in the black-and-white photograph. I said his name under my breath as I vacuumed a seashell pattern into the carpet.

Killian. Mr Killian McIntosh.

My art history professor.

He had dark eyes, smudged circles under his eyes. His shirt in the picture was white. His hair was black and longish in the back. He looked like a painter, although I'd never really thought about what a painter might look like before. I'd been watching him all semester, but hadn't really seen him.

In class, he talked about The Masters. Capital on the The and on the Masters. He showed slide after slide of the Impressionists. One water lily looked like another to me. I couldn't tell my Manets from my Monets.

Why hadn't he shown us his work?

Why hadn't he shown slides of these?

That night, I dreamed of him painting me. The same crystal colours that he'd used for those girls on the easel. A pale rose to my cheeks. A cigarette in one hand, even though I didn't smoke.

At home, my mother said I could damn well vacuum her carpet if I could vacuum Ms Lawson's. I wanted to tell her that Ms Lawson was paying me. Instead, I plugged the machine in without a word, and the whole time I worked, I imagined Killian fucking me.

He would tie me to the brass bed with the rags he used to wipe drops of paint off the floor. He would tie my wrists over my head and he would fuck me, the way nobody ever had. And when he was done, he would flip me over and fuck me again. I'd come in a bright swirl of colour. I'd come like the paint he squeezed out of a tube, his fist around me, pressing so tight.

'I've never seen that,' my mother said, admiring the fan pattern I made on her pristine white rug. 'You make a good maid.'

As soon as she said the words, I knew that I was going to

move out, get my own place. Maybe a tiny room on the top floor of a Victorian in San Francisco. Or maybe an attic room, if I could find one. I could be a maid in the city if I wanted to.

But perhaps I would be something else. I would be an artist's model, and I would hold myself completely still and silent while a stranger painted me. He would never have to chide me to sit up straighter, to keep my pose. I would be immobile until he told me what he wanted next.

Ms Lawson called me that afternoon. She wanted me to come a day early. To clean the whole house, not just the three rooms. A party, she said, and she needed help. She would pay me double. I wore my first outfit. I don't know why. Together, we cleaned the downstairs, where she lived, and then I went to the trio of rooms, and cleaned them better than ever.

Finally, I pulled the steps down to the attic.

Night had come while I'd cleaned. The room was dark. I felt for the light switch, jumped when I heard the click, then smelled the smoke. Someone was there. He was there. In a way, he had always been there.

'I'm sorry,' I said when I found my voice. 'I'm usually done before you get back.'

'You like the pictures,' he said, and I saw that they were all facing forward now, all the canvases I'd been too awed to touch. Women in different poses. Stunning, quiet creatures.

But when I looked again, I saw that they were not women. There was just one woman.

There was just … me.

The pictures were in a row now. And I could see the motion, the full-on fan dance that he had captured, canvas by canvas. The feathers moving. The pasties shaking. The light and heat and tremor of feathers, flesh, and fringe.

Killian sat on the edge of the bed, the smudges of fatigue under his eyes, a cigarette burning in his hand. He smiled, and I felt my throat catch. This was what being beautiful must feel like, I thought. The way he looked at me, inspecting me and finding me pleasing. I had that urge to curtsy.

'But I've never posed,' I said. I spoke the words to see what he'd say.

'I know,' he said.

'I've never –' my voice broke, as I walked to the wall of pictures, as I looked at each one. The hair that had covered the model's face – my face – was thrown back in the last painting. Was that the look I had when I came?

'I've never,' I tried again, but Killian came forward. He turned me to face him, he put his arms around me. Had I been so stoned I hadn't known he was watching? Had I missed the signals? I waited for him to lead me to the bed, but he didn't. Instead, he motioned to his closet. I went carefully, slowly, still feeling as if I might be sleep-walking. On the top shelf of the closet was a box that I took down with shaking hands, and opened the lid. Inside were gloves, the pasties, the pretty panties. While he watched, I stripped and dressed. I felt his eyes, I felt his brush. Rather than be the model for his paintings, his paintings had been the model for me.

I did not do a bump and grind. I did not strip once more. Killian took me on the bed like that, his hands moulded over my limbs. Fingertips running down the net of the garters, lips on the curve of my throat. He kissed me, and I swallowed hard and looked into his eyes, feeling him fumble with the button of his slacks, feeling him push my panties aside.

'From the start of the year,' he whispered to me, 'I saw you. Dancing.'

'Dancing?'

'In my head.'

I sucked in my breath as he pushed inside me. I felt the fabric of his trousers against the net of my stockings. I arched my back and met his body with my own. Dancing. He'd imagined me doing the burlesque show that his paintings featured. One after the other after the other. While I'd been lost in a silver grey world, he had been seeing me drenched in colour.

He gripped my wrists and held me down. His thrusts speeded up, and my breathing matched his rhythm. This was fucking. So different from me with my vibrator in a basement room. This was the sway of the fringed pasties on my nipples, the satin of the panties on my ass, the scratch of his evening shadow on the soft skin of my cheek.

The pleasure built, and he pushed one hand between our bodies and touched my clit, taking me where I needed to go. Taking me over, and just as I came I turned to look at the last painting, the only one that showed my face. I locked eyes with myself and I – we – came.

The last time I went to the boarding house marked the end of the semester for me. He was gone.

'Tenants come and tenants go,' Ms Lawson said. She seemed relieved that her house was free of artists.

But the painting was there waiting for me. On the top shelf of the closet, where only a good maid would think to run her fingers.

Just Another Night In Paradise
by Lauren Wissot

For the past dozen years I've been aware of my role as an undercover agent in the mainstream world, a gay male born into female form, passing as a straight chick like a 19th century, light-skinned black pretending to be white. Yet heterosexual relationships have never felt normal or the least bit real. Not when compared to primal homo lust, lip-synching with the genderqueers, weekends spent bonding with the boys on Fire Island. Female desire is something I've play-acted but never known. What I do know is that ever since I was a teenager I've had a thing for rough trade – cocky, arrogant, dominant men who take no bullshit and seize control. Men like me in other words. Guys whose bodies I can live vicariously through, if only for one night.

So when I heard the Paradise club was the place to go to view aggressive, buff, bis hustlers in all their 'full Monty' glory I practically foamed at the mouth. I called my best friend Brandy (a gay guy like me, albeit one who loves camping up her biological girly form – a female drag queen!) to check her plans for Friday night.

'Wanna see male strippers in Times Square? The *Village Voice* ad says the Paradise has six shows on Friday. The guys are gay-for-pay so they'll fuck girls for free!' I enthused like a hyperactive kid.

'The ad says that?' Brandy replied, exhaling pot smoke.

'No, my sister's friend was there last week. He says the

guys are gorgeous,' I added, hoping to seal the deal.

'OK then,' Brandy purred. 'But we'll have to meet at midnight so I can get my beauty nap first.'

'Deal!'

By the time Friday night arrived my stomach was knotted in anticipation. Wearing a silver mini-dress and knee-high boots, I met Brandy outside the seedy strip club (or, as the newspaper ad for the Paradise read, the home of 'classic male burlesque'). We handed over fifteen bucks each, passed through a turnstile, and into a small, dimly lit, theatre where the first thing I noticed was how empty it was for a Friday night – only half full.

We took seats towards the back as a boy band song filled our ears. The screen, which had been playing bad porn, rose to reveal the wooden vaudevillian stage, and the music suddenly changed to something awful as the first dancer was announced. The PA was loud and clear. 'Let's welcome – Rocco!'

Rocco, a dark-haired, alt-porn reality version of Daniel Craig, took the stage in blue jeans, a black fishnet top and tight jacket, making me breathless as he stalked the runway. He removed his see-through shirt and stroked his hairless chest, turned and flexed the inked wings on his back, making eye contact with virtually all the lust-filled gentlemen. I was still gripping the arms of my cheap chair as Rocco went backstage to get hard for his second number. But when his next song came on I cringed – some cowboy rap tune. What on earth was he thinking?

Moments later I understood as the gorgeous stud appeared in a black cowboy hat, matching leather vest and chaps. He tipped his hat to the audience. I wanna be a cowboy! Brandy nodded approvingly.

Looking incredibly buff and oozing sex Rocco did his best to turn on the crowd, but unfortunately he wasn't turning himself on. He was only semi-hard.

'Brandy, I'm going to help him out,' I whispered naughtily.

30

Discreetly I rose and walked to the side of the theatre. Leaning against the wall I began to slink inconspicuously towards the front, trying to play it cool as I prepared to run my tongue seductively over my upper lip when he glanced my way. Unfortunately, he was too busy working the men with the tips to notice me, and before I knew it he had disappeared behind the curtain with a tilt of his cowboy hat.

Dejected, I remained standing as the next dancer was summoned. 'Please welcome Nick Savage!' I expected a huge dark Fabio in Tarzan costume to come swinging out on a vine at any moment. Needless to say, I was horrified when a little, skinny British-looking guy took the runway. He looked a bit horrified as well. I returned to my seat.

'That's Nick Savage?' Brandy wondered aloud, as shocked and disappointed as I was.

'Bathroom?' I suggested. Brandy and I gathered our things and headed for the men's room. Brandy watched the door as I peed, then we took a seat on the bench outside the lounge where within seconds the majority of the strippers had us surrounded. We ignored an annoying brunette's half-assed attempts at being amusing until a grating blond joined him and I realised we were being double-teamed by bimbos. It was time to pull out the heavy artillery.

'Yeah, I'll go home with you guys,' I breezily told the blond. 'If I can watch the two of you together.'

'You want to watch us together?' he asked, startled.

'Are you paying?' the brunette asked.

'I don't have any money.'

'Then I don't do that.'

'OK.' End of subject.

'So that's the only way you'd go home with us?' the blond continued, undeterred.

'Uh-huh.'

Finally, the bimbos gave up and Brandy and I breathed a sigh of relief. That's when I glanced over to see another dancer heading towards us.

'Well, look who's here!' I greeted, smiling like a Cheshire

cat.

'Hello.' Rocco immediately swaggered over, took my hand and gave me a kiss on the cheek, introducing himself. Then he took Brandy's hand in his own. 'I'm Rocco.'

'This is Brandy,' I answered enthusiastically before Brandy had a chance to say anything at all.

Rocco smiled widely, eyeing me from my long brown hair to my black knee-high boots. 'You look good,' he nodded as a statement of fact.

'Thank you.'

He put his foot on the bench and leaned in closer. 'How are you?'

'Good. How are you?'

'Well, I made no money this week. It's been awful. There is just no one here.'

'I know. The place is pretty empty.' He turned on his heel and plopped down on the bench beside me. I stood up to take the more dominant position.

Rocco looked me over once again like he was preparing to dig into a six-course meal, making me incredibly nervous. He broke into a huge grin as he continued to stare me down. Then he leaned back, sniffed the air deeply. 'You smell good, too,' he stated.

'Thank you,' I answered, blushing at his straightforward cockiness.

Rocco rose and nonchalantly peeked into the lounge. He moved back towards me as he ran his hand over the hard bulge forming at his crotch.

'Now he's hard?' Brandy laughed.

'You couldn't get hard for your show but now you can? You're a little late!' I teased. Rocco flashed a wicked smile before walking back into the lounge. Brandy and I hung around for a little while longer before deciding to return to the theatre in search of the next big dick.

I was following Brandy when, out of nowhere, Rocco intercepted me and pointed to the bathroom.

'Go in there.' Confused and excited, I obeyed Rocco's

orders as he trailed after me. 'Keep walking.' I continued all the way into the stall at the end of the bathroom. 'Close the door.' I turned to see Rocco feigning the need to wash his hands as he kept a lookout for any clients or dancers. I shut the door.

'Sit down on the toilet,' he called to me. He had to be kidding! There was no way I was actually going to sit on a strip club toilet! 'Up! Now!' he commanded.

Things were happening so fast I didn't have time to contemplate what exactly was going on – only when Rocco unzipped his pants did I realise where things were headed.

'You're going to get in trouble,' I whispered. Rocco dominated me with his gaze as he pulled out the full ten inches that the audience hadn't got to appreciate earlier. I was stunned and thrilled by his size.

'Oh – you're going to get in trouble,' I whispered once again; it was all I could think to say. Blowing Rocco in the dirty bathroom had been the furthest thing from my mind all evening.

When Rocco grabbed me by the hair, forcing my mouth onto his cock, I realised that blowing him in the john was not the game plan he had in mind either. Nope. My mouth was going to get fucked. I opened as wide as I could and let him use me. He jerked my head up and down and forced himself in so deep that I couldn't breathe. Even if I had wanted to cry mercy I wouldn't have been able to – the sound would have been stifled by his dick. I tried to suck to slow him but it was impossible. He just fought against me by thrusting harder, holding my head in place with the power of a vice. I started to panic, reached for his hips like a drowning victim grasping for a life preserver. I was as incapacitated as a slave in bondage as I gave myself over to his cock, prayed he'd come before I choked.

Suddenly, Rocco's cock deflated between my lips. I wasn't sure if he'd ejaculated or if he'd stopped himself on the edge of his orgasm. Under normal circumstances I'd know if someone were to come in my mouth, but Rocco's cock had been so far back in my throat that I wasn't sure if I'd swallowed or not. My head was reeling from lack of oxygen and it was all I could do to stare at the pink member as Rocco took it from my aching mouth. He continued to hold my head as he wiped his cock clean with toilet paper. He tilted my chin up, gently ran his finger along my lips. Instead of meeting his eyes, I watched as his dick disappeared back inside his blue jeans. He zipped up his pants, turned and disappeared. Shaken, I gathered my coat and purse and opened the door.

'Hey, the sign says "No sexual activity permitted," you two!'

Fortunately, the reprimanding voice belonged to Brandy. She was speaking to Rocco as he exited the bathroom. But by the time I joined her he was nowhere to be found.

The Duck, The Mouse And The Bride
by Daphne Bing

It's not like I drank a lot. Well not normally anyway. But every now and then I had a couple and they turned into a couple more and then my internal policeman went on leave and anarchy ensued. Sober, I was too shy to even catch a guy's eye without blushing. Drunk, I was dragging him to bed before he'd even registered I was interested in him.

But it wasn't just my sex life that was affected. The night I agreed to learn and perform a burlesque dance for a donkey sanctuary charity I was less than sober. In my defence, the cocktails were free.

At the class our teacher, Helen, or Miss Fluffational (yes, really) wasn't too terrifying and sensibly suggested we all started by getting into costume. These weren't the ones we were going to wear on the night but they helped us feel sexy and elegant. Of course my outfit gaped forlornly at my chest as if something was missing; well it was: a pair of tits to fill it.

'Ahh,' said Helen sympathetically throwing a glance at my offending vacuum. 'Fabulous legs, darling, but I think we might want to do something about the boobs.' She went into her trunk again and pulled out a blue satin number for me. It was a miracle worker; padded boobs and padded bum. I gazed at myself in the mirror. For the first time in my life I had a curvy figure and, with my long legs, I looked good. Something inside me stirred and I started to wonder whether I might actually enjoy this. Two hours of parading and dancing later my unfit body disagreed; this was more like boot camp in heels and a corset.

I still turned up for the next lesson, though, in which we were told to think of ideas for our routine. To help us, Helen asked each of us to name our favourite heroines, as inspiration for the sort of characters we might want to be.

So that's how I found myself on stage doing a comedy burlesque routine as cartoon character Mandy Mouse. And – this is the bit I'm really proud of – I was sober. It was tempting to down a few, but Helen had said it was 'inadvisable' and, knowing how bad I could be when drunk, she was probably right.

Before I went on stage I was so nervous that only the thought of the charity stopped me running off. But once I got up there the support from the crowd gave me a confidence I'd had never had before. My eyes were drawn to a cute, dark-haired guy, and I gave an extra shimmy and wiggle every time I caught his eye. At the end they actually stood up and cheered my elegant, funny little Mandy Mouse. I could have kissed them all, and afterwards I did get through a fair few at the after-show party. I was on a high, feeling sexier than I ever had before. And so, of course, I had a few drinks.

I sashayed around the dance floor and eventually found the cute, dark-haired guy I'd spotted while I was on stage. I discovered that his name was Paul. I'm pretty sure he'd been the first person to stand up to cheer me, so I was already in love with him, and the moment we danced together it was obvious he was interested too.

I didn't want to wait to go through the normal courtship ritual; I just wanted sex as soon as possible. So we were very soon outside, snogging in a doorway and getting very heated. It was not the most private of places (unlike where Paul's hands were) and I was vaguely aware of an audience. Well, we were right by the night bus stop, and I was dressed as a burlesque version of Mandy Mouse. Paul didn't seem bothered by the attention, but I thought we should find somewhere more private, and there was a dark park about two minutes away.

The grass was damp, but by the time we found a spot we really didn't care. My knickers were off and thrown to one side, making the chances of finding them again pretty remote. Paul's trousers were down and he was fumbling in the dim light with the condom wrapper. I heard the rubber twang and a duck squawked nearby. Paul paused and swore, 'Shit, oh shit!'

'What?' I asked nervously.

'That was the condom. My only condom,' Paul whined.

'Can't you go and get it?'

'After it's hit a duck?'

'I still think you should get it.' Childhood memories of watching *Blue Peter* presenters lecturing on the dangers of litter to animals surfaced in my brain; my middle-class upbringing, I'm afraid. I was really worried.

'Condoms can't be good for ducks," I said. "Supposing ... well supposing it gets stuck over the duck's beak?'

'It squawked. I don't think it could have squawked if it'd twanged around its beak.'

'Well, it could still give it a bad tummy, couldn't it?'

There was silence for a few moments. 'You really want me to wade into the lake in the middle of the night in case I've given a duck gut-ache?'

I shook my head as another sensible thought fought its way through the alcohol to my brain. I wasn't on the pill and school lessons on STIs took over from the *Blue Peter* presenters. 'We need it!' I wailed, really worried now.

'I'm safe if you are,' he whispered, nuzzling my ear.

It was tempting; very tempting. I was feeling so incredibly horny and tomorrow was another day ... The duck squawked again; its judgement was more sober than mine – or was it the mental link between ducks, chicken pox and the really nasty syphilis rash I'd seen in some book that persuaded me? I shook my head mournfully; I was almost in tears. 'Best not'.

It was only after Paul had stomped off across the park that I remembered something. I should have called him, but I was still worrying about the duck, so I grinned drunkenly to myself. Lying on the grass, staring at the sky, a noise broke through the peace, a flutter of feathers, and something that sounded more like a yelp than a squawk.

Paul emerged through the gloom again. 'I couldn't find the right duck, or the one that got it was hiding it. Maybe it's on a promise too.'

'I think it's probably broken by now.'

Paul nodded seriously. 'Or around a very little duck willy.'

A duck squawked again. 'You shouldn't have been rude about his manhood,' I remonstrated; I was really concerned for the duck's sensitivities.

'Duckhood.'

'What?'

'It can't be a manhood on a duck, can it?'

'Suppose not.' I nuzzled up to Paul again. 'You know we could use the condom I brought earlier and put in my cleavage, just in case?' OK, there was part of me that wanted to highlight the fact I had a cleavage that night, thanks to my costume.

Paul was not so impressed. 'You've got a condom in your cleavage and you've had me fighting ducks to get my one back?'

'I didn't want you to think I was easy.'

He laughed. 'Look, the grass is bloody damp; I have an army of ducks out to get me and I think we know each other pretty well by now. Any chance we could go to my place or yours?'

I thought for a minute. Would the sort of guy who would try and rescue a condom from a duck turn out to be an axe murderer? I figured it was unlikely, so we walked hand in hand back to his place.

'What's your perfect woman?' I asked, my drunkenness making me bold.

Paul grinned. 'A burlesque Mandy Mouse, obviously.'

'No, really.'

'OK. The sort of woman who likes to put on a display of how horny she really is.'

I frowned, not quite sure what he meant. He gave me a

wicked smile. 'I love watching and being watched. I bet you'd love it too.'

'Well it was better than I thought it'd be tonight.'

Paul grinned and shook his head, which told me that I didn't know what he really meant. I soon found out.

When we arrived at his place his flatmate was there, toast in one hand and mug of tea in the other. He spluttered a 'Hello' and eyed me up and down lewdly.

'I think we have a mouse in this flat,' he said.

'I've just come round for a coffee ...' I responded, embarrassed.

'Yeah, right. I'm Pete by the way, and you are?'

Paul grabbed my arm and pulled me down onto the sofa, 'About to be very busy,' he responded on my behalf. He cuddled up and started stroking my arm. Pete went back to watching the TV but I caught him giving us the occasional glance, particularly when Paul started groping me. In fact, he was acting like Pete wasn't there at all, and even started tugging at my clothes. At first I was horrified, but then, to my surprise, it really started to turn me on. He pushed my top down and started sucking hard on my nipples while I buried my hand down the front of his trousers to find a stiff cock. With his head down I had a full view of Pete staring at us and massaging himself. When he realised that I'd seen him and wasn't complaining, he smirked and made it more obvious.

I was now hornier than I'd ever been and was revelling in making a display as Paul tried to pull my costume off; with the corset, it was quite a job. But soon enough I was naked except for my mouse ears and my heels.

'You don't mind, do you?' Paul whispered. A bit late if I did!

Paul pulled his clothes off and moved on top of me. Pete was masturbating openly now. I wantonly let my legs fall open and he moved to get a better view. With camera phone in hand he started to film us. Instead of objecting, Paul pulled aside to give him a better view.

Paul then pushed himself between my legs and finally

entered me; I moaned and put my head back to see Pete. He was now naked too, his cock waving at an obscene angle, but for the moment he was ignoring it and fiddling with his phone. I had a rush of excitement as I realised he was sending the video clip to someone and that at some point I was likely to get his attentions too. After only minutes of fucking like we'd been celibate for months, I started to come loudly. Paul wasn't far behind. He lay on top of me sweating and panting for a while before Pete came back to join us.

Paul got off me and allowed Pete to grab my legs, roll me over onto my front and pull me up onto all fours. He rubbed himself up and down my crack a few times and I moaned and pushed back. Paul stood and watched. Pete's hands took over and he used the liquid now dripping from me to lubricate and probe my anus. I was slightly nervous, but didn't have long to think about it as his fingers were replaced by his cock and he slowly eased in. I squealed as he gained entry then put his hand around my hips and pulled me hard back onto him, grunting loudly. This was not the drunk but loving sex Paul and I had just had. This guy was being animal-like, and I loved it.

Somewhere a door slammed and I realised someone was entering the flat. Pete didn't stop, but from the way Paul greeted the newcomer it was clear it was another flatmate: Warren, a huge, gorgeous black guy. Warren lost no time in joining us and I found an enormous cock pushing its way into my mouth. I hungrily accepted him and started to suck noisily. Pete's pummelling pushed me hard onto Warren and I gagged, so Warren buried his hands in my hair and held me tight onto him meaning I could hardly move at either end. I noticed that Paul had his camera phone in one hand. In the other he held his rapidly recovering cock.

Pete finished with a shudder but before I could relax Warren pulled himself out of my mouth and took Pete's place behind me, mercifully entering my cunt, not my arse. I didn't think I could take another one up there that night. Warren's large hands held my waist and bounced me up and down while

40

the others panted gently, watching and filming us. Warren groaned in frustration. I couldn't move quickly enough on him so he pulled me onto the floor. One hand squashed my face into the carpet while he knelt behind me and dragged my hips up towards him. He moved hard and fast into me and I found myself responding again as he fucked away. When he came he almost screamed. Frustratingly, it was just before I reached my own climax and I moaned wantonly, craving more.

Pete was lying on his back next to me so I straddled him. He massaged my tits and pinched my nipples hard. I'm not sure when Paul joined us, I just felt his hand pushing me down hard onto his flatmate, and then he started probing my arse, which was still sore, but I was so aroused that I quickly relaxed. Then Paul did what I thought would be impossible and penetrated my arse while his mate fucked me. The feeling of Pete in my pussy and Paul up my arse was intense so it was probably only seconds after this double pounding started that I came loudly, pulling the two guys deeper into me. They came soon after, to Warren's cheers, and we all collapsed in a heap.

Paul stroked my back. 'Come on, let's go to bed so I can have you to myself.'

The sun was streaming in through the windows when I woke up and Paul was kissing my neck, which is pretty much my favourite thing. We were soon having loving, gentle sex. I suppose there must have been something about the wildness of the night before that had broken down all my inhibitions. As a result, I felt incredibly close to Paul, not at all embarrassed. I even had breakfast in the nude, with my ears still in place and all the guys waiting on me.

'Anyway … that's how me and your grandfather first met and fell in love.'

Emma smiled lovingly across the dinner table at her granddaughter, whose face had been ashen for the last half hour. OK, Phoebe had asked how her grandparents had met, but she'd expected a romantic story to set up her for a good night's sleep before her wedding day. She decided that night

41

that 86-year-old women shouldn't have those sort of memories and, if they did, there should be a law against them sharing. It wasn't proper; it wasn't decent; it was so wrong.

Out Of Bed On The Right Side
Olivia Darling

The alarm clock rings. The worst part of the day. I open one eye to confirm you still have both of yours shut. I snuggle close into your warm side and place a kiss on your shoulder. You stir and snort your way into wakefulness. I love the bewildered look on your face as you struggle to shake off a dream.

You have to get up. Fast as you're able. To linger would be to put yourself in danger because I don't have anywhere to be but in your arms this morning, and if I can persuade you to stay then I will. My leg creeps over yours. With the fingers of one hand I tip-toe across your chest. I tighten my thigh and give you a squeeze that says, 'I'm game if you are.'

But the office awaits. There are other people who require your presence this morning. People who just won't get things done unless you're there to watch over them. You stand up suddenly and skip away from my hand, which is outstretched to touch your bare buttocks.

You head for the shower. I hear a bellow of indignation as the water comes out cold. Then it settles down and you're talking to yourself more softly. Singing a snatch of a song. My mind drifts to a hotel room and a shower big enough for the two of us.

You sashay back into the bedroom with a towel around your hips. You put a glass of juice on my nightstand and tell me to open my mouth. I glance up suggestively to where your dick strains the front of the towel, but you have something else for me: a square of chocolate that you place on my tongue like a dutiful nurse.

'Say aah.'

I quickly shut my lips around your fingers and you close your eyes and let me suck them for just a second. But there's nothing more on offer. You have to be out the door by seven fifty.

I sit up in bed and cross my arms over my chest. I frown and pout but you reel off the names of people who come higher on your list of priorities than I do today. You pull a pair of underpants out of a drawer with a magician's flourish and deftly hop into them, like his rabbit.

'They really have to go,' I say, admiring the loose elastic.

'They're vintage,' you tell me.

You select a shirt and strip it from the hanger to cover your big broad chest before I have a chance to do the same with kisses. Then it's socks on. Trousers. Belt. In front of the mirror you flip up your collar. Tie.

That's my favourite tie. I chose it. It was the week before your birthday. I wandered into Selfridges after a boozy publishing lunch, in search of the perfect gift. We hadn't known each other long. What about a tie? I thought. How's that for original?

Ahead of me in the queue, a young guy preparing for a job interview wanted something 'classic'. The assistant picked out a nice neat navy with a thin white stripe that looked like a fault in the weave. For you I had picked out laughing whales swimming nose to tail across a sea of azure blue. It reminded me of the grinning fish you wore the first time we had lunch, when you smiled that killer smile of yours and I made up my mind I had to have you.

The assistant folded it into a long, narrow box and reached for some tape.

'Don't seal it,' I said. 'I want to put a card inside.'

Back home, in my bedroom, I opened up the box and pulled your new tie out. Quite chic, I decided. But a very boring present.

So I whipped all my clothes off and pinned my hair up out of the way. Then I took your tie and wrapped it around my own neck. Nothing fancy. Just the knot I used to use for school. Fat end over the thin end, around and back and through the loop. It took a while to get it the exact right length, so that the pointed end covered the neat square of my pubic hair as if indicating treasure beneath.

In front of my bathroom mirror, I posed with my digital camera, contorting my body to show just enough but not too much with the tie hanging straight down the middle of my curves. I tried to make my pose business-like, as though I were just walking into the office when, whoosh, a hurricane blew away my knickers. Well, wouldn't you know …?

I spent hours on my laptop, adjusting the colours and cropping my face so that only my smiling lips could be recognised. I was quite pleased with the composition. The white tile of the bathroom hinted at assignations in restaurant ladies' rooms. Their utilitarian plainness was the perfect foil for my pale pink skin. No other colours there but the pop of your blue birthday present between my little round breasts, with their eager, rosy nipples. Click. Print.

When I gave you the birthday present, you insisted on me replicating the pose. Then I danced for you, only the tie preserving my modesty. Not that I wanted my modesty preserved.

And now you've got the tie on. And I know what you were thinking about while you knotted it.

'Will you never be late for work?' I sigh. 'Just ten minutes. Come on; you are the boss, after all.'

You plant a kiss on my forehead, pull away and smile into my eyes.

'Sooner I get to my desk, sooner I can come back to you,' you tell me.

Now that sounds like a plan.

Room Service
by Katie Fforde

Helena was not optimistic. Her husband was arrogant, overbearing and no longer fancied her, but her mother had taught her it was a woman's duty to keep her marriage going and so that was what she would do.

It took quite a lot of planning. First of all she had to sneak off and learn the techniques, although with Leonard's work ethic she didn't often have to lie about where she was. Then she had to find the perfect venue – there was no point in this going off half-cocked (so to speak) because she'd skimped on the hotel. But at last she found it. Small, luxurious and ruinously expensive, it was in a discreet part of Knightsbridge. Although her mother was long dead, Helena felt she would have approved.

Finally, she ordered a corset tailored to fit. Had she realised it would take so long to arrive she'd have ordered it before she booked the hotel, but three weeks had seemed ample. In the event she had to send some frantic, pleading emails to the corsetiere, begging her to hurry, that her marriage depended on it. It was delivered just in time.

Helena arrived at the hotel early, in plenty of time to have a lovely scented bath, relax and feel sexy – this was crucial. And yet, in spite of a foray into the mini-bar (fortunately well-stocked), she found it difficult to summon up any sultry emotions. She needed the clothes, so she got out her tissue-wrapped parcels.

First she put on the suspender belt. Lacy and black, with scarlet ribbons, it was divinely pretty. Then the silk stockings; also black, very sheer, with seams and little red bows at the tops, to match the suspender belt. Then the knickers. Full, silk, and trimmed to match the other items, they were pretty and sexy, but tasteful. Leonard had a prudish side – she wanted to excite, not shock, him. These clothes were perfect. All she needed now was the corset.

The corsetiere prided herself on producing beautifully-made, perfectly-fitting, historically-correct corsets. She had wrapped it in scented tissue and put dried rose petals in the box. Helena unwrapped it. It was silk and velvet with black Nottingham lace, threaded with scarlet silk ribbons. She gave a sigh and hugged it tightly to her chest.

With it came instructions. 'A Victorian Corset does not include a brassiere'. Well, that was all right. She had some lovely nipple tassels – that would make it all sexier. Just thinking about it made her stir a little. She regarded the corset. Which way up? Because it ignored the breasts it seemed more or less the same either way, a long strip of bones and silk. It was easy to work out that the ribbons went at the back and the hook and eye part (referred to in the instructions as 'the busk') was the front, but only when she found a discreet label did she discover which way up was which.

Now what? How on earth would she do up the back? It was hard enough doing up the front, as the top kept popping out as soon as she did up the bottom bit. But now, although it was on, sort of, the laces at the back were hanging loose. It wasn't doing what a corset was supposed to do at all! Time was getting on. Getting dressed was no longer a leisurely, sensual procedure, but becoming frantic. Desperate, she put on the fluffy bathrobe provided by the hotel and rang room service.

'Could I have someone up here to help me with something?' she asked, her voice high with anxiety, making her sound as if she were perched on a chair, frightened of a mouse.

Waiting for the person to come was a bit nerve-wracking,

but she'd seen <Hotel Babylon> on television – their staff were perfectly used to strange requests from their guests. And, sure enough, five minutes later there was a knock on the door and the most attractive young man Helena had ever seen came in.

'Er ...' She'd been shown to her room by a similarly gorgeous young man but it hadn't occurred to her that the hotel might employ nothing but young men like these.

'I was sort of hoping you'd be a woman,' she said.

'I'm afraid we have no women on duty at the moment,' said the man, who had the hint of a Continental accent. 'I could ask for one to come from one of the other hotels in the chain, but it would take a little while.'

There was no time for modesty. 'All right. Maybe you can do this for me. I want you to do up my corset.' Boldly, feeling like someone on Gok Wan's television programme, she let the robe fall and turned her back. 'Pull on those ribbons as hard as you can. I want a really tiny waist. And we haven't got long!'

He was a trouper. He got the point instantly, gathering up the ribbons and tugging hard. Helena nearly fell over backwards onto him.

'Hold onto something – hold onto the bed!' he urged.

Helena held, now feeling more like Scarlett O'Hara. She quite liked that feeling. She enjoyed feeling like a minx who probably needed a good spanking. Just briefly, she allowed herself to imagine what it would be like to be spanked by the young man who was tugging at her back. She found the idea very sexy, but how would the reality be? Maybe Leonard would spank her – anything to spice up their moribund sex life!

'How much tighter do you want it?' he asked, and she jumped, as if he'd just asked her how much harder.

'As tight as it'll go, but I must be able to breathe. I need to dance in it,' she explained.

'There, have a look at you.' He turned her towards the full-length mirror, his hands on her hips. But for the first few seconds she found herself looking at him, standing behind her in his dark suit, looking down at her reflection in the mirror. Some part of her – and she knew it wasn't her heart – gave a little spasm, then she inspected herself.

Her waist looked amazing. She looked amazing, and a glance up at her helper's face told her she wasn't the only one who thought so. She glanced at the clock.

'Thank you,' she said breathlessly, and not only because her corset was so tight. 'Now you must go!'

Leonard knocked on the door at exactly six. He was surprised to see her, but he didn't look pleased.

'What's all this then?' he demanded abruptly.

'I've arranged a little treat for you,' she said, feeling despondent. 'You go and sit over there. I'll bring you a drink. Then you just sit back and watch.'

She was wearing a very pretty net skirt and boots that laced up the front, black gloves to her armpit and a feather boa. Over her corset, to hide the nipple tassels, she wore a little velvet bolero jacket. Her hair was done up on the top of her head and a single ostrich feather curled over the top. She held an ostrich feather fan.

Before she started, she poured two shots of Scotch into his glass. She put on the music, dimmed the lights and then took up her pose.

Ten minutes later Leonard stormed out of the room, horrified by his wife's antics.

Back in the bedroom, utterly humiliated, Helena stumbled to the mini-bar, pulling out bottles at random, fighting tears. The waiter who had helped her came rushing in.

'What happened?' he demanded.

'He didn't like it. I've failed,' said Helena, and tipped back a miniature bottle of vodka, not even bothering to put it in a glass. She looked in the fridge again and grabbed a bottle of brandy. She was drinking for oblivion.

'Don't drink that, it's not good. Go and sit down.' He walked across to the fridge, took a bottle of champagne from the mini-bar and flicked off the cork with a discreet hiss.

'Here,' he said, handing her a flute a few moments later. 'Drink this up, and then perform for me.'

'It was a striptease. Look.' She pulled the bolero aside, revealing the nipple tassels. It had been her botched attempt at getting her tassels to twirl in different directions that had so disgusted her husband.

'Good. Show me. You have studied. Now perform.'

'Don't you have to be doing something else?'

'I went off duty an hour ago. Now dance.' He sat down on the dressing table chair and prepared to watch.

Already feeling better, she pressed play on the CD player and music filled the room.

Maybe it was the alcohol, maybe it was because she didn't really like Leonard any more, or maybe it was because she felt she had nothing left to lose, but she really got into it. She stood before him, her breasts held proudly, and slipped the jacket off one shoulder. She shrugged herself back into it again in a second. This was the Gypsy Rose Lee – the movie – school of stripping – very little was actually revealed.

The jacket came off though, and the nipple tassels wobbled and shook. She removed just one glove but then pulled it on again. For the last few bars of music she turned her back on him, flicked up her skirt and pulled down her knickers, giving him just a glimpse of her bottom before covering it up again. She turned round to face him again, panting a little, from exertion and from excitement.

'You are a very naughty girl,' he said sternly. 'Come here.' A frisson of fear and excitement made her breath even shorter. She went towards him.

'Now,' he said, 'bend over!' He indicated his thighs pressed together to make a firm base. She could easily had said no, but she found she didn't want to. She bent over his knee, her heart racing. Carefully he pulled up her net skirt, making sure it was well out of the way before tugging down her silk knickers.

She gasped in anticipation and he restrained her hands. Then he spanked her, slow measured slaps, hard enough to

50

hurt but not so hard as to be agony, although she was grateful when he stopped.

He turned her over in his arms and kissed her, at the same time pulling her knickers right down out of the way and finding her moistness with his fingers. 'Ah, you are a naughty girl! You enjoyed that.'

He picked her up, deftly pulling back the bedcovers, and dropped her onto the sheet. 'You, young woman, are about to be totally undressed.'

He took his time. Helena wondered if he'd been on a course; every garment that was taken away left a caress. First, her boots were unlaced and pulled off. For her stockings he used his teeth, nibbling her toes as he passed them. Her nipple tassels were eased off and the sting kissed better with nuzzling lips. Her knickers hadn't made it to the bed, so soon she was just wearing her skirt, ruffled round her waist, framing her body as if it were a picture.

He knelt down and put his head between her thighs, his tongue between the lips of her vagina. She curled her fingers into his hair and moaned.

He left her while she was asleep. When she came to she found herself alone, the room beautifully tidied. There was a note on the pillow.

'I've arranged for the bill to be put on your husband's credit card. I will be in touch. With love, your Paul.'

Helena sighed deeply, totally satisfied. It wasn't what she'd planned but it had been oh so much better. Even if Paul didn't get in touch she would always remember him. But now she had to get up, go home, and face Leonard. She wondered if she'd manage it without a very smug smile on her face.

Callipa The Stripper
by Elizabeth Black

Kelly powdered her nose and inspected her face in the mirror. Just the right amount of rouge and her look would be complete. Glancing at the flyer the Cat's Eye Club had handed out only a week earlier, she couldn't help but smile. That smile had sold a lot of tickets. She was already well known at the burlesque club for her bump and grind in the chorus line. But after her performance this evening, she was going to be the act of the year – of the 1920s, even! Tonight, she would make heads turn with her new solo show.

Gentlemen and Rakes, meet Callipa the Stripper!

'You're going to wow the crowd tonight, Baby,' Hugh said, patting her on the back. 'And don't you worry about the police. I'll take care of them.'

'Of course you will, sugar. What else could I expect from the chief judge in this town?'

'The League of Decency will soon be nothing but a memory to you and the girls here. I'll see to that. Now, how about giving me a little sugar?' Reaching around to give her breast a pinch, he nibbled her ear.

'Behave, Hugh. I have to go on stage in a few minutes.'

'You have at least ten minutes. Time for a quickie.' He gave her breast another squeeze. 'Have I ever told you that you've got the biggest titties I've ever seen?'

'All the time. You squeeze them like they're your personal

hacky-sacks.'

'They are, darlin'. Now, let me nuzzle them …'

Turning to face him, Kelly took his head in her hands and guided him to her full breasts. His mouth found her hard nipples, wrapping around them and sucking hard. When Hugh got amorous before her act, Kelly loved to give him the run of her body, knowing there was nothing more exciting on a dancer than the smell of sex. And not just for the audience. Smelling his come on her mixed with the scent of greasepaint, turned her on like nothing else.

Barely able to contain her arousal, Kelly guided Hugh's hands from her breasts to her ass. In one movement, he pulled her onto the make-up table, shoving aside brushes, powder boxes and cream rouge. Kelly spread her legs and automatically reached for his trousers to unbutton his fly. She wanted to feel his heat inside her.

Grabbing the bottle of oil she normally used to remove her make-up, Kelly dribbled a little of it on her hands. With one quick movement she grabbed Hugh's trousers and lowered them to his knees. Underneath, he was naked. Taking Hugh's hardness in one hand, Kelly stroked and pulled, the blood pulsing in his dick making him hard and warm. More than ready, she guided him to her pussy.

Hugh slid right in as if he belonged there. Kelly wasn't exclusive by any means, but Hugh was her favourite lover. He was fun, and always ready for action. Pumping away, he grunted in her ear. When he was horny he could be a beast, which made her feel sexy and ravished. His hot breath burned her throat as he grunted. There was only one thing sexier than Chief Judge Hugh Tennant pumping away inside her, pulling his dick upwards until he massaged her clit. It was Chief Judge Hugh Tennant going down on her.

Pulling out without coming, he covered her breasts and belly with kisses. His mouth travelled from her nipples to her belly button until his lips reached her bush. She felt his tongue against her pussy lips. Always driving her crazy at first by not lapping her erect clit, he sucked on her pussy lips, pulling them into his mouth. After what seemed like hours of excruciatingly aroused agony, Hugh's lips found her erect clit. Immediately, Kelly's body tightened at his touch. Clenching her pelvic muscles, she begged for his tongue against her, rubbing against his mouth to spur her orgasm on but it wasn't enough. As if he read her mind, he licked two fingers and slid them into her. With his tongue on her clit and his fingers inside her, she felt the familiar pulling deep inside as her orgasm approached. Grabbing his head in her hands, she guided him as he licked her clit, and came hard, bucking against his face. His fingers moved in and out of her, pulling and tugging, until she could stand it no longer.

This is the best orgasm I've had in days! And all because I'm debuting my nude act tonight!

Suddenly, the door swung open. Startled, she pulled away from Hugh.

The Cat's Eye Club's manager, Billy Templeton, took one look at the pair and span back into the hall.

'Damn it, Billy, don't you know to knock on a lady's door before entering?'

'If you were a lady, I'd knock.'

'Smartass.'

'You two done? I've got a show to put on, and that show's on stage.'

'Just a good luck fuck, Billy,' Hugh said. 'You remember those, don't you?'

'I don't live in a monastery. Are you two decent? Can I come in yet?'

'C'mon in, Billy. We're about as decent as we're going to get.'

Billy entered the room, raising an amused eyebrow at the recovering pair. Seeing both of them dishevelled but dressed, he walked to a chair, turned it around, and leaned on it.

'You are a sensation, Kelly, or should I say … Callipa? What a stroke of genius was that? What a name! Callipa the Stripper! The house is packed. We should've turned people away, but it's all money, so they're packed like sardines in the back of the room. One look at your fun bags tonight, baby, and the crowd will go wild. I can't wait to see it! The cops are out there too, along with that stick-in-the-mud League of Decency idiot Jim Greeley. He's got no idea what's in store tonight. He took the bait. He won't be able to do a thing about it, and you, baby, will pay our bills for months.'

Standing to her full five foot eleven, Kelly placed her hands on Billy's shoulders, if only to get him to stand still for a moment. A bundle of energy, Billy Templeton's body buzzed with the excitement from the crowd that yelled and joked in the house. They wanted Callipa now, but they would have to wait until the end of the night. She was the closing act.

'You calm down, Billy, or you'll give yourself another coronary. I practised the dance all week. I know the rules. Only lower the fans when I'm behind the scrim, and once the scrim is pulled away, don't move.'

'That's the key, Baby – don't move. Not one muscle. As long as you stand perfectly still, you can't be arrested, even though you'll be buck naked. That's the new law – they call it 'tableau' – nudity is allowed so long as you're completely still. Won't that bust Jim Greeley's chops? I can see him in audience now, chomping at the bit because he sees a nude woman and can't put her in shackles. Haha!'

Hugh pulled the Callipa ad from Kelly's mirror. 'Wasn't this the best advertisement ever? 'Callipa the Stripper! Wowed thousands of men west of the Mississippi! Now making her East Coast debut at the Cat's Eye Club!' So what if it's all a lie? Billy made it all up, baby, and I wouldn't have it any other way. Look at that crowd! The men have lined up for blocks to come in here and see *you* – how does that feel?'

'It feels wonderful, Hugh. I'm going to wow them tonight. And afterwards I'll give you a private fan dance.'

'Totally nude?'

'Of course. You won't be able to resist me.'

'I never can resist you, baby. It's a date.' Hugh gathered Kelly in his arms and planted a kiss on her full lips. As her arms wrapped around his broad shoulders, his hands found her ass and kneaded her flesh. Hugh had a weakness for a tight ass, and Kelly's was the tightest. Wanting to melt in his embrace, she allowed his tongue to slide into her mouth for a few stolen moments.

'Have I ever said you have the most luscious cheeks?'

She pulled away, and kissed him on the forehead.

'All the time, Hugh. Now, sweetie, you can't be seen here. Watch from my private balcony.'

'Not until I give you a good luck present,' Billy grabbed a large box from one of the chairs. 'You're gonna love this. A professor buddy of mine made it for me. He's an inventor, and he's very forward-thinking. I had him make this for you to wear tonight.'

Taking the box, she tore at the wrapping. *I love presents. Wonder what's in the box? Could it be jewellery? Not if it's made by an inventor ...*

Moving aside crepe paper, she pulled a metal contraption attached to straps out of the box. Confused, she turned it around in her hands.

'I give up, Hugh. What is it?'

'It's a hands-free vibrator. This isn't made for medical purposes, but then again none of the vibrators made these days are. Just strap it in position, and let it do its thing while you're on stage. It's small enough that no one will figure out what it is.'

She found a switch and turned it on. The room was filled with a loud buzzing.

'How do you expect me to dance wearing this noisy thing?'

'Come on, baby. The audience won't notice. The orchestra and the crowd will drown it out. Just wear it.'

Shrugging, she slid her legs through the straps and positioned the vibrator over her pussy. Once it was comfortable, she turned it on. Intense vibrations immediately sailed through her pussy.

Damn, this thing is powerful! I'm going to come again!

Not wanting to come until she was on stage, she turned it off.

'I love it, and it doesn't look too obvious. How'd your professor friend make it so small? Have you seen most vibrators? They're huge!'

'He's a genius, I tell you. Likes making things compact. You like it?'

'I love it. Now you have to go. It won't do for you to be seen here by the wrong people.' She gave Hugh a big, wet kiss, which she knew shook him from head to toe.

'Kelly, you're up next.'

Billy saluted her, and she knew she was ready to go. This was the moment she'd envisaged for months. Starting out as a chorus girl at the Cat's Eye Club, Billy Templeton had taken to her right away. He ran a tight ship and wanted his acts funny, sexy, and never-ending. The moment one act was over, the next was on the stage. But tonight, and only tonight, for Callipa the Stripper, there'd be a pause while the band played a catchy tune. This time, let the audience froth at the mouth in anticipation of the hottest burlesque act ever.

So excited that she broke out in goose-bumps, Kelly watched the crowd through the curtain. She always liked to gauge the crowd before she began. Men passed bottles back and forth, enjoying something alcoholic. Kelly suddenly wanted a shot, knowing that the liquor would calm her nerves, but stage fright was a good thing. It meant she cared which made all the difference when it came to performing.

Jim Greeley sat stone-faced in a centre row. The man's scowl brought fear into the hearts of many people, but Kelly couldn't have cared less about him. He was a spoilsport, pure and simple. Surrounded by his goons in cheap suits, he looked like a schoolyard bully who was about to get his comeuppance.

The spotlight went on in front of her, and she knew what she was supposed to do.

'That's your cue, darlin'. Go wow the crowd!' Billy whispered in her ear.

The band slowed to a gentle beat. Reaching for her crotch,

she turned the vibrator on.

Holy moly, that feels good! And Hugh was right. The orchestra and the crowd are making so much noise I can't even hear it buzzing.

Holding her fans in such a way that they hid her body, she took one step on the stage.

The crowd howled. Shadows of horny men leapt up and down. The smell of cigars and pipe smoke floated in the air around her. Dipping and moving the front fan towards her back, but not before the back fan covered her body, she took a few more steps onto the stage. Vibrations pressed against her clit, making her wet. This was going to be one hell of a dance.

Curious to see how the League of Decency would handle her act, she glanced into the crowd. Jim Greeley leaned forward in his seat, hoping to see a little too much skin. *Why does he bother with this little burlesque house so much? Is he a closet pervert? For someone who protests so much, he sure shows a lot of interest.* His goons sat on either side of him, eyeing her up as if she were a slab of meat.

If only Big Ole Jim Greeley knew about the vibrator, he'd have a fit.

Twirling on her toes, she danced as she had hundreds of times in practice, but never before an audience. Waves of pleasure rose from the vibrator to her pussy, making her thighs shake. The fans hid her body but not her long legs. When she faced the back of the stage she lifted the fan that covered the front of her body. Away from the prying eyes of horny men and the League of Decency, she waved the fan in front of her head and, upon turning to face the audience, again hid her body from eager eyes.

'Show us your tits!' someone cried. Hoots of approval greeted the heckler. Kelly dipped and lowered the fan to show a bit of shoulder. The crowd went wild. She danced, keeping time to both the music and the rhythmic throbbing in her pussy. The catcalls encouraged her to add a little bump and grind. When she reached centre stage, she faced the audience, twirled her hips, and bumped her pelvis forward as the drums beat in time to her movements. She pressed her legs together as the vibrator buzzed against her clit.

I'm going to come, right in front of hundreds of horny men.

Dancing in front of the scrim, she twirled like a ballerina, fans a blur. As she danced behind the scrim the spotlight went out and a backlight went on. Only her shadow was visible, and she raised both fans over her head. Her nude silhouette was visible, showing her breasts and hard nipples. Wiggling her ass, she spun again, driving the crowd insane with excitement.

'Drop the fans, babe!'

'Get a load of those nipples!'

As she danced away from the gauze scrim, she moved her fans to cover her body once more, and the spotlight followed her movements. A few boos rose from the crowd, but the cheers silenced them. She spun until she was dizzy; from the heat of the stage lights, the pulsations of the vibrator and from the cigar and pipe smoke. Money and flowers showered the stage as visible compliments. Spinning and dipping, she continued her frenzied dance, letting the fans lower just enough to show a bit of shoulder or hip, but never enough to show her entire body.

Now came the moment everyone was waiting for. She danced again behind the screen and the spotlight turned off. Holding the fans over her head, she showed off the contours of her body. She pressed her legs together, the buzzing of the vibrator doing its work on her pussy. Inhaling deeply, she felt her orgasm build. At that moment, the spotlight turned back on, and the scrim rose. Kelly tried to catch her breath. Feeling much more tired than she had expected, she stood motionless, save for the vibrations in her pussy, feeling the desire in the crowd as the spotlight revealed her nude body in all its glory.

Her body tightened as her orgasm came over her, so intense that she could barely keep still. Enjoying the waves of pleasure, she focused on her audience. Men hooted and hollered. Jim Greeley stood red-faced in the front of the crowd, pointing a finger at her and barking at a cop, who only stood by and shook his head. If she didn't imagine it, the cop winked at her. He must have enjoyed her act and wasn't going to let Jim Greeley ruin his fun. She felt exhilarated. The crowd loved her. The League of Decency couldn't touch her. Smelling the cigar and pipe smoke, she closed her eyes and enjoyed the love of the crowd, but then the worst happened.

A tickle developed deep in her nose. *No! Not now!* The smoke irritated her nasal membranes and, though she tried with all her might, she couldn't stop it from happening.

Kelly sneezed.

Her breasts bounced with the force of her sneeze. Her entire body jumped. Not only did she sneeze once, she sneezed four times! She dropped her fans. The cops jumped at the stage, but were held back by the bouncers. The lights went out, and bedlam took over the club.

'Kelly! Here, quick!'

Billy led her out of the wings and into her dressing room before the cops could catch up with her. He shoved her clothing in her arms, and led her to her closet. Hugh was already on the stairs, guiding her away from the cops and the League of Decency.

'It's a raid!' Hugh said. 'They've been waiting for this all night.'

'I'm so sorry, Billy.'

'Don't you be sorry for nothing. That's the best crowd we've ever had. Did you see some of those cops? They smiled at you. Now get running, and don't come back until I call you.'

Hugh led Kelly down the stairs to a hallway that ran under the road and into the basement of the Catholic church. The Cat's Eye Club had been a nunnery until the 1880s, and that secret passage had been used by the nuns to escape during times of war.

Quickly changing into her clothes and taking off the vibrator, Kelly pulled on Hugh's arm until he told her what was going on.

'That was the prank, Kelly. Jim Greeley couldn't touch you, until you sneezed. When your body moved, his cops

60

moved. But not all the cops were on his side. I know all of them, and most of them wanted to see your act. So, you pulled a fast one on the League of Decency. I'm sure the other acts will get arrested, but they did nothing wrong, so no charges will be filed. I'll see to it that you avoid charges as well, my lovely fan dancer.'

'I hope Billy asks me to keep that act going.'

'He will, trust me. You brought in the biggest crowd the club has ever seen. And your sneeze couldn't have been timed better. You'll be the talk of the burlesque crowd for months. Billy'd be crazy to let you go. Hell, I'd be crazy to let you go.'

They hugged, and Hugh opened a bottle of wine.

As Hugh and Kelly drank a toast to her debut, she knew her act would continue for months. And it would all be under the watchful eye of the League of Decency, who couldn't do a damned thing to stop her.

Burlesquetual
by Aimee DeLong

Denny hands me tickets for free drinks from the bar.

'There's going to be a lot of people in tonight,' he says. 'How d'ya feel about a crowd?'

'I like it,' I say.

Hank Bukowski's at the show tonight. He sits at the bar, his sturdy fingers caressing his wine, regretting the subtle curve of a long-lost breast. So Hank likes a little burlesque. Who knew? This is the Bukowski that stayed in New York, and didn't run back to the sedate and tawdry sunshine of LA.

He's staring at a woman with blonde hair like a poodle, and candy-coloured lips, sipping on a Diet Coke. Her legs are crossed and foot arched. She's a performer. I'm a performer. We are going to perform on the same bill. Me and poodle-candy. She is sexy. We will be sexy together at the burlesque show.

The bouncer yells at some girl who rushes past him without flashing her badge of alcohol authorisation. Her face is not embarrassed, but oblivious. This is a swingers' bar, can be a bit overwhelming. One never knows if one is being hit on directly, or for appearances. A sitcom lesbian couple, one part toolbelt-butch, one part femme hottie, tries to pull my boyfriend away and make him dance. With both of them? Sounds tedious. The femme hottie stares at me with a sultry decadence during the entire process and runs her wistful fingers through her two-inch, black, cropped hair. Andy looks at me with that mixture of fluster and flattery that a 16-year-old boy might have when being paid attention that he's not sure what to do with.

'I don't care,' I say. 'If you wanna dance with them, go ahead.'

'I can barely dance with one person; what would I do with both of them? Besides, they were probably trying to get to you anyway.'

'Don't know what to do with women, do ya?' I ask, joking about how often Andy gets approached by men. He's one of those. The hot straight man who is skinny and stylish enough to attract the hot gay men and repel the hot straight girls who are insecure about their weight.

I walk over to Poodle-Candy to find out what her real fake name is. I have on a slinky black halter dress with a large cut-out in the fabric between my breasts. My feet are strapped into a pair of shiny crimson heels. I can feel the heat of over-used, over-heated, badly-lit bulbs on the round caps of my shoulders as I manoeuvre through all the ambiguously sexually-oriented swingers.

'Hi,' I say coquettishly.

Her eyeballs glance up from her coke, lips still cock-sucking her straw. She's attached to that Diet Coke. As she realises that I'm a fellow burlesquer, the straw slides out and down, her pout, still pursed. Damn, she is hot. She's the kind of woman that makes a girl like me almost look forward to my thirties. She looks like a vaudevillian Cyndi Lauper, all pink, and poofy and sizzling. But she is real cool too.

Her lips unclench from the memory of her straw. 'Are you China Doll Cherry?'

'Yes. And you're Carnivorous Candy?'

'That's right.' Her voice sounds like the way it feels to have a woman snake her finger along your arm. I can imagine what that would feel like, anyway. I turn my head and notice Hank taking in the whole scene, his gaze angled at our legs.

'Do you want to head downstairs and change?' she asks.

'Sure, have you seen the other girls?'

Candy shakes her head no.

We trail along together past Bukowski, past Denny, past the dancing lesbians, and past the girl who survived a boisterous scolding by the bouncer. I give a goodbye-for-now-wave to Andy, who's sitting at a table in the corner lusting after his own glass of scotch. He's ignoring all the be-my-boy-toy-stares from his gay admirers with an authentic aloofness.

I glance up at Candy as she pulls off her top. I mean, I'm going to be seeing her breasts quite a bit tonight, anyway. I should probably get acquainted. In mid-inconspicuous gander I hear some heeled shoes galloping down the stairs. It's Fanny Frosting and Mademoiselle Annabelle. And Fanny is distinctly breathless. Annabelle looks like she's just come back from a vacation of sexual escapades. These two always seem to be floating about each other's necks and skin. Some sort of intoxication wafting through the small space between their noses and lips. We all hit that zone where it's just burlesque from here out. The B-spot.

Although some girls' B-spots are a little easier to reach than others.

As I wander to the back room to find a mirror, I catch Annabelle heartily indulging in some of Fanny's frosting, all of which I can view quite explicitly due to the reflection in the mirror. I try not to act shocked or intrigued as I stumble back into the other room.

I glue pasties on my tits. The basement makes them cold and rigid. The skittering hum of Betsy and Annabelle's voices is agitating and titillating at the same time.

After they rejoin Candy and me, I watch them powder shimmer on each other's backs. Coy looks dart around the dressing space. I become paranoid as a result of their lesbian lover banter. Their hesitated hisses. I think they're talking about me.

'Hey! Are you two talking about me?' I prod, keeping things light.

'We're whispering sexy secrets to each other,' says Fanny Frosting.

'Tell her your Spanish name. It's super hot,' says Mademoiselle Anna Belle.

'Marrrrr-ia Sosa.' Anna Belle's tongue rolls, the underside of it glistening with saliva.

I become relieved that Fanny and Frenchy aren't slandering me, although a little reputation isn't always bad. When I put my fishnets on, all the plum and silver glitter I just finished rubbing onto my legs falls through the holes and settles in snowy fashion to the floor.

Often, I push my pasties into my breasts to make sure they're well fastened. The sequins feel coarse. I check my ass in the mirror. My cheeks hang out just below the deep electric-blue frills of my panties. My eyes sting and bulge from eyelash glue. I wasn't careful enough about that. Abandoned in my ritual. The fake lashes stand stiff from my eyelids, curling out and up. A butterfly erection.

I position each breast within each cup of my bra so as not to disturb the pasties. I know I'm up next and my adrenaline is curdling in my stomach. I can't fasten the hooks of my vintage jacket, and Carnivorous Candy has to do it for me as my breathing quickens pace.

'I'm not good with time pressure,' I divulge.

'You'll do a fabulous job,' she breathily reassures me.

I climb the stairs from the chilly air of the basement into the radiation of the crowd. I count the steps in my head. Tedious and welcome. In my black patent leather ribboned shoes with the sleekly shafted heels, the tap of each ball patters the climb.

On stage. Don't remember how I got there. The flash of light sinks in between my strands of teased hair. I can feel the hue. Gold. I fondle each piece of clothing individually and deliberately. Unclasped. Stepped out of. Rolled down. Groped. Twirled around. The bra glides down the umbrella back. Opens. My legs slide apart for the splits. The wider they pull apart, the louder the howls. Everyone loves a flexible woman. My hips do obvious things.

I can hear every wash of yelling. I might call them laughing groans. One for the removal of stockings. One for spreading of the legs. One for the swing of the hips. One for vintage velvet falling to the ground. One for the thighs. One for the tits. One for the bra that glides down the umbrella back. Open. One for the legs. One for the legs. One for the ass one for the ass one for the ass one for the ass. And. One for the finished product.

The audience is appreciative. Beaming. I suppose. Clapping. Swollen hollers. I walk through them with a perceptive grin.

At the end of the night I spot Andy dancing with femme hottie.

And Bukowski's outside the window smoking a cigarette. I could use a little nicotine.

On my way out of the door, I'm approached by the bouncer.

'I would like to give you an oil massage,' he says.

'Are you a masseur?' I ask.

'Yes,' he assures me.

This, I think, is a dubious claim.

Dominatresque
by Carmen Ali

We were lying in bed when he said, 'I'd like you to dominate me.'

Usually, we liked it rough, but with neither of us in control. Now he wanted to surrender completely.

I asked what he wanted me to do.

'Use your imagination,' he replied …

A few weeks previously I'd been to a burlesque class and had been amazed by how much it increased my sexual confidence. We'd learned all we needed to know, from how to take our gloves off sensually to shaking our nipple tassels. The teacher had also taught us how to tease.

'Pretend you're about to take your stockings off,' she'd instructed. 'Then stop, look at your audience, start to take them off again, and then look up, until you finally pull them off in a sexy, elegant movement.'

I'd never used the burlesque class for anything; I'd just kept it in the back of my mind.

I went to a domination class.

It was another world. Mistress Sadie taught us how to whip and where to whip and she taught us to word things in a certain way. 'Don't say "I want you to do this", tell him he's *going* to do it,' she'd explained. 'Don't give him the option to refuse.'

She also taught us safety. 'Watch your slave every second. Domination is also about responsibility. He's under your control. Give him a safe word in case he wants to stop the play, a random word he wouldn't usually say during sexual play, like tangerine.'

I was planning to mix the two classes together to create the ultimate burlesque domination session.

I practised my act whenever he was out at the pub, letting him think I'd forgotten about him asking me to dominate him. He had no idea it had been on my mind constantly. And tonight it was time for the reveal.

After setting up the stereo in the kitchen and leaving the back door open, I dressed in front of our bedroom mirror, admiring the transformation. I smeared on lust-coloured lipstick and created shimmery dark eyes; long black lashes with sex-flush cheeks. Teamed with a red and black bra, nipple tassels, waspie, knickers, stockings and spiky shoes, I knew I looked hot. I lit candles on the table in the garden and waited …

The door creaked open as he shouted, 'Hello'.

'In here,' I yelled back, trying to sound normal to enhance the surprise.

It worked. He took one look at me and his jaw dropped.

'Come into the garden,' I said.

He did as he was told.

'Sit on the grass.'

He looked puzzled, but did as I asked.

I pressed the play button on the CD player.

The music started to play. Sweet old burlesque music.

I strutted over to the bench and stood in front of him, dancing with my shoulders and hands and hips and staring into his big blue eyes while I eased one glove off with my teeth. I pulled it off and ran it up my thigh. He followed its slow journey. I removed the other glove and teased it under my breasts, slapping his hand away when he reached towards me, and moving to sit down on the bench. Leaning back and looking him straight in the eyes, I kicked my legs in the air as my teacher had taught me. Then took off one shoe and threw it at him. It hit him on the leg and he looked at me with a mixture of annoyance and lust. I was just getting started. I took off the other shoe and pretended I was going to throw it at him again. He winced slightly and I threw it into his hands: an easy catch. I gave him a cheeky smile.

I took off my stockings, so slowly that if it hadn't been a teasing burlesque show it would have been painful to watch. It probably was painful for him.

I'm sure he wondered what I was going to do next but I wasn't going to rush things. Instead, I started to fan myself on the bench, wearing an innocent smile. He started to speak to break the tension but I hushed him, then turned so that I was sitting on the bench facing him, with my feet on the floor. Picking up a bottle of champagne, I put it between my legs and undid the silver cage, looking at him with every twist of the wire.

Twist. Look. Twist. Look.

I eased up the cork until it flew into the air, making a loud pop then quickly put my thumb over the top, stood up and shook up the bottle until it started spraying all over him. I got sprayed a bit in the process but he was completely soaked. His trousers were dripping and his hair and shirt were drenched. He laughed. I laughed inside. I handed him the bottle and bit my lip with a cheeky look.

I had my back to him and started to undo my waspie, looking over my shoulder as I did it, making him wait. I took it off and threw it to the side, still keeping my back to him as I danced with just my arms, then started to move my legs and grind my hips with a lascivious sway, then moved to some cheeky bending over …

I stopped and put my finger to my mouth as if I was thinking. I took hold of my bra and started to pull it off one shoulder, looking at him inquiringly, as if I needed confirmation. It was all part of the show. We both knew I was going to take it off and he looked at me with adoration and excitement as I did.

I covered my breasts and gyrated in front of him, until his breathy, 'Please,' made me take pity on him. I moved my arms away to reveal sparkly black nipple tassels.

With a shimmy and a twist, the tassels twirled as my tits bounced around. My boyfriend gazed up at me, spellbound by the sight. Just as the music stopped, my tassels stilled and I reclined on the bench, smug with my performance. He clapped. My own boyfriend was clapping my show as if I'd been on a stage. I lapped it up.

'Wow that was amazing,' he said

'Now it's your turn.'

'What do you mean?'

'To give me a show,' I said, as if it were obvious. 'Kneel on the ground.'

He looked back at me, slightly confused.

'Kneel.'

Something in his brain must have clicked. He knelt on the ground. I let out a small, slightly evil laugh.

'If you want this to stop at any time, your safe word is 'burlesque'. Understand?'

'Yes,' he said, meekly.

'Yes, Mistress,' I corrected him

'Yes, Mistress.'

'Now, crawl and pick up my stockings with your teeth.'

He crawled on his hands and knees and retrieved my two stockings in his teeth as he had been told.

'Take off your trousers and put the stockings on.'

Still on the floor, he removed his trousers with difficulty, and put the stockings on with even more difficulty. It was hilarious to see a man doing an elegant thing with such complete lack of elegance.

'Fan me.'

He fanned me as I reclined on the bench again, feeling like a princess.

'Now remove my knickers and put your head between my

legs.'

I was going to get off first: that was for sure.

He did as he was told and was soon lapping at my pussy while I grabbed his hair. He sucked at my clit, nibbling and licking. I closed my eyes and enjoyed the feeling of power as much as the heat of his mouth. He probed my hole with his tongue, grabbed onto my legs and clawed at them – then stopped and looked up at me as if to ask permission to scratch me. Under normal circumstances, he wouldn't have asked. I raised my eyebrow at him and he carried on. He would get his punishment soon enough.

He licked either side of my lips as if he was licking a beautiful, honey-laced lollipop, then stopped licking and breathed on me. I ached with the exquisite agony of wanting to orgasm. As if sensing this, he teased me further, kissing and sucking my thighs. I threw my head back and closed my eyes, jolting as he moved back to my clit and flicked his tongue on it lightly.

It was time for his next surprise. I reached behind the bench, picked up another bottle of champagne, opened it and sprayed it all over both of us, while I came spectacularly; I squirted onto his face, holding him down there with my legs. The champagne dripped down my body in small droplets and I quivered as I felt it run over me.

I picked up a black cotton dress from behind the bench and put it on. I wasn't going to be naked while I dominated him. I would feel less in control. Giving him a stern look, I made him lie face down on the bench, tied his hands and legs to it with duct tape and went into the kitchen. I returned holding a whip, a shaped root of peeled ginger and a bowl of cold water. I dipped the ginger in the water to moisten it, since I'd read that lube could blunt the sensation.

'Here's something I made earlier,' I said. He gasped as I inserted the ginger into his anus, leaving a pre-carved lump sticking out of the end, so his butthole wouldn't swallow it. I waited for the ginger juice to seep.

'Look at me.'

I wanted to see the tears streaming down his face and the beautiful turned-on look of someone trying to resist pain. Sure enough, when he turned to look at mistress straight in the eyes, his eyes were watering.

'This is called "figging",' I said. 'What do you think?'

'I'd prefer a fig in there,' He quipped.

When slaves get sarky, they don't get rewarded. I looked at him as if to say, 'How could you have the audacity?' He knew things were going to get a lot worse from now on.

I picked up my whip and whipped him. I didn't even start softly. He was beyond that level of sympathy. I whipped him over and over: hearing a grown man scream was turning me on so badly I could feel my pussy dripping with silky juices.

'How does it feel to have a root of ginger in your arsehole while your mistress whips you?' I asked

'It burns,' he replied.

'Clench.'

He didn't clench. I whipped him again and he clenched his anus around the ginger and screamed again. It really must have been hurting his cock and his balls in that position too. Ah well.

I whipped him harder and harder. Hearing that satisfying 'thwack' sound it made was driving me crazy. He was still looking back at me, gulping as if he was about to shed full-blown tears. I couldn't imagine what the ginger must have felt like. I hoped I would never find out. But I knew the risk. Having done all this stuff to him, I was sure he would decide he wanted to do it all to me some day soon. I knew I would probably enjoy it, though, in a fucked up, twisted way.

I stopped. He seemed to relax. Perhaps he thought the pain was over. He was wrong.

'Close your eyes, bastard,' I said.

He obeyed and I hovered over him, holding the whip. It must have felt like an eternity to him. In reality it was about a minute. In that minute I listened to him breathing slowly and deeply, bracing himself.

Until, finally, I ended his torment with another searing

slash.

He didn't scream. Perhaps he was toughening up.

Now we couldn't have that, could we?

I went into the kitchen and returned with a tray.

I removed the ginger from his arse and untied him. He pulled up his boxers and sat on the grass opposite me.

'How do you feel?' I asked.

'Sore.' He looked at me with affectionate loathing.

'I know,' I replied in a blasé tone.

I leaned over and kissed him. He kissed me back, but I could tell he was dying to pin me to the floor and get me back for the way I was treating him. He resisted, though, and it was me pushing him to the ground, lying on top of him. I grabbed his hair and smacked his head against the ground. I bit into his neck and twisted his nipples, my tongue still dancing with his tongue all the while, our lips joined together.

'Wait,' I ordered. As if the prick was going to go anywhere.

I returned with two water pistols. I put them down on the grass and resumed the kissing session. We kissed for ages, the way teenagers do. I could feel him harden and took his cock out of his boxers, leaning down to place my mouth on it, but stopping just as I could see he was expecting my silky mouth around him.

'Beg,' I told him

He looked at me.

'No,' he said, with conviction. He looked at me as if he was testing me. I slapped him hard across the face, first left cheek then right. Then I lifted up my dress and sat on his hard cock.

'You fucker. You should follow my orders.'

'I wanted to see what happened if I didn't.'

I hit him again. Backhanded. He smiled, grabbed my hair, pulled me down towards him and kissed me. I put my hand round his neck, maintaining my control, and used the other hand to pin down one of his arms. I fucked him, rolling my hips back and forth, sometimes pulling out almost to the tip then plunging deeply down, other times simply rocking against him and using him as my sex toy.

I decided to degrade him with words as well as actions.

'I wish I had some stocks so I could put you in them and invite all our friends round. Then we could throw rotten tomatoes and other festering things at you. I could invite all the women you've ever slept with. That would be awesome. Or maybe we could try hook suspension. You could be strung up while I laid below masturbating and you could do nothing about it. Or what about some electric shocks? I could tie you down and watch you squirm.'

He listened to every humiliating word and seemed to get more aroused by the second.

He deserved a reward.

'Roll over,' I said.

He rolled me over and soon he was on top of me.

'Be a little bit rough,' I encouraged him.

He knelt in front of me and pushed my legs apart, thrusting hard. I giggled at the sight of him fucking me while still wearing my red and black stockings.

'I can't believe you did all that stuff to me.'

'Good.'

'I want revenge.'

I handed him a water pistol and gave him an inviting look. I picked up the other one.

We stayed there fucking; silently, each tensely waiting for the other to crack and use their toy.

Eventually we went for it at the same time and that's when the sex became chaos. Pure al fresco intimate chaos. We sprayed and screwed and kissed and bit and grabbed and touched and laughed and sprayed.

This was a night of extremes. He'd been my slave, but at that moment we were fighting on equal terms.

The water pistols ran out and we were both drenched to the skin. My dress was stuck to me, emphasising the curves of my body. He was wetter, though, thanks to his earlier experiences with the champagne and the pond.

'Roll over,' I half ordered, half begged.

As I straddled him I felt like a goddess, riding my man's glorious cock in our own garden, feeling the air on my skin. I wasn't cold, even though I was wet; adrenaline overrules anything else during sex sometimes. And now it made me want to dominate him once more.

'Stroke your cock. I'll be back.'

I picked up one of the candles from the table and brought it over then slid back into my place above him.

'Unbutton your shirt.'

He unbuttoned his clinging shirt to expose his smooth, toned chest.

I slowly tipped the candle sideways, watching the anticipation in his eyes. I waited. And waited. And finally, just when I knew he thought I was bluffing, I dripped the hot melted wax onto him while we fucked faster and faster. I leant back and grabbed his balls in my other hand while the candle wax drip, drip, dripped over his front. His face wore the tell-tale signs of imminent orgasm. He grabbed my waist and pulled himself in deeper; I pulled downwards on his balls and dripped a seemingly endless stream of wax over his chest and thighs. He shouted my name as he came, and we collapsed on the floor, wet, tousled, exhausted and satisfied. We lay on the grass holding hands.

'I love you,' he said.

'I love you too,' I said.

Then, with a stern look, I slapped him full on the cheek.

'Now crawl into the kitchen and make me dinner ...'

Oh, My Mother Was Frightened By A Shotgun, They Say
by Richard Bardsley

She sits on the sofa. The TV's on – a documentary about some guy who sat on a rollercoaster for 47 days and got a world record out of it – but she's not watching it. She's thinking about the people that have been to view the house over the last couple of days. It's being sold privately on the internet, so there's no estate agent involved, just folk who make appointments and then turn up.

Hi, how're you doing?

Great thanks. How're you?

And then Jenny and Greg or Erica and John or Michael and Martin or whoever it is introduce themselves and she says, *Well, come on in ...*

With no agent involved, they really could be anyone; murderers who want to dress up in your panties while reciting *Paradise Lost* – or just plain old nosy Marys who make a pastime out of looking around other people's homes. It's just the way the process works and you don't think twice about it.

And this is the kitchen. The worktop's a quartz composite that doesn't chip.

Oh wow, that's great.

But they obviously don't think it's that great, or someone would have bought it.

Today there was just a single guy viewing. Paul was supposed to be coming with his partner, Janine, but it turned out she had an emergency at work. Something about the way Paul explained it made her unsure of Janine's existence. She tried to engage him in conversation but his replies were laconic (*Right. I see. OK. Yep*). As she showed him upstairs she felt conscious of the fact she was walking in front of him, just above his eye level, the creases folding in her white capris as her ass bobbed from side to side. She showed him the closet in the landing first, rather than going to the bedroom.

He smirked and pointed.

That the master bedroom through there?

Sure.

They went in. He ambled around the bed, his hands nonchalantly clasped behind his back, and looked out of the window.

He's a cocky one, that's all, she thought. One of those arrogant guys who get a kick out of making you feel awkward. He turned to face her, his head angled slightly with that smirk again, as he nodded to her.

I gotta be honest with you.

Yes?

I've seen all I need to see.

I'm sorry?

Then Paul started shaking his head, and whatever was going on inside it. He sighed.

I'm not feeling it. The house I mean. I'm just not feeling it. It was Janine's idea to come, really.

Oh.

I just thought I'd be honest, up front, rather than take up any more of your time.

OK. Odd, but OK.

He made his way over to her and offered his hand. She hesitated for a brief second, then met it with hers. He grasped her firmly, as if she was a business associate or a buddy, regarding her with a look that beamed trite appreciation.

Thank you. I'll show myself out.

The TV cuts to a break, the change in volume to the louder

commercials jars her, and she finds that she has been thinking about that placid arrogance of his. What she could do with that; what she has done with that in the past. Paul is the kind of guy she used to go for, though it never lasted.

Nonetheless, she thinks of him a little more intently when she is in bed a while later, then falls asleep.

She looks at the clock. It is 4.14 am. Then she hears the noise again – a shuffling, a dull thud from downstairs, then a creak on the fifth stair. She springs out of bed, opens the drawer, wraps her finger around the trigger and stands a few feet away from the door. The steps continue up the stairs until they are directly outside her room.

She shifts her position, readies herself. Her blood pressure and adrenaline well up in her neck. She feels dizzy. The door opens. She fires at the silhouette.

Click.

The figure collapses, as if gravity has suddenly increased a hundredfold, grunts through clenched teeth. She watches as it tries to writhe through its rigidity, on the floorboards.

Jesus, Tia, it says, then moans gutturally.

Bobby?

She leans closer and sees her husband's face in the moonlight as he flops onto his back.

Honey. You tasered me.

I – I thought you were someone else.

No shit.

Bobby grasps her ankle.

You're nude, he says.

And this is how it begins; 50,000 volts of electrical cord linking a butt-naked wife and her fallen spouse, who has returned home a day early after falling out with his brother.

These things don't develop overnight. It takes time, reflection, subtle intimation, acknowledgement. A certain predisposition – even latent – certainly helps. But once agreed, all it takes is action.

78

There was definitely something about that night. In retrospect.

It would just be role-playing.

Pause. Coffee sips. Watch the waiter walk past.

Are you saying you want to try it again?

Something like it. We don't have to.

I want to.

Hands meet across table. A foot rub against the leg. Clandestine smiles.

When? How?

Bobby breaks into his own house during an agreed time frame on a Sunday evening wearing a ski mask. He is chased into the back yard – beautifully secluded by mature valley oaks, honeysuckle and creeping figs, notes the couple's downloadable brochure – and eventually tasered with a (slightly) reduced voltage as he runs past the gazebo by a wife wearing a torn police uniform, stockings and Gucci heels, which she digs against his chest as he struggles in the flowerbed. Tia goes to cuff him and when Bobby resists she pulls the trigger again, sending another shock down the wires. She watches his strange struggle, then rubs the glistening dew that seeps through her panties onto Bobby's face, rubs it there until his muffles quieten down and his cock gets hard. After a while, she drags the subdued offender back into the house for questioning.

The whole thing would be ridiculous if it wasn't so fevered, and both enjoy the night more than they imagined they would do.

Life continues in the usual manner. People trot through the house but no offers are forthcoming. Bobby stays late at the office. Tia is busy with her graphic design business.

Meals, shopping, pilates, movies, drinking, friends, driving, routine, reliability, safety.

One day, their suburban life affects the other one. While cleaning, Tia knocks a glass of water over the taser as the

79

batteries are on charge. It buzzes for a few seconds, gives off a desultory blue spark, and dies.

The following day they are at Delilah's Twelve Bore 'n' More Store, and they overhear another couple.

What about this one?

I don't like the look of that. That other one, there, that's better.

Tia nudges Bobby as the woman takes the taser from Delilah and proceeds to handle it. She's like Angie Dickinson in *Police Woman* as she points it at her husband (boyfriend, lover; whatever he is, he looks embarrassed). Then the woman becomes aware of her audience. She smiles at Tia, eyeballs Bobby, before turning back to Delilah.

When it's Tia's turn, Delilah recommends a model with a long range. Then she asks if they would like to subscribe to the email newsletter.

You have to know how to handle these things properly in all situations, says Delilah.

The newsletter is waiting on their computer when they arrive home. It's the usual mix of information and sales. Tia decides to search for something else – at least, she finds her fingers are typing. It takes a while, but she finds what she wants.

Delilah was right, there are lots of situations, aside from the burglary thing. Muggers or flashers in back alleys. Good cop, bad cop interrogations. Old fashioned (albeit nude) duels offer the pleasure of voyeur, victim or both. Night-time stake-outs. Girls with guns on man-hunts. Prison breakouts. The Scarface scenario. Etcetera. Little pockets of active communities all over the country.

And apparently electricity conducts more pleasantly if a person is covered in olive oil.

Tia doesn't tell Bobby. A few days later, though, he says, *Honey, guess what I found on the internet?*

I think it'll be good, she replies.

They sign up for a meet called Annie Get Your Gun.

Enter preferences and safe-word, tick below for consent,

read form. A confirmation email will be sent to you with more information about the evaluation process.

They're driven to a place just outside the city, a Victorian house with a wrap-around porch set in sumptuous grounds (previously a regional Quaker centre, of all things), and meet in a low-lit wood-panelled hall. Seven other couples sit in a semi-circle, men on the left, women on the right. All are dressed for the opera, as instructed. In front of them, placed on music stands either side of a miniature theatre stage, are signs declaring No Communication.

The warm beginning of an orchestra plays through some speakers, followed by the sound of Betty Hutton singing one of the numbers from the film:

Oh, my mother was frightened by a shotgun, they say ...

A platinum blonde emerges onto the stage dressed in a cowgirl ensemble. There are leather chaps over her bare legs; a thick holster belt around her midriff with ruched panties underneath; a tight red rhinestone waistcoat encompasses her breasts; a Lone Ranger-style mask covers her eyes.

...That's why I'm such a wonderful shot ...

A gun in each hand, she quickly aims them in the direction of the audience to kick-start her burlesque routine, and she hams it up, shimmies like an old-time starlet.

When I'm with a pistol,
I sparkle like a crystal,
Yes, I shine like the morning sun.

She walks down the steps that lead from the stage and glides through the attendees, wiggles her snake hips around the men, shakes her tits in the women's faces.

But a man never trifles,
With gals who carry rifles,
Oh you can't get a man with a gun.

The cowgirl then apes stalking the audience, fires the guns at a few of them, which shoot a liquid that turns out to be milk. She gauges their responses, blows Monroe kisses, as the song builds to its finale.

Oh, a man may be hot,
But he's not,
When he's shot,
Oh you can't get a man with a gun!

On the last word of Betty Hutton's recording, the cowgirl drops the pistols to the floor, pulls two tasers from her holsters and shoots Bobby in the chest. The lights are immediately dimmed as he falls from his chair.

Then there is the sound of a scramble. A velvet bag is pulled over Tia's head. A hand on her arm motions her to rise and, as she does so, two prongs dig against her bare back between the V-cut of her dress. Tia is led from the hall.

She hadn't expected them both to be first and doesn't know what will happen next. Not exactly. Just that some of the options she's previously chosen will occur, ones which promise the fulfilment of some kind of perfect symbiosis. It will take some time to understand, but eventually the thrill of obedience will fuse with the threat of that brief, searing immobility, its subsequent capitulation, and wallowing. In the meantime, however, there is the knowing-but-not-knowing. The when-and-where. And now, the who.

There are strangers in the house.

The Performing Breasts
by Marcelle Perks

Although Lydia knows the theatre is jam-packed, with the curtains closed and the lights dimmed, she can fool herself she is alone. The audience sits tight, with their mouths closed, so still with anticipation, their bodies are mentally screaming at her. It's what performers like, this hush; as if what you're doing means something. You're melting and exploding all at the same time.

Dada dada da da DAA! It's her music, the plaintive strains of *Light my Fire*. The curtains glide open and the spotlight falls on her as she sways her way to the front of the audience. She looks dignified in a long black feathered evening gown that makes a little sound as she walks. It shimmies its way right down to her calves. Her breasts and hips move in unison, two halves of a perfect whole. Her hair is fashionably raven, swept back in a glossy parting over her face to fall in perfect waves down to her shoulders. It's worn as if it was a diamond necklace. There's something doll-like about her glamour, her cheeks un-rouged. The paleness only accentuates her perfectly made-up eyes, the stained red lips. Every ounce of her speaks desire. When she moves, it's controlled. If she was kissed, surely it wouldn't dent her lip-line.

Fi-EEERRR! She turns away from the audience. A coy flick of her hair and her gown drops. From somewhere to the left there is a murmur of approval. Underneath she is even more alluring. Her corset is cream silk, edged with antique black lace. It fails to hide the uplift of her naturally full breasts which threaten to spill out at any minute. The tight lacing at the back ensures that the breathing process becomes in itself a pneumatic heave, a show. But then every part of her draws a stare.

Almost breathless, she dances her way to centre stage, pressing her breasts forward for the audience. A few men near the front lean forward eagerly, heads bobbing to the almost swimming motion of the hips. She nods, smiles secretly to a special someone. Now she's in the sacred place. That stab of happiness that comes with audience recognition. She sways her hips even more generously. Now they are clapping. The theatre is filled with gutsy slow hand claps as she twirls in time to the music. Her breasts are held fast by the bodice, just. Now they're seeing something. All of her being seems to have become pressed into her bosom. She longs to take off everything and reveal herself. Not yet; still has to play the game. Da DA! Da DA! She undoes her bodice, taunts the audience with the opened straps, smiles. As the music builds to a crescendo, she rips off the bodice but – da DA – the hall is plunged into darkness; her trademark signature for ending a striptease. Let them think about what they saw for just a second. Or imagine it.

Thrilled with the exertion of it all, she makes her way back to her dressing room. A bunch of red roses is waiting for her. She doesn't need to open the card, lingers a little as she takes off her finery, knowing that Ethan loves to see her dressing down. A little whisper as the door opens. She giggles, knowing there is no lock. That anyone could come in for something. It's the guy she never dreamed could be sexy who drives her crazy. Ethan is every inch the gentleman and even the way he moves is well-mannered. His hair is foppishly wavy, grey eyes twinkle like an unexpectedly good looking professor.

His eyes widen and he smiles at her. 'You were fabulous, as usual, out there.' He pats her hip through the corset. 'Everybody loved you.' She kisses him, feels as if all of her is being cradled in his hands. Somehow his palms are always hot, and have the capacity to soothe away any ache, magic her into orgasm. She stands up, knows he likes her to do a private dance for him alone.

This time, she reveals her breasts at once. They hang, heavy and pulsating, in close-up very real. She runs her fingers over them, lets him see her deliberately stroke and caress them. Her nipples, normally never on public display, harden and stand out, pink and glistening, from her pale flesh. Half-dressed, with the bottom part of her coyly packed in lace, she's the sexiest thing he's ever seen. He kisses each breast in turn, greedily licking each nipple; feeling every part of their round mass. She throws off the rest of her bodice, the expensive knickers end up on the floor.

The teasing is over. Their eyes lock as they exchange kiss after kiss after kiss. She can't stop looking at him, wanting him. They are curled up on the sofa, a hot panting mass of excitement. His eyes are liquid in the half-light of the dressing room. She kisses his nose, his forehead, wants every part of him. She's jittering with sexual excitement and her own juices are beginning to slide down her leg onto his waiting fingers. Ethan finds and tweaks the bud of her clitoris and she reacts as if stung with pleasure. Juice floods out from the pressure under his fingers. When he fingers her opening, it's like her sexual consciousness comes on-line. Suddenly, she's aware of hidden muscles, of how her vaginal wall contracts and quivers to his every manipulation. All the time he's looking at her face, and she fights to gain control and not cry out and come instantly.

Both of them are moaning out loud, past caring. There's no time. It feels like she is turning her insides out, aching for him. She just has to clamber on to him, do that leap to feel the precious jut of him inside her. She wants to hold on to that sensation as their slippery genitals grate on each other for a moment, but his penis slips in and then it starts. She pushes her hips down onto him and feels his cock penetrate even deeper. It feels absolutely right. A pushing, tugging motion they do tirelessly. They cling to each other and she sits a little deeper on his penis, feels it springing off her insides, work a naughty hidden spot. A few more precious strokes and her vagina spasms, for a second she is weightless, everything is white hot energy. The room is filled with the sound of their moans dying …

For a week or two after the birth, she remembers the peculiarly specific grip of contraction pain, but in the hectic days afterwards the memory fades. Everything else about the birth is a permanent memory: the exact temperature of the birthing pool; the midwife's kind eyes; the way her daughter is a total stranger the first seconds she is placed into her arms.

Little Heather is so slippery she's half afraid to take her, then something magic happens and Lydia presses Heather closer to her chest. Her breasts become the most comforting place for her newborn daughter, where she not only feeds, but hears the comforting familiarity of her mother's heartbeat. Now it's not how they look, but how her breasts feel and smell that matters. Mother and daughter revel in close skin to skin contact and the sweaty, milky joy of breastfeeding. The previously unused area of her neck and chin becomes an area she can press against her daughter when she holds her close to her face. Ethan couldn't be a prouder father.

But Lydia's perfect stage-performing bosoms don't quite deliver. When Heather is three days old, she notices the other women sport huge nipples, as large and unmissable as bullets. Her own remain unchanged; still large, proud, but not up to proper mothering. It turns out that well-endowed women have more problems breastfeeding. Heather is fussy, constantly hungry and needs to be held all the time. Lydia cries with frustration to Ethan.

'Why, are my tits so fat and useless?' No corset can help her now. She should be producing 120ml of milk a day, but only makes half of that. Ethan strokes her, takes Heather and tries to shush her into an uneasy sleep.

'Don't worry so much, darling,' Ethan helps Heather latch onto a nipple, but even so it's a struggle. The hungry baby cries and squirms; everyone is frustrated. A slim, efficient midwife looks on disapprovingly.

'Keep it going, but if she's still fussy by tonight then we'll have to start with formula. Heather's lost just too much weight.'

It's such a pressure to perform, to produce milk. There is no trick or exercise she can do to make it happen. She drinks strange teas and lots of milk to boost her supply, but nothing works. She can give out a meagre 50ml or so, and then that's it. When she pumps breast milk Heather sucks it up at once, and is unhappy when forced to finish off a feed with formula. Lydia has never been hotter and sweatier in all her life. Showering is almost a waste of time; as soon as she is dry within minutes her upper body is coated with a sheen of sour milk. Holding the baby close to her and breastfeeding is actually hard manual work, every touch and embrace brings her to a sweat. A baby that needs to be constantly held becomes a dead weight. She can't even imagine wearing her fine, lacy undies. Her body is permanently feverish, aching, longing for sleep. Her once so responsive nipples feel fake, deadened.

Ethan no longer looks at her breasts with desire. He tries to plump out the nipples with a syringe to make them more prominent, massages the generous outer curve to force more milk out, but it can't or won't come. In another age Heather would have died of malnutrition. Lydia gets rid of all of the old photos of her stage days, which display her boastful, prominent breasts, with their nipples pointing upwards, as high as the moon.

Lydia worries constantly, but perseveres. For five months Heather gets breast milk topped up with formula; but it's exhausting making time for getting her on the breast, then pumping, sterilising everything, starting all over again. But the day comes when Heather just wants the bottle, and she's left with breasts a little bigger, that sag as soon as she takes her bra off. And a little kickback, the layer of fat around her middle that materialised not during pregnancy but after she stopped breastfeeding. Now her curves are in danger of dragging her down, of pulling her centre of gravity through the floor.

Lydia longs for the time when she could spend three hours languidly getting ready for a show; now she's in and out of the shower as quick as she can scourge the shower gel off. Almost never gets the chance to dry her hair properly. She feels naked in the street without her carefully applied make-up, her raven tresses, but Ethan laughs off any insecurities.

'You look better without make-up, anyway. And we're saving a fortune on make-up!' He looks at her dead centre in the face, 'Anyway, we've got better things to think about.'

In the mirror she's not sure how she feels about her mommy face. It looks both older and younger at the same time. She's so tired there are permanent shadows under her eyes, but Heather brings her a kind of inner contentment that gives her a dreamy, far away look. Maybe she'll go back to her burlesque shows, perhaps she'll lose weight, but none of these things are possible, not yet. She is both the spirit of her old self and a new mother constantly melded with her child. Somewhere between the two lies her sensual self.

Now it feels different when Ethan touches her. All day she is attuned to Heather's possessive snuggling, to using her body as a big soothing bed of comfort. And she knows that for her child, every little part of her is magic; whether holding her hand, tugging at her hair, it's all manna. If Ethan pats a hand on her shoulder, it feels odd. She is now used to little people with quivery heartbeats. To sleep rather than talk. Her body is not automatically programmed for sensual response; when Ethan wants sex he has to try a little harder.

In her mind she's on stage again, the music playing her song. Her outfit has never been so skimpy and it feels as if she can feel the warm glow of the lights right through her corset. The audience is a dark insect blur that she doesn't so much see as feel. All eyes are on her, and her breasts are weightless. Her arms and legs move and twirl without stopping. For the refrain she does perfect high kicks that draw an appreciative roar. Although she's alone it feels like she's in the middle of a winning football crowd; everybody loves her. The energy runs right through her legs, tips her over with desire; she could just burn up.

When Ethan wakes her, he's no longer the doting Daddy. His eyes stare at her, feral and full of suppressed longing. He leads her downstairs to the bathroom, pushes her inside and locks the door.

Dozens of red rose petals float lazily in a warm bath and the room is awash with fragrant steam. Six scented candles glow with promise and two glasses of champagne froth and hiss on the side. Ethan smiles at her, places a comforting hand on her.

'I think you deserve some me-time in the bath.' Gently he takes off her night robe, nuzzles her shoulder, 'Let me help you to relax.' Lydia lets herself be undressed, led into the bath. When she sits down, her breasts float up and her tummy disappears under the water. It's such a luxury to just sit, be tended to. Between her thighs she feels pleasantly warm. Her pubic hair becomes slick and dark under the water. She splashes her already-cleaned face, lets the water trickle into all the areas of exposed flesh. Then she raises her legs a little so that Ethan can get a good look at exposed vagina, runs a hand over her breasts. With him standing outside the bath, she feels absolutely displayed, and completely desirable. Her curves fill out the confines of the bath.

Ethan hands her a glass of champagne, but kisses her forcefully before she can take a sip. Some of it falls into the bath. They both laugh.

'Down, boy,' she says, but he doesn't stop. His tongue reaches into her, hands pull at her hair. They kiss deeply, tongues exploring, doing their little dance. He's on his knees pushing his face onto hers. Ethan begins to pant. He stands up, and with one hand he undoes his jeans. His penis bobs up, absolutely hard, not over-long but pleasantly thick. She reaches out, touches it, feels for once as if she's one of the audience obsessed with another's sexual parts. She rubs her hand over the foreskin and starts to rock herself in the bath.

'Ah, ah …' Ethan is already moaning. Both of their nipples become hard, hot points. They're conscious of the spit in their mouths.

He stops her, pushes her back down. 'This is all about you,' he says. His eyes bore into hers, and gauge every reaction to his ministrations. With a firm hand he feels the outside of her breasts, cups under the generous flesh and rubs circles around her nipples. It's instantly pleasurable, and leaves her gasping, unexpectedly light-headed. She thinks he'll leave it there, but he moves on down, dabs into her now-larger belly button. Massages her tummy where she grew his child. There's not just raw desire between them but shared experience. Tonight she's his lover as well as his wife.

She sees in his eyes how much he's enjoying this. That nothing will stop him now. His eyes are open so wide he looks drugged. His hand goes down, splashes her a little as he hones in on her genital area. She's almost shaking when his finger finds its way between her legs, immediately pushes itself inside her.

'Ohh.' She immediately bucks, and bath water splashes everywhere as she tries desperately to get more of his fingers into her vagina. Her delicate inner skin, so traumatised by childbirth, is now even more sensitive and vital. He's building up a rhythm and she gasps while his penis presses uncomfortably into the side of the bath.

She's an amazing sight, out of control, thrashing in the water. He looks down at her, his eyes glistening with pleasure. His hand once more massages her stomach.

'Move your legs up high,' he says. 'I want to access all areas.' He arranges her so that he can put his face right down to the engorged lips of her vagina. Even the lips on her face are prickly with desire.

It's almost painful for her when his tongue replaces his fingers. Waves of pleasure ripple from her pelvic area down to her stomach. He spits out the taste of rose, concentrates on her blossoming clit. Now she's crying out. It's not the laps of his tongue that get her, but the warmth of his saliva trickling down rudely to her bum. She thrusts her open legs at his face, giving little cries of excitement. He buries his tongue in her clit while two fingers push relentlessly into her vagina. The pressure begins to mount in her pelvis, and she bucks her hips ever more wildly.

'Aahh ...' her cries fill the room. Her body is wracked by orgasm, her eyes wide open as if with shock, her nipples standing out; her hair sticks up where it has been splashed wet.

Ethan has never seen her so excited. He can bear the pressure in his penis no longer and stands up, crouches over her so that his penis is inches above her breasts. He notes they look even better now that the nipples have darkened post-pregnancy, now that he really knows them. Every part of her body reminds him of something they have experienced together.

Instinctively, he grips his penis; painstakingly, expertly works the shaft. Her nipples stand out, hard and brown above the water, enticing him to press his cock even harder. Deep down in his balls he can feel it coming, that rush of hot energy that engulfs.

'Oooh, ooohhhh!' As his orgasm hits, he aims for Lydia's breasts, and comes even harder when he sees the arc of come land thickly on one nipple and dribble all over the front of the beautiful breasts that he knows so well. It's a wonderful performance – and a very private one that only he can enjoy with his darling wife.

Private Dancer
by Portia Da Costa

The card on the little easel says 'Madame X'. The easel is vaguely familiar but the name isn't. It sets up the strangest little shiver in my imagination, an instant jolt of tightening in my loins. What's going on? What *is* this? I smile and sip my wine, waiting. Well, whatever it is, I think it's going to be interesting …

The wait isn't long, and she appears at the edge of the impromptu performance area like an image from a fantasy, a vision in blue. Her body is swathed in an enormous feather boa of midnight, sapphire and silver, and the delicate mass of feathers ripples and dances as she sashays forward, fluttering with every step, every breath. Then a familiar, brassy, stomping tune strikes up from the sound system, and she flings the marabou wide, exposing her costume and herself in all their glory.

I start back in my seat, almost choking on my wine, sideswiped by her magnificence.

She's a showgirl, a beautiful burlesque diva, an icon of glitz and kitsch and glamour, a figure both mysterious and brashly, openly available.

My dick's like a rod of iron in my pants.

Flirting with her boa, she circles her domain, owning it with every bump and sway of her hips, every salacious yet imperious glance in my direction. She's wearing a blue satin eye mask, in keeping with her ambiguous title, but her eyes are bright and direct and constantly on me as she moves. They glitter with all the fire of the sequins and sparkles that trim her mask, and every item of seductive clothing that graces her body.

No sylph is she. No willowy Las Vegas twenty year old. She's lush, ample, majestic. A banquet of gorgeous jiggling flesh that's both crammed into, and almost bursting out of, her fabulous costume. Her breasts nearly bounce out of her jewelled bra as she bumps and grinds, and her thighs are broad and inviting, gleaming tantalisingly beneath the fine casing of fishnet that both conceals and reveals them.

And her arse ... Oh, her *arse* ...

As she bends over, facing away from me, flirtatiously framing it in the boa as she glances suggestively over her shoulder back at me, it's all I can do not to surge up out my seat, plunge towards her, and grab those delicious rounds of flesh and squeeze them and handle them through her naughty ruffled panties.

I gulp down some of my drink, my heart thudding wildly, my cock thudding too.

Gyrating slowly, she turns towards me, then moves forward, jutting her hips with every step. Light seems to dance over her and shine from within her, shooting from every spangle and crystal on her blue silk bra, her hooked and laced waist cincher, and her frothy, frou-frou knickers. Boa dangling around her shoulders, she runs her fingertips up and down her arms, one after the other. The music pounds as she shows off, even *presents*, the spectacle of the shimmering satin gloves that embrace her fingers and forearms. She seems to intimate that she might remove them, gift me with the inestimable sight of her bare gleaming skin, but then she tilts her head imperiously, and gives it a shake as if to say, 'How dare you even dream something so outrageous?'

And instead she teases and taunts me with the boa.

First hiding her goodies with it. Then using it to exhibit them.

She drapes the soft, floating feathers over her shoulder, and teases it slowly, slowly over her corseted midriff, her breasts, her shoulders. It ripples like a cold, blue flame and my fingers tense, longing to be that boa gliding over her, enjoying the touch of her costume, her silky skin, her stupendous body.

As she shimmies, the feathers shimmy. I swear I nearly come in my shorts.

But there's more.

Staring into my eyes as she performs, she deliberately widens her stance, flicks the boa between her legs and slithers it back and forth, as if caressing her pussy with it. Her mischievous wink and the way she licks her glossy lips make me feel faint. Then, with a swirl of her hips, she whips out the fluffy, flirting length, and hurls it at me.

I'm amazed I can catch it. I'm amazed I can even think straight. It's like my vision's gone red with lust, and my mind has turned to mush. Literally moaning aloud, I cram the soft fluttering mass of feathers against my nose and inhale, desperate to draw in the scent of her sex. But all I get is a whiff of a familiar cologne, and an enormous tickle in my nostrils. As I sneeze violently, she breaks her persona for a moment and giggles behind her mask.

But then it's all business, and she's sliding her fingers up and down her gloves again, as if they're my cock and she's slowly taunting it. She exhibits them to me like the prize for my good behaviour … or maybe bad behaviour. Delicately teasing and tugging at each finger of her left hand, she eases the silken tube off her arm, her wrist. Tug, tug. Beat, beat. The instant it slips off her hand, she catches it, twirls it, and flings it to me, another trophy.

I'm in the middle of kissing it, and trying not to think about cramming it against my crotch, when she addresses the other glove, tweaking it off as saucily as the other, but this time tugging it with her teeth. Watching my eyes, watching my reaction, she twirls the glove, kissing a fingertip of her free hand, boo-boo-be-doo style. God almighty, she knows exactly what I'm thinking. The second glove comes sailing high, towards me, and she turns away, dipping in time to the slinky rhythms, and shimmies her frilly-pantied arse in my direction.

I'm almost beside myself. What will she do next? What will she take off? What will she keep on? How much can I take?

Strutting her stuff, she tantalises and taunts me, sliding her newly naked fingertips over her arms, her waist, her thighs. Her luscious flesh shudders as she shakes and rhythmically undulates, and I want to hurl myself into her sweet abundance and abandon my soul.

As the horns wail and the percussion thuds, she turns away from me again, glancing coyly and yet invitingly over her shoulder. She doesn't miss a beat as she manipulates her costume, and suddenly her waist-cincher is loose and she's sliding it to and fro, from side to side across her back like a bathing belle posing with her towel.

A flick, and another spin, and she's facing me again, holding the edges of the mini-corset, then flirting first one side of it open, then the other side, offering me glimpses of the milky, satiny skin of her delicious midriff.

With another enormous flourish, she throws it wide, her rib cage lifting to offer her breasts to me like juicy fruits in the cups of her glittering, sequinned bra.

And I'm hungry. I want those fruits. I want to rub my face between their abundant ample curves. God, I want to rub my cock there, I want to come on her lovely painted face and see pearls of my semen splatter her jammy lipstick and dangle on the ends of her enormously long false lashes.

Oh, baby, I think I'm starting to lose my mind!

I reach for my wine and realise I've drunk it, and I don't remember when.

The basque whirls towards me and lands at my feet.

Not long now … not long now …

I nearly shoot my load when she wiggles her bottom and reaches deftly for the catch of her bra.

And then it's tease, tease, tease …

She unfastens it, and lets it swing from her shoulders, and I catch my breath, and clutch my crotch with my fingers as I catch a glimpse of her splendid breasts swinging free. It's just a tiny flash of flesh, but it's enough to make me moan. Over her shoulder she smiles creamily, like a goddess.

Then while I'm still gasping, she performs a sensuous ripple with her entire body, throwing forward her chest and letting the spangled garment fall. It slides down her wrists, she flings it away, and throws her arms up in graceful triumph …

The Big Reveal!

Magnificent, her rounded breasts assault the very air, proud and full and tipped with twin, glittering circles, blue jewelled pasties. Intellectually, my brain knows what these little bits of burlesque nonsense are called, but the knowledge is in a corner, inconsequential, not part of the rampaging howl of lust that fires my blood.

She stands there, her pose perfection, her masked expression arch and all powerful, her rounded limbs a poem, her belly and bosom luscious and fecund. My mouth drops open, my hand tightens on my groin. I just can't help but squeeze myself. It's several moments before I realise the music is over.

Her arms drop slowly, her hands soft, the lowering like a ballerina, a swan queen. My throat is tight and I almost feel tears in my eyes. I'm totally in awe of her.

'I think you've got most of my costume … do you think I could have it back?'

Her breathing is a little uneven – the dance was strenuous, after all – but the huskiness speaks of a different energy, or maybe the same one, quite undiminished. I walk towards her, but she doesn't reach for the boa and the cincher and the gloves …

She just reaches for me, her eyes dark and fiery behind her mask.

And then we're kissing. Messily. Hungrily. I'm aware that I'm ruining her gorgeous make-up but I don't care and neither does she seem to. She devours me as savagely as I devour her. My hands crush her almost-bare breasts, the sequins and crystals on the pasties digging into my palms. The sharp

96

sensation only adds spice and strangeness to holding her glorious, generous, familiar flesh.

Moaning in her throat she grinds her pelvis against me, using the movements of her routine to arouse me with touch now, as well as sight. I'm beyond control and I want her in a way that defies reason. She understands this, and reaches down to unzip my flies. I sob when she takes me in hand rubs me against the pretty blue ruffles of her flirtatious panties. We struggle. We rock. We grapple with her clothes and mine. Those saucy showgirl knickers are snug, and beneath them are fishnet tights, even snugger.

'How the fuck are we going to do this?'

Like an adolescent confronted with his first ever set of female underwear I tug at the ruffles and the tights, almost choking with the blind desire to bare her and plunge into her.

She just laughs and, pushing me lightly away, she effects another elegant heel pivot, and bends with grace and a cheeky grin over the back of an armchair. Then, with apparently no effort at all, she slips down the panties and the tights and parts her thighs just enough for me to enter.

And enter I do, like an express train, powering into her beloved pussy from behind, groaning aloud at the heat and wetness of her welcome. She's so ready for me, aroused as much as I am by her dance.

I fight for control. I fight to remember my own name. I fight my own desire just to fuck and fuck and fuck and, thinking of her, I slip my hand around and across her belly to find her mound. She's shaven, more or less, so no stray little pubes could peek out of her costume, I suppose, and slipping in between her thighs my finger instantly finds her clit.

She bucks and howls now. So ready. So hungry. So quick, quick, quick to climax under me. I shove and thrust. I jerk and heave. I come, half blind with love as she ripples and ripples and comes around me.

'Oh my love,' I gasp and empty myself inside her.

A while later, it still feels like a bomb's dropped and we're stretched out on the carpet naked, bits of costume scattered around us.

'So, how did you like your birthday present, Mr Curtis?' Susan says pertly, running her fingertip suggestively round the areola of one of her nipples. The surrounding skin is slightly pink, and she idly picks off a bit of rubber adhesive from the rosy flesh.

'You were sensational, Mrs Curtis,' I growl at her. 'Although, I must admit this wasn't exactly what I imagined when you said you were taking a dance class.'

'Well, it was either this, or yogic-dance or keep fit for the over-forties …' Her hand strays again towards my cock, which seems to have absorbed some of her energy and staying power and is well on the way to a stiffy again, '... but I thought that Burlesque for Beginners would be much more fun … for both of us.'

My hips start to move of their own accord, rising to her hold on me. I can't exactly rock them with the grace and elegance that she possesses, but what I lack in finesse I certainly make up for in raw enthusiasm.

While both of us laugh again, I shimmy into place … and we bump and grind.

Laura The Laugher
by Jeremy Edwards

The plush seat of the nightclub chair felt physically seductive to Regina. Yet even as her bum sank comfortably into luxury – a relief after a day spent running all over campus – she was acutely aware of her psychological discomfort. Why the editor of the university newspaper had sent her to interview a 'neo-burlesque' star was a mystery but, whatever the reason for the decision, the assignment was a keen source of irritation for Regina.

She was by no means a prude. She acknowledged her own urges, and when they became distracting she addressed them, effectively and expeditiously. But she dismissed any larger fascination with sex just as easily as she dismissed all other forms of frivolity.

Frivolity. Regina cringed as she remembered that not only was her interviewee a specialist in titillation, but her act actually revolved around *jokes*, of all things. She glanced once more at the blurb she'd printed out from the web:

Laura the Laugher is a Neo Burlesque star whose speciality is erotically-charged laughter. In a twist on the historical marriage of comedic and erotic elements in burlesque, Laura has created an act in which the laughter becomes *the sex ...*

What the hell was that about? Regina couldn't fathom it and she doubted that sitting through Laura's act would enlighten her any further. If it weren't for her sense of obligation to her editor – and the indisputably nice feeling of the chair against her rump – she'd be tempted to bolt and forget the whole thing. She consoled herself with the thought that Laura the Laugher was on first, so all she had to do was survive one stupid performance, conduct a bare-bones interview, and flee.

She looked around at the other members of the audience. The club was nearly full, which she had to admit was remarkable for a Thursday night. Apart from those at her own table – a good one, thanks to her press pass – almost every chair was taken, as were the majority of the bar stools. And almost every face seemed to be alive with anticipation. People were even dressed up, though not in the way Regina was dressed up; greyly professional in deference to being 'on assignment'. This silly event was being treated as some kind of important night out, she realised, with a touch of incredulity.

She took a sullen sip of her ginger ale and occupied herself by mentally scoring the piped-in light classical music. Soon the house fixtures dimmed, the light classical became lighter and lighter until it was inaudible and a sort of gloaming established itself on-stage.

Regina saw two male forms, crisp silhouettes in the near darkness, float in from the respective wings. The shadows stood still, faintly whimsical in their silhouetted bowler hats. Impressed by the drama, Regina forgot her disdain for a moment. A slender spotlight, an oval the colour of watermelon flesh, suddenly illuminated the centre of the stage from its front edge to the hefty purple curtain at the back. A gap developed in this curtain, through which walked – no, emerged – the most self-possessed woman Regina had ever seen.

Laura the Laugher.

She looked fancier in her near-nudity than most women looked in ballroom gowns. The two-piece silk outfit that glimmered around her breasts and hips – it seemed too grand to be called a bikini – was two or three shades of watermelon deeper than the empty areas of the spotlight, a colour which would probably fall somewhere between 'flamingo' and 'vulva' on the Dulux chart. Hundreds of individual pieces of silk had been sewn intricately together to form the garment, mimicking the texture of feathers and creating a ticklish effect for the observer.

But Regina wasn't ticklish.

Laura, her stance at once statuesque and soft, turned to the left and to the right, taking in the still-shadowy male figures at each end of the stage. Her sensuous shoulderfuls of dark hair were paraded as she glanced each way and the pink spotlight caught the sweet outline of her pixie-esque nose. Then she faced forward, her eyes absurdly, but beautifully, large with promise. And she laughed – a merry trill.

It was quite brief, but it rang across the room and sizzled down Regina's spine, coming to rest at the small of her back. Laura followed it with an even briefer trill, and Regina found her buttocks shifting involuntarily. She felt embarrassed … yet curious. What was funny? And why did the pretty, irrelevant laughter seem to resonate with every cocktail glass and beer bottle in the nightclub – and with Regina's bones?

A warm male voice from stage right broke into her thoughts.

'Did you hear the one about the bed?'

'No,' said a similar voice from stage left, perhaps half a key higher. 'It hasn't been made up yet.'

It wasn't very amusing, but Laura pretended it was. An emphatic 'a-HA-ha-ha-ha-ha-ha' burst from her lips – as though the gag had surprised her, despite hours of rehearsals – and the spotlight intensified slightly. Laura's cheeks glowed a bit brighter and the tight skin of her tummy looked scrumptious where she pressed it with delicate fingertips. A subdued wave of sympathetic chuckling surrounded Regina as the audience laughed, not with the two-dimensional comedians, but with the three-dimensional goddess at centre stage. The ambient laughter was heavy and sexy, like sticky limbs awakening on an August morning.

The sweet kiss of ginger ale tingled in Regina's mouth, a

pleasant disorientation.

'What's the tallest building in town?' This time it was Stage Left Man who served the ball into play.

'The library, 'cause it has the most stories.'

Laura's face lit up with delight: 'Ha-ha-HA-ha-HA-ha-ha-ha-ha-ha!' As before, the pink light intensified and a shiver of glee coursed through Laura's torso, visibly travelling from her throat to her navel.

A shiver coursed through Regina as well, and lodged between her legs. Again, the room murmured with collective chuckling. As it tapered off, Regina thought she heard one or two stifled moans. She felt her clit give a twinge.

'Why did the turkey cross the road?'

'Because it was the chicken's day off.'

Laura bent her knees, then slapped them with mirth, shimmying very subtly as the laughter rippled through her. 'Oooh-hee-hee-hee-hee!' she sang, each syllable a precious comment. The spotlight flashed in her cleavage like cartoon lightning and Regina saw the Laugher's pink-feather breasts vibrate with the dignity of minor planets. 'Ooh-hee-hee,' Laura reiterated, as if summarizing. Her eyes danced; and when they refocused, they seemed to be staring right at Regina.

Regina felt as if one more 'hee' would make her soak her panties.

Regina felt that maybe there was something to this, after all.

Regina waited breathlessly for the next joke.

'If two's company, and three's a crowd, what are four and five?'

'Nine.'

Laura's knee-bend was a deep one this time; a display of flexibility that looked raunchy as hell in combination with the expression of uncontrollable ecstasy on her face.

'Eeeeeeeeeeeeeee-hee-hee-hee-hee-hee-hee –' she shrieked – indefinitely, it seemed to Regina, who only realised that one cascade of laughter had ended because another, equally intense, began.

'Eeeeeeeeeeeeeee –' Laura stamped her feet, folded her arms across her chest and writhed in a sultry, slow rhythm that formed the perfect counterpoint to the frenetic sixteenth notes of her giggles. Regina felt hypnotized by the sound and by the fascinating motion of Laura's hips, where the corporeal echoes of the laughter appeared to be most concentrated.

The corny riddles came faster and faster, and Laura would break up at the next one just as she'd disembarked from the previous crescendo. Each burst of delight was delivered with exquisite artistry and musical precision by every muscle of her highly-trained body: she stalked and danced, tittered and howled, her entire form expressing the eclectic rapture that was her stock in trade. When an invisible stagehand pushed a plush-seated stool through the curtain, Laura, amid a particularly strong gale of laughter, spun it around like a partner, then straddled it lewdly as she bounced through the final paroxysms of her gust of jollity. When she stood, Regina strained her eyes to see if the velvety fabric on the stool showed signs of the wetness that she imagined was developing in the crotch of Laura's silk knickers.

Regina's interview stockings seemed to crawl on her thighs like snakeskin waiting to be slowly shed. Her pussy was a vortex of sensation and she knew that if she were at home it would be one of those evenings when she'd thrust a hand into her panties in a businesslike fashion and fondle her clit into an explosion. And that it would be satisfying in a not-very-satisfying kind of way.

But she wasn't at home; what she was feeling was anything but businesslike; and her clit, removed from all direct contact save the half-hearted tension of underpants, was getting the fondle of its life from a stranger on a stage. And Regina knew that she wanted to watch Laura laugh until the beautiful performer came like a hyena in heat.

By the end, Regina wasn't even hearing the riddles, though they were no doubt articulated with perfect clarity. She had learned that it didn't matter what the joke was – that all that mattered, in fact, was that the joke be a weak one, so as to ensure that the bumper crop of erotic laughter would be purer than any prompted by a spark of actual wit. Laura's laughter was a freebie, an act of generosity, a reward for nothing. It crossed Regina's mind that many a theatrical producer would have loved to have Laura in the audience – except that then the audience would have taken notice only of the Laugher, and not of the play.

For her grand finale – triggered by yet another stale punchline that Regina ignored – Laura rolled on the ground in a full-fledged frenzy of artistic giggles. Then, situating herself with her lovely tummy to the floor and her silk-sheathed arse gleaming in the spotlight, she hammered her fists to underscore peal after sturdy peal. To top this, she flipped over and spread her arms, kicking her sleek, bare legs in the air and making herself a kinetic portrait of wide-open womanhood. As Laura's laughter shouted itself to the ceiling and down again, her crotch became the electric centre of Regina's attention. Still remaining on her back, Laura now switched from a kicking to a pedalling motion, working her limbs like an inverted, hilarity-drenched clown on a unicycle, her feathered gusset anchoring the action of the surrounding flesh. Her wild, giddy voice carried with it every other voice in the room – including Regina's. Together, all present comprised a sea of euphoria, an ocean held in place by a palpable sexual tautness.

Then the Laugher jumped to her feet, a woman composed and in control. She bowed like an orchestra conductor and disappeared behind her curtain.

The laughter in the room was overtaken by applause. The comical shadows made discreet exits and the house lights went up. Regina gasped when she found she was alone again – and she had never been so aroused in her life.

When she'd arrived, the management had shown her which door to proceed through after Laura's act in order to keep her interview appointment in the dressing room. While other patrons moved casually toward the bar or the toilets Regina rushed in the opposite direction as desperately as if she were trying to catch a train.

'Best I've ever seen from her,' she heard someone say as she hurried past.

She flashed her press pass at the hipster who sat on a stool in the corridor, breathing one burning word out to him: 'Laura.'

He nodded to the left, toward a black door set into a black wall.

'She just flew by ten seconds ago. Probably had to pee.'

Regina blushed, daring to hope that the stagehand had correctly read Laura's urgency – but incorrectly read its cause. In her imagination it was nothing as biologically mundane as an eager bladder that had sent Laura rocketing into the privacy of her dressing room in the wake of her onstage exhilaration. Regina wanted to know that Laura, hyper-alive and trembling from her performance, was one giggle away from a thunderous orgasm, and that the Laugher had raced to her dressing room to bring it upon herself without further delay.

As she navigated past the hipster she was then suddenly afraid that Laura would be doing precisely what she hoped, but that she herself would be excluded: locked out, her interview relegated to the lobby and its subject cool and professional, fifteen minutes hence … when nothing would matter any more. Feeling a need that scurried from her pussy to her knuckles she rapped hungrily on Laura's door.

The hesitation was brief, but Regina thought she could discern the noises of slick digits being extricated and elastic snapping back into place.

'Come in.'

It startled her to realise that, until now, she hadn't heard Laura speak – only laugh. Did she imagine it, or did even the polite neutrality of Laura's voice come in echo with teasing titters?

The dressing room was femininely fragrant. Regina might have feared that it was her own beseeching scent that coloured the atmosphere, giving her away; but this was a sweeter, rounder aroma than her sharp, familiar tang. Unsure of her words, she could only chuckle foolishly.

Laura smiled from her seat at the make-up table and chuckled back. The vibrato played on Regina like a thousand intimate, exploratory fingers.

'We have an interview scheduled, yes?'

Regina nodded. 'Is – is this a bad time?'

The star smiled again, this time as if at some secret joke. She shook her head to dismiss Regina's concerns.

'Please don't mind if I'm a bit – keyed up. It's always that way after a performance.'

'I guess it would be,' said Regina. The essence of Laura's pussy was making her dizzy.

The Laugher's bum shifted on its seat, the silk feathers on the hips fluttering under the fluorescent lights.

And Regina lost it.

'Can I touch you?'

Laura's eyebrows went up a fraction of an inch.

'Oh my God.' Regina felt as if she were choking. 'I'm sorry. I'm –'

But her hostess cut her off with a laugh – a large, loud, Laura laugh, which knocked Regina down to her knees with her hands clasped between her legs. Her reporter's notebook dropped to the floor, forgotten.

Laura laughed anew – more delicately, so that it felt like a kiss. And Regina watched Laura's hand stray to the most alluring point on her shimmering stage knickers, where it teased the ripe plumpness.

Then Laura stood. She walked gracefully toward Regina and squatted effortlessly in front of the journalist, her muscular thighs bouncing lightly.

'You made my show, reporter. Sitting there all alone with your cute little notebook and your ginger ale … front and centre, looking so out of place.'

Regina felt naked. She blushed a blush even deeper than before.

'Did you sense me playing to you tonight? Straight to you, only to you?' Laura punctuated these questions with mellifluous, tinkling giggles, and the questions seemed to require no other answer from either of them.

The star's hand drifted to the front of her confection-pink knickers again.

'When I won you over, my sweetie, I thought I was going to come right there, on stage.'

Regina whimpered. She clutched the dampness under her skirt.

'I saved it for you,' Laura said gently, as she took Regina's free hand and placed it where she needed it. Laura's next laugh was impossibly soft, more a coo than a chortle.

'Can you feel how close I am?'

As Regina stroked the wet silk, Laura's laughter became richer, and soon the small room reverberated with her bliss. Regina noted that the other woman's ticklishness was psychological, not physical: when the hand that pleasured her went beneath the feathers, the laughter artist's flesh remained stable, churning with a controlled rhythm rather than the quivering chaos that Regina was experiencing from her own touch. The Laugher's wetness was a warm comfort to the reporter's fingers. Regina felt herself floating in the smell of Laura's arousal, in the magic of Laura's increasingly excited trills. She had looked lost, Laura had said; and lost was exactly how she felt now, only in a wonderful way – lost like a tourist who knows that some bright adventure is around every confusing corner. Exploring the unseen territory within the performer's cunt, Regina was high on the thrill of bringing the soap bubbles of Laura's laughter up from the cauldron of her privacy, her clumsy fingers agents of glistening ecstasy. Each stroke seemed to elicit a new river of glee, as if the Laugher were a wellspring whence came a hundred flavours of joy. And touching Laura's clit seemed to make all the flavours flow at once.

'Oo-EEE-hee-hee-hee . . .'

When Laura's entire body began shaking, she had to hold Regina by the wrist to keep her hand from losing contact. Laura's eyes were even more brilliant than they'd been in the watermelon spotlight and her gaping, laughing mouth was the sexiest thing Regina had ever been close to.

'Oo-EEE-hee-hee-HEEEEEEEEEEEE . . .'

Regina was barely aware of her other hand, the one that was jammed into her own drenched panties, until it dutifully showed her the reflection of Laura's climax. And she felt even more like a tourist upon realising she'd never known what a really good orgasm was. Her legs felt as if they'd ejected themselves from her stockings, and the hard floor of the dressing room caressed her bottom like the softest of chairs. Between her thighs was an oven of happiness; she wrapped her whole being around it as its radiance painted her, inch by inch.

She closed her eyes as Laura kissed her. For several seconds a delicious mixture of satisfaction and hunger ate at her lips. Then she recognized that something was being pressed into her hand. Her notebook.

She opened her eyes just as Laura was beginning to laugh again.

'Now I'm afraid I don't have time for the interview.'

Regina's face broke into the relaxed smile of someone who definitely didn't give a flying fuck on a unicycle about any interview.

'You'll have to come back tomorrow, OK?' The Laugher stood up, adjusted her knickers and gave a practice shimmy, silk feathers dancing across her hips, bringing each one to life like a hopeful clitoris.

That night, Regina laughed herself to sleep in the dark.

The Rebirth Of Venus
by Christiana Spens

Victoria sat in a dark corner of Soho, slightly hidden in an alleyway from the neon and the strangers who flooded by in their frantic sway to tunes of sleaze, caught up in crimes to shock and mock and tease.

'Do you work here?' a man asked, pointing to the gutter by way of euphemism.

'No, I play here,' she said, signalling the guitar she held in her right hand, and he walked on by in search of other entertainments.

Busking had its drawbacks but it wasn't a bad way to watch the world spin by. She started playing some more, noticing the sky deepen greyer with rain clouds, threatening to drench the already-damp Dean Street, its sodden debauchery rising like steam, a cold autumnal breeze disturbing the heady fumes of waiting cars, steamy kitchens and smoke of cigarettes and herbs and drugs, all mixing into the proud and decadent airs and breaths and sighs of sultry Soho.

Victoria took a deep breath and sang it all back: lyrics melted into the soul of the place and the tune floated like ash in the wind.

Edward was leaning on a doorframe across the road and the song woke him from a mid-afternoon slumber. He was smoking on the edge of Old Compton Street, a little drunk, but fully aware of the girl with red Pre-Raphaelite hair and a guitar, a black ribbon tied round her neck, pale skin and a soulful voice, an expression so vacant it could mean anything: a face good for playing poker and playing dead, playing sweet and playing sad.

He finished his cigarette and lit another, listening all the while and watching, hoping to be noticed but not. After another cigarette he walked over to her as she finished her little version of *Rock 'n' Roll Suicide*.

Edward didn't know what to say, being less a speaker, more a looker. A painter with pretty eyes, beauty was his currency and his cause: small change, also.

He dropped a five-pound note into her trilby – she smiled, slouched back against the wall of a pub and said, 'Thank you'.

'You should have a garter to tuck that into.'

'Is Bowie such a turn-on?'

'It's not the song, it's the lips.'

She smiled again. She hadn't meant to serenade him but it was working anyway.

'Do you sing anywhere else or is the gutter your only gig?' he asked.

'I'm singing at a burlesque night tonight, actually.' She had a young but husky voice; a voice against the elements and an early preference for Marlboros, not lollipops.

'Can I come?' he asked.

'Yeah but I'll want more than a fiver for that.'

He fell for the tease; she handed him a flyer. Five hours later he was there.

Bethnal Green Working Men's Club: bingo in the room downstairs and stripping by the bar … entertainment for all the family.

When Edward wandered into the dimly-lit dive he looked around for that girl. She wasn't there and the shadows were instead inhabited by groups of the strange and the beautiful, the kinky and the coy. He went to the bar for whisky and kept looking around, curiously and childishly. The show started: sleaze and tease; tall hats and short skirts, nipple tassels and coquettish eyes, corseted busts and abandoned rules. Dancers appeared and disappeared, hid and revealed, danced and entranced …

And then at last the red-haired girl entered and took the stage and sang her sultry song. Cabaret, this time, more excuse to pout and move and seduce the room. Edward moved closer to the stage and watched her lips move. She was kissing her song and her audience's vanity, whispering dirty secrets into the twilight zones of their imaginations.

And then she was gone – with a smile and applause and a coy sharp exit – and it was dark again. Edward wanted more. He was too distracted to notice the opening of the next act, 'The Rebirth of Venus', a girl dancing behind a giant oyster shell, slowly moving, stripping to the sultry song with long golden hair and an ethereal presence. As she stripped the girl with red hair emerged at the back of the room. Venus's twin; a black ribbon around her neck again, wearing a wraparound dress of pale cream silk with little saffron-coloured flowers and green leaves sewn into the fabric. Her cream kitten heels were trimmed with pale blue satin and a gold bracelet was on her right wrist; there was an orchid in her hair. She looked as if she had wandered in lost from another age.

'You came?'

'Couldn't help it.'

She smiled naughtily with darker eyes.

Not far away, the Venus stripped bare behind her oyster shell, teasing the audience with her smile divine and white breasts and soft eroticism. Edward handed Victoria a glass of wine and watched as she sipped it, unwittingly falling for an age-old trap as she fell for a new one. She had never been with an artist before.

The night was young, foolish and impressionable, as were Victoria and Edward, who left the burlesque night not long after a scantily-clad Venus disappeared into the oblivion of a blackout and a kiss became a touch became a pull to a quick exit. They kissed on the way to the tube, too long so it had already closed by the time they reached the station. It was cold but Victoria didn't feel it, her body warm with excitement and lust, her surroundings forgotten on account of the night's distracting delirium; Edward's hand slipped into her dress and she pulled him closer and kissed him more intensely as he pressed against her, touching her breasts then her hair, hidden in another alleyway not so different from the one in which they had met. Delirious with affection and each touch stimulating and stronger; even the dry air and sirens of the East End failed to penetrate their private intoxication.

After some time forgotten, Edward pulled Victoria back into the night and cold breezes, slightly cooling her flushed cheeks, and he hailed a cab.

Edward's flat was closer and emptier than Victoria's. Paintings and photographs were propped up against the walls: nudes and lovers and sensations obscure; people caught up in colourful misdemeanours; drinkers, criminals and suicides; girls quiet in trappings of liberty and prostitution, serving cruel attentions but painted with a compassionate gaze.

Edward was an unknown artist, young and spontaneous, insecure as he was proud, but with no problems in expressing every desire and distress and delight. He had brown hair, messy but stylish, an athletic body and the glow of one who runs fast and kisses well.

Inside the flat Victoria kissed him again, then smiled and sat down on his sofa, suddenly shy, it seemed, or provocatively restrained; it was hard to tell. Edward followed her pace and rolled a joint. Victoria watched the delicate flame light up the dim room. They smoked together and she asked about his pictures.

'Who's this?'

It was his ex-girlfriend but he said, 'A friend.'

'Do all your friends pose nude for you?'

'Only my best friends.'

'Can I be your new best friend?'

He laughed and said, 'Yeah I'd love you to.'

He passed the joint to her but she put it down on the edge of an ashtray and sat on his lap instead, kissing him again, high and placid, sexual and controlled. Where Edward had first seen innocence now he felt experience; where he had first seen beauty, now, in each movement, he felt brutality; and where her face, so pale and young, had met him with a child's gaze, now those dark eyes looked down on him disaffectedly. She was easy but she had a hard look. With each touch and kiss he felt he knew her less, because actually he didn't know her at all.

She unfastened his belt as he untied the ribbons that held her dress together. The fabric fell to her sides to reveal her naked breasts, pale skin, rose nipples and soft shoulders. She moved down his body as she pulled his clothes off and started kissing him there, her tongue teasing him then commanding him then controlling each movement, the arch of his back and the frantic movement of his hand in her hair –

She stopped and looked up at him and said, low and softly, 'Don't touch my hair', then started sucking him again, enjoying the taste and his warmth and his body moving with her pace and her kiss and her strength as she lost herself in the rhythm, rubbing him softly then harder as he started to moan, his head back, his hands tense and strong as he gripped her breasts and squeezed her left nipple as she sucked harder and he came and came and she swallowed, content in the way his body suddenly calmed and his skin was softer and damper, and he held her closely and kissed her, abandoned.

He kissed her breasts then moved down, feeling her waist and her hips and his hand between her thighs. She was wet and open as he rubbed her, gently at first; but she wanted it deeper so he got rougher, and she sighed happily and her back arched. He started kissing her, holding her down as ecstatically she sighed, his lips coated in her, his mind obsessed with each sensation, each second and each sigh as she lost control to him, moisture pouring as if tears or blood or wine. He was hard again and climbed on top of her, his hands feeling her arse and her waist as she pulled his head into her breasts. He fell under her control again, feeling more subservient as she wrapped her leg around him, and he forgot himself, fingering her again as she moaned, coming, and held him closer and harder, and he slipped inside her, fucking her hard and then harder, his hand grasping her breasts then her face and mouth, pressing into her, lost in his ecstasy, lost in her, as he came again and her eyes closed and she smiled and held him and he wrapped himself around her and blacked out into her darkness.

The next morning, when Edward awoke, Victoria was already up. She was naked and standing next to him with a cup of tea.

'Milk and sugar?'

'Sugar, just half …'

He was tired and happy. The light that poured in was bright and harsh, consuming his room. He lay back and remembered the night before, looking at Victoria's pale body and red hair still tied up, and a black ribbon still around her neck, looking serene and sexual at once: easy and restrained, open and closed, new and yet familiar. And then it occurred to him that he didn't even know her name.

He didn't ask her until much later, after he had photographed her lying on his bed, her expression still serene, her look still dirty, her body still sweet.

He asked for her phone number and pretended he didn't know how to spell her name. She looked at him with her inviting, daring, insolent eyes and an almost smile:

'O. L. Y. M. P. I. A.'

Olympia stayed forever in the prison of a frame and Victoria left her there, a picture of Edward's fantasy and her own, in search of a new picture, this time of her own making – a muse to put in her own frame, an affair to immortalise, and people to set free.

Titillation
by Alcamia

When Madame Satie introduced me to the Hot Kookie Bazoukie Crew, the girls all stared at my third nipple. A few of them asked to touch it, and I presented it to them in my cupped hand like a pet. I couldn't wait to feel so many fingers stroking and palpating.

My third nipple is like the switch to my sensuality, directly wired to the pleasure centre between my legs. Fondling this nipple agitates my clit and the harder the playfulness, the more I echo with sexual pleasure. My third nipple is so much more alive than my other two, as if all their sensitivity has been condensed into this one small fulcrum of delight. The girls love to play with it, and some even pounce on it with their lips and tongues. I never find that offensive, because I enjoy it so much. All of us girls are the same. Within the Hot Kookie Bazoukie Crew we share a secret sisterhood, and it's all about the breast.

When I was young I hid the nipple beneath baggy clothing and I forged notes for PE so that none of the girls would see it. But, of course, they did, and I was ribbed like mad. I affected a nonchalant air, though, because I knew I was different, and they would never know the depths of pleasure I experienced beneath my clothes. Boys would whisper about me, staring and pointing, and the first shivers of satisfaction from the caress of the male eye began.

Later, I would stand outside Satie's burlesque school

quivering with erotic excitement, hoping that one day Satie would notice me. She possessed the faded elegance and allure of a bygone age with her thick waved hair, bustle at her back and indecently large breasts, cleavage dotted with heart-shaped beauty spots. She was a perverse burlesque hybrid, tainted with nuances of both the gothic and Mother Earth. I loved what she represented to me – a hurly-burly, sexually-liberated creature.

Her burlesque troupe drew huge audiences. Curious women with desires they were too afraid to express at home, but which they loved to see acted out by the bold actresses on stage. And men. Because men have always been enamoured of the breast. What man does not want to fondle and suck and fecklessly cuddle against those warm, responsive pillows?

Satie's students were of all shapes and sizes, but they had one thing in common; they were chosen by Satie for their fabulous 'breastfulness' and bubbling, punchy attitudes. It was extremely rare to be chosen for the Hot Kookie Bazoukie Crew because Satie only took girls who met her exacting standards – they had to have outrageous baps.

One day I followed her inside the theatre, which serves as both the Hot Kookie Bazoukie school and the venue for its performances, and I hid behind the curtains. Constructed in the 1880s, the old theatre possessed a brooding atmospheric intensity, as if all the sexual vibrations and essences of masturbating men and women had seeped and been absorbed into the floors and seating. It was personal and small and the tables reached right up to the stage so that the girls could interact with the patrons. I was impressed by the rich red faded carpets and upholstery and the aromas of decay, perfume and women, and I stood in the darkness intoxicated, watching the girls on stage doing high kicks and balancing acts on chairs, while Satie rustled up and down the stage, shouting orders. The variety of bosoms intrigued me. From the hard white porcelain eggshells of China Doll to Madame Africa's entrancing ebony beauties, which gleamed like cocoa beans, the theatre was a shrine to the lustrous 'breastfulness' of women everywhere. After that, I followed Satie in whenever I could manage it, standing, mouth agape, in the shadows.

One day, though, I wasn't careful enough, and Satie crept up behind me and smacked my hands away from under my panties.

'Oh I thought it was you again,' she said. 'Really if you must be a voyeur, be more open about it. After all, there's nothing to be ashamed of. It's simply titillation.' I stared, entranced, as her bosom swelled up like a balloon from her tight corset, exposing a crescent of nipple. She was invulnerable to any self-consciousness.

'I can dance and I have a secret,' I said boldly.

'Oh, really? And what's so special about your bazoukies that makes you think I'd even consider them?'

'I'll show you,' I retorted, reaching down to unbutton my blouse.

'No, darling. Come along tomorrow night before the show and we will see.'

The next day, when I tapped on the dressing room door, Antoine opened it. Antoine was Satie's dresser and shadow. He was a violently sensual man with hooded eyes and the sinuous flexibility of a salsa dancer. Satie was sitting at the mirror studying herself closely, her infamous breasts hanging pendulously from her kimono. They were huge, tight and globular, with bright pink nipples. She was exploring herself with the same intent concentration with which I explored my own nipple and clit, running her hands over her voluptuous body.

'What do you think, darling? They're not as fabulous as Mirabelle's, are they?'

This was true. Mirabelle's specimens entranced me. One was like a huge, oversized teardrop and the other so small and perfect it was like that of a girl in the first days of womanhood. Satie gripped her breast and the nipple expanded in her hand.

'No two sides of the body are ever exactly the same,

darling. But such differences make women unique, don't you think? Perfection's so boring.' She continued to squeeze the breast as if weighing it. Then, tearing her gaze away from herself, she glanced at me. 'Right, doll. Take off your clothes and let me see this secret.'

I felt a savage, throbbing hunger clutch at my pussy as I gazed at Satie's bosoms and thought about the unveiling of the nipple. But my wild exhilaration was tempered by a peculiar erotic fear. Antoine stood in the corner of the room, watching me silently, as if presenting a challenge. The movement of his eyes over my skin, tangible to my flesh, was like a fuse to touch-paper, triggering the nipple, causing the clit to clamour in response. It was as if Antoine knew the power he had over the breast. He parted his feminine lips and his tongue flicked out to touch his perfect cupid's bow. I wanted to devour him and have him devour me. The fact he was witness to the unveiling of the nipple filled me with a quivering excitement. But I also felt captive, suddenly, in the small room, and I backed towards the door. Antoine ran to it, pressing against it to prevent me leaving, pushing me away with his hand, his fingers purposefully pressing my breasts. I stood glaring at him, attracted to him.

'Antoine will just stand there until you show me,' Satie said. 'Hurry up, or I shall be late on stage. In twenty years of performing I have never been late for a show.'

I stared Antoine in the eye, my arousal making me bold. My fingers fumbled with my buttons and one popped free and bounced across the floor. Satie stood up, the kimono falling from her shoulders. Now she was stark naked and, reaching forward, she felt under my blouse and grasped my breasts fiercely in her hands, her fingers tracing my areola. Instantly, I felt them respond, leaping, firming, a concentric heat sparking as she found the third nipple, above my breasts and slightly to the right, and circled it.

Satie's pink tongue moved restlessly around her lips. 'Oh! What have we here?' She pressed closer to me, breast to breast, and she lifted and peeled the blouse from my shoulders.

'Ooh, you are so wonderful, darling. Let me feel you all over. Ah, you are so firm and warm, just like a pillow. I could lay my head on you. I could lay my mouth next to the hot part of you.' Then she giggled. 'But, really, you are much better than a pillow.' And I felt her warm fingers under my skirt, against my stockings, rising up my thigh; a gentle form of titillation which left me breathless with warm desire – not the same kind of desire as that for a man, but desire nonetheless. I had never felt attracted to a woman before, yet the thrill of my 'coming out,' and Antoine's voyeuristic presence, added to the excitement. Satie expertly palpated my breasts, a little in the manner of a medical examination, but much more sensually, and Antoine studied the performance with his erect penis clearly visible through his pants.

'So, you have three nipples darling. How delicious! And such a nipple it is, it's splendid. You are perfect.' Evidently, she could feel the alert response of the third nipple, for she added, 'How curious! This third nipple seems to have much more personality than the others!'

I am glad Satie was the one I unveiled to, because she understood the complexities of the nipple. She kissed me on my closed lips, but it was not the kiss of a lover but a fellow conspirator. When she stepped back I felt a shiver of surprise to see her arousal, her huge taut, pink breasts and moist gaping sex. She tweaked my nipple in a gesture of farewell.

'You'll do marvellously, darling. Antoine can paint an eye or something pretty around it. Does it not ignite you, darling? Oh, I can tell it does. You're shivering. Is that because Antoine is looking at you so lasciviously?'

She turned to Antoine. 'She has the most extraordinary prominence, doesn't she, Antoine? Show him the tit properly, darling.'

I boldly thrust out my breasts and Antoine, in the manner of a spider capturing a fly, darted forward and seized on the nipple, fastening his lips around it and sucking it greedily.

Satie laughed. 'It makes him feel horny. I think we must call you Lady Titillation. You will need special costumes and

119

an act designed to arouse, and most certainly you must have the nipple pierced to give Antoine more to play with.' I saw a salacious glaze appear in Antoine's eyes and I didn't know whether to be aroused or repulsed. Personally, I was astounded by his ribald behaviour.

'You are luscious,' he whispered, pressing his mouth hard to the third nipple, until it became so tight and hard I thought I would have to slide my fingers down into my panties to stroke myself. 'It invites sucking.'

My third tit propelled me into the stratosphere. I was born to be a burlesque performer. I was a brazen libertine and I adored the punters' eyes on my nipples. The Hot Kookie Bazoukie Crew women enjoyed a unique fellowship and their open embraces and flirtatious innuendo opened me up to a period of joyful experimentation. We compared our breasts in mirrors and touched and fondled them at every opportunity.

Antoine always arrived early at the theatre because he couldn't stay away from the girls. He was bewitched by the breasts and his eyes were always on them. The girls spoilt and mollycoddled him. They sat on his lap and nibbled his nipples and pressed his penis through his pants. In actual fact they played with him like they might a pet, but Antoine was a pet with a bite, and I knew it. I wanted that bite on my third nipple.

On one occasion I was sitting in my chair before the dressing room mirror when I raised my legs high on the table and Antoine's eyes fluttered all over me like a butterfly, alighting here, there and everywhere. I let my dressing gown slide open and I saw his eyes seeking what lay underneath. I desired Antoine, but I feared the intensity of consummating desire with him. You see, I knew Antoine possessed the ability to ignite me, and I thought that if that happened I would burn up, curl up like a piece of blackened paper and expire from lust.

'I do so love your breasts, Ava,' Antoine said. He fingered my corset and smoothed his hands over the satin. 'I dream about them all the time. And this … well, this is what wet dreams are made of.' He tickled the third nipple and, reaching down, his tongue salsa'd over it. Instantly, my clit struck up a vibration and I felt the resonance reach like an invisible hand up inside me. I bit my lip and tried to squeeze my legs together, but I couldn't control my reflexes. It was curious, as if someone was turning on a faucet. The more he stroked the nipple the wider the faucet opened, and I felt the expansion of my sex and the pulsing flood of my internal juices. It was then that I fully understood the danger Antoine presented. He had his fist on the handle of the mechanism which controlled me. Suggestively, he poked out his tongue, and, outlining my lips with his finger, he pushed it inside my mouth.

'Try that once more,' I said, 'and I'll eat you.' I bit down on the finger and sucked it between my luscious lips and his eyes were watchful. They lingered on the nipple and the nipple twitched in response. The sexual power of Antoine tugged at me like a dog tugging at a lead. I wanted to know how it would feel to have him suck my tit really hard, and how the clit would respond to such voracious suction. Bending down to fasten my shoe, I arched my back so my breasts were thrown forward provocatively and I exposed the nipple to Antoine.

'It is so much larger than the rest, Ava.' He brushed my breasts with the back of his hand and he squeezed them with the same thoughtfulness with which one fingers fruit on a market stall. 'I must have you. I must see what happens when I press the right buttons, so to speak.'

I did not move away, I invited him. I was too aroused to be angry. I sat in my chair with my legs spread wide and a moist blossom staining my panties, wondering about which button Antoine would like to press first. He must have seen the wet invitation. He sat beside me and, taking out his gold magnifying glass, he leant and studied the specimen tit carefully. Through the lens he could see every detail of it, and I watched with mounting sensual alarm as his concealed penis writhed in his lap.

'I shall make you splendid. There will be nothing like it. I shall frame it in a diamante heart or perhaps a pentagram. It will be the star of the show.' He rubbed the nipple vigorously to harden it and then took his time touching glue to each diamante droplet before pressing it to a nipple. Actually, his hand lingered much too long. Sometimes he wet his finger and ran it around the areole and I closed my eyes while the clit and tit rang in harmony and small spasms of liquid indulgence raced through my aching hole and spread pools of lustful want onto my chair. It never failed to turn me on when Antoine applied the sequins. I wriggled and squeezed my legs together and my hand resting in my lap triggered my orgasm.

My corsets are made with strengthened bodices. They tug in my narrow waist and push up my breasts to artfully expose or conceal the nipple. When Antoine fastens the corsets he pulls the strings so tightly I feel breathless. He likes to watch the breasts swell above the ruches, ruffles, ribbons and bows, exposing the upturned tit. On occasion he paints an extra nipple just above my décolletage, opposite to the real one. The faux nipple is such fun because it is sometimes amusing to confound the audience, and especially the men, who like to have a quick tweak on it. I have dresses with heart-shaped cut-outs around the breasts and costumes which provide picture frames for Antoine's works of art.

One day before the show Antoine came into the dressing room and slid his hand into my hair. Then one long fingernail slipped under one of the ribbons and he rubbed his finger against my bare breast.

'You're not like the other girls, Ava. You are unctuous. You are like a tempting sweet with a very soft, but naughty, centre. I love sweet centres you can suck on.' His gaze was boldly suggestive as it fell on the nipple. 'Shall I suck on you, Lady Titillation?' Ignoring him, I placed my foot on the dressing room chair and rolled my stockings up before I clipped them in place.

I've watched Antoine through the crack in my dressing room door and I've seen him press my corsets to his nose as if he is eating cunt, so he can breathe the scent of me. And he has picked up my nipple tassels and rings and, unbuttoning his shirt, he has placed them on his own nipples and walked around, his luscious, muscular cock peeping out from between his leather pants. It is as if by inserting a part of me into his skin, he can assuage the obsession he has for my tit. I cannot resist him. I dream of tangling Antoine in my strong dancer's legs and holding him there. Once I orgasmed with Antoine's finger embedded in the dripping lusciousness of my greedy slit. He'd brushed close to me, capturing my plump sex, and squeezed it, holding his hand there, breath warm on the nipple. The pain of the squeezing excited me and I felt as if I was fighting my way up through thick waves of warm water.

As part of my performance, China Doll slips a silver chain through my nipple ring and parades me around the stage. I adore all the tugging and pulling and the sensitive tit swells to attention, hardening and tingling to the applause. As the girls fondle the nipple during the act, it is easy for me to rub against the chair and prompt my furtive orgasms while I smile sweetly into the audience.

Tonight, though, it is not China who will parade me around the stage; it is Antoine, and suddenly I feel as if I am the participant in a dangerous game. He brushes against me as I peep through the curtains, the long nylon hair from his wig brushing my face.

'You look very good as a woman,' I say angrily.

He is artful in his tweaks and jerks of the glittering leash. I want to say, how dare you? Instead, when the moment comes, I grasp his mouth and I pull it down onto my nipple and I make a great public performance of moaning and shrieking with delight as Antoine's taut tongue swirls around and caresses the tight bud and his sharp teeth nip. The crowd erupts around me in tumultuous applause and Antoine's finger slides beneath my skirt and, finding me wet and unctuous, ingratiates itself into the cavity. Finding my ripe hot clit, he titillates me until I come.

I sit in the dressing room and I remove my make-up. The nipple is pink and swollen and it seems to glare at me, demanding attention. I am so intently studying it, I do not hear Antoine behind me. I only feel the tug as he slips the leash onto the nipple ring.

Antoine is obligingly naked, his cock ramrod hard and jauntily upturned. I shiver, delicious tremors of anticipation racing up and down my spine, the chain jingling and pulling on the nipple. Antoine has a key. He slips the chain over the door handle and locks it with a tiny padlock, then he hangs the key around his neck. I have only to reach for it, but I doubt that I will.

The tongue flicks and the mouth fastens on the third nipple. Antoine knows exactly how to titillate, and how open or closed should be the faucet to best augment my excitation. He explores the dimples of the nipple, as if tracing the contours of a map, tapping the tit until the tap causes the flutter inside me. Next, he probes and coaxes with the very tip of his tongue in stabbing movements before he fastens onto it. The hard sucking on the nipple agitates the clit and then the cunt begins to resonate deeper and more disturbingly, as if the turning of the faucet also opens the vagina. Antoine is literally sucking the orgasm out of me, extracting a profound, shocking response from some deep, hidden part of me.

When he buries his face in my sumptuous mound so he can suck my clit, guess what happens? It is like a reversal in the circuit as the nipple fizzes and tingles and a momentous orgasm explodes through the vent of my volcano, overflowing and molten, around Antoine's lips and nose. Then, as I straddle his lap and he slips his cock deep inside me, finally, his teeth bite once again at my nipple, the switch that is wired to my deep core, and as the thrusts ripple through me, then comes the overload, the explosion I'd so feared and longed for. But it does not consume me. Rather, as I shatter into bright pieces, his fist clenching and palpating breast and tit, I simply thrum with a deeper, more scintillating newfound pleasure.

He knows exactly what the nipple wants. He is a master in

titillation and he strums on the nipples like a musician on a harmonica. Sometimes he plays the music on the tit and sometimes on the clit. I allow the nipple to lead the show and I wonder what it will do as an encore.

Catch Me If You Can
by Nikki Magennis

When I'm up there under the lights with my tassels twirling
and the 24-carat smile frozen on my face, I pick someone.
Someone sitting in the lightspill at the end of the runway,
someone quiet. Not one of the whoopers or the ones whose
mouths hang wide open like they're trying to inhale the whole
damn atmosphere in one gulp. My preference is someone who
looks a little uncomfortable. A guy with the hint of a healthy
blush tickling his gills. I lock eyes with him. Give it a bit of
sauce-and-wink. Shrug my shoulder like I've got a little
suggestion to make. Give me a shy one with nervous eyes and
maybe a little quirking dimple, and that's it, I'm hooked.

And then I wheel the character out – the bearded lady, the
mermaid caught in the fishing net, the spacegirl floating in the
most peculiar way, whatever. So long as I have someone to
latch onto, to hook my eyes on, I'm good. I dance for him and
forget the sea of eyes that follow my tits like they're watching
a fast rally at Wimbledon. With luck, we'll turn all the
arseholes into angels by the end of the night anyway. Marcia
will have them eating out of her hand, despite her subversive
tattoos, and Joelle will win the hearts of the most misguided
leerers – flutter her diamante lashes and blow them a kiss like
she's lobbing a perfumed hand grenade.

'Sell 'em sex and hand out love for free,' Joelle is inclined
to crow after every show, when she's all sweat-slick and
pumped with adrenaline.

After the show that night the dressing room was the usual glitter-filled bomb site – damp towels and discarded costumes littered the floor and Marcia's clove cigarettes tinged the air with their pungent smoke. We were sharing our post-performance bottle of fizz and the other two were bickering over who'd got the most gasps from our sunburned, booze-drenched audience. I was uncharacteristically quiet.

'Coming upstairs?' Marcia asked, but I shrugged and took another swig of lukewarm cava. Marcia narrowed her hot brown eyes and sucked her teeth.

'You're acting strange, little Vi. Someone upset you?'

But upset wasn't the right word. Someone had unsettled me, and it was giving me a peculiar mix of butterflies and wanting – like I had something tugging at the ends of my hair, fingertips, nipples. Just enough to disorientate me, not enough to hurt.

It was his look. The one I'd hung my attention on right at the start of the show; the one in the shabby pinstripe suit. His face was narrow and delicate, with big, serious eyes. Could have been a composer, or a scientist, maybe. Someone who watched, who listened, who took their time. He smiled, sure, and he clapped at the appropriate points like everyone else. But his gaze was never amazed. He just sat there with his eyes on me, as I ducked and twirled and worked the floor. How can I put it? He watched me *deeply*. Not that I could explain that to Marcia. I smeared cold cream on my cheeks and reached for a tissue.

'Want a little pick me up?' Marcia's voice hovered by my ear. She was holding a paper wrap, a tiny envelope in her palm, and her other hand traced circles on the nape of my neck.

'Not right now.'

'Suit yourself, angel. I'm off.'

Marcia marched to the door and banged it open. She never did anything quietly, which is why I took no notice of her shout as the door crashed against an obstacle and rebounded, and didn't catch the brief, murmured exchange she had with the guy who was standing on the other side.

And I suppose that's why, when he came up behind me and I suddenly clocked those fathomless green eyes fixed on me in the mirror, I nearly wet myself.

My hooker. Still gazing at me, but no longer smiling.

Now, the thing is, although I do technically strip when I'm on stage – as in, I remove every item of beaded, sequinned, costume, peeling and unpeeling and pulling apart the zips and buttons and bows – in a funny way, I always feel less naked as the clothes fall away. I pull off my bikini top and dazzle the crowd. I let my knickers drop and the applause covers me. I am dressed in stage lights and wolf whistles and the hum of appreciation.

Sitting there that night in the deserted back room, under the glow of a 40 watt bulb, with my face smeared in cold cream and my tired, sweaty body wrapped in a dirty silk bathrobe, I felt truly naked. Not because of what I was wearing, but because of the way he was looking at me. It was as though his eyes slid underneath – underneath everything. And though he didn't speak for a long, long minute, I felt like we were already pressed up against each other, so close you couldn't have fluttered an eyelash between our bodies and hearts.

'You were stunning,' he said at last. My hand floated to my hair and I cringed as I realised his words had made me primp like a teenager.

'Thanks,' I said weakly. He was close enough that I could smell the air around him. It smelled fresh, like a cold spring night with the stars already out. And he was looking around with that same calm curiosity that had given me the butterfly effect earlier on. His gaze had fallen on the tangle of netting that I used in the mermaid skit. Draped over a chair, embellished with the fabric starfish and seaweed that I'd stitched on haphazardly, it looked like the handmade prop that it was.

'You liked the act?' I asked, trying to rub off stray smears of cold cream, then wishing I hadn't as my face emerged pink-faced and scrubbed underneath.

'Yes,' he said, reaching to tug at a sequinned sea-urchin. 'Fabulously inventive.'

His fingers tangled in the netting, and I immediately translated the image into his hand tangled in my pubic hair, imagined him opening me up so delicately and precisely. I swallowed. This was a punter, I reminded myself. We got a few who'd try to sneak their way backstage past our amply-armed bouncer, Bernadette. Usually they carried their teeth home in a paper cup.

'How d'you get back here?' I said, crossing my fingers under my robe and praying this wasn't some stray stalker with a mermaid fetish.

He grinned at me. 'Charm.'

I laughed. 'Congratulations. Bernie doesn't charm easy.'

'I guess I must have the golden touch,' he said, and I wondered exactly where that soft mid-Atlantic accent came from, just as he reached out to brush a lock of hair behind my ear and made me shiver.

His hand lingered and I held myself as still as stone while his knuckles bumped gently against my cheek and stroked along my jaw, very softly. I watched him in the mirror, his wide shoulders and his crumpled trousers hanging from sweetly slim hips. Everything about him was easy, loose, and cool, apart from that gaze. I met his eyes in the mirror and was dazzled by their soft moss green, so when he tugged at the collar of my robe I only dropped my shoulders slightly and let him pull it aside.

He'd seen my oh-la-la finale already, naturally, and two scallop shells were covering my blushing nipples, so I shouldn't have felt quite so bare. But under the glitter and the fake tan, my heart was tripping over itself.

'Still got your tail on?' he asked, and I couldn't tell if he was teasing me or not. I wore a gold hobble skirt for the mermaid skit – sateen with velvet scales and a stiffened tail fin in painted cardboard. I could walk in it, but with difficulty. After the act I'd rip open the velcro slit at the side so I could move freely, turning it into a flappy long skirt, and that's what I was wearing that night under my robe. The loose hanging fabric fell almost to the floor, brushing the tops of my gold-dusted bare feet.

Without a word, he reached down to tug at my belt and pulled the knot apart. He moved slowly enough for me to protest, but I didn't. The robe fell away and my fish tail glimmered. The fins at my ankles quivered.

'Don't swim away,' he said, smiling. 'Or I'll have to wrap you in that net.'

I laugh-gasped. 'Just try it.'

He raised an eyebrow. 'That's not a bad idea.'

Now we were playing the game, and his breath was warm on the side of my face, I felt the power surge back into me. Just like the moment on stage when you know the audience is following right at your heels, I felt the crackle of certainty spark through my veins and mix with the butterflies already going wild in the pit of my stomach. I was wet, and trembling, and licking the gloss off my lips.

He'd reached out for the net – I realised I didn't even have a name for him – and with a wicked half-smile he tugged it towards us. Was this wise? I opened my eyes wide and my mouth wider as he hefted the black strings in his hand and wound them round his knuckles.

'May I?' he asked, as gracious as a silver-service waiter.

In the act, I float around the stage with an industrial fan blowing my long black hair out so that the strands swim around me. The lights are deep blue and all the movements are supple – I take the audience underwater with me.

In the dressing room, I sat with my body limp and sweat-cooled under the soft white of the fluorescent tubes. The man circled me with the net, looping a square over my wrist and wrapping the ropes around behind, binding me to the chair.

In the act, I catch a fisherman's hook between my teeth and pull, swimming backwards upstage until the shadow of a boat's hull falls over the crowd. It's a projection, of course, sliding across the ceiling. Me luring the fishermen to their watery graves.

He wound the net around me again, so that I was fixed tight and the cords dug into my skin, criss-crossing and cutting me into tiny diamonds. Between the lace geometry of the netting my body was portioned into scraps of bare flesh – and my hands and feet were tangled hopelessly among the felt seaweed and trailing cords.

'Hold fast,' he said, giving me the most beautiful smile.

'I don't think I have much choice,' I muttered, wriggling about to prove my point.

He stilled me with a hand on my chest, laid flat right between the scallop shells.

'It's fair,' he said. 'I was fixed in my chair all evening getting hooked on you.'

'And now?'

'And now you'll sit still while I play with you.'

So I did. While he shifted aside the scallop shells to reveal my pale, naked breasts, I said nothing. When he flicked at my nipples so that they poked through the netting, I held myself as quietly as I could. But when he bent his head to my crotch and stuck his tongue into the centre of a diamond to lap at my clit, I couldn't help but start to flail. The tail fins flapped ridiculously against the legs of the chair and the net strained against the curves of my arms and hips as I twisted about underneath it. He was down there with his delicate mouth, coaxing and sipping at the pip of my cunt, sending me reeling as the net tightened around me. I moaned as the pointed tip of his tongue slid deeper, curling into my wanting nook, promising fullness and heat and force.

'Will you fuck me?' I asked. He pulled away from me and I thought for a swaying, horrible moment I'd broken the spell, that the net would magically evaporate and leave me cut loose, free and disappointed.

But he was busy again, tugging at my hips, sliding me forward so that I was balanced on the lip of the chair with the net clinging yet harder to me. His face was thick with concentration as he grabbed at the net and tore at it, ripping

131

larger holes where he wanted to reach through. Those precise, delicate hands were strong enough to break the flimsy strings and I fixed on them with absent-minded surprise as he unzipped himself, swift and certain, with a movement like a soldier going for his gun, pulled his prick free and held it in his fist to show it to me. The skin was dark, and it stood thick and proud in his hand.

'Please,' I said, and I didn't know any more if I was winning or losing, because the nets were holding me and his cock was bumping against my thighs and sliding inside me with a long, insistent rush. He fitted deep in me, and we held each other hard.

I had him trapped between my legs, and I hooked my feet over his hips until he was meshed in the net, as tangled as me. We could only make the smallest of motions. His cock kissed my centre, rocking back and forth into my dark, welcoming heart.

We rolled against each other, locked tight and bound together, repeating those small inner bumps and kisses until his hips started to swing more wildly and I felt the chair creak under us. At last his mouth met mine and we plunged our tongues into the hungry depths of each other as we fucked harder, lifting the chair up onto two legs with every stroke. His hands were on my breasts, scrabbling at them through the black threads and plucking at my tender nipples until they zinged with shocking pleasure. I could have rolled him in the seaweed and dragged him under, down to where the water was dark and thick and inescapable, where the swarms of fish would nibble at our toes while we fucked forever on the seabed.

'I'll cover you with gold,' he said, his voice a rough whisper as he sank into me deeper and deeper again. 'I'll tie strings of pearls around your throat.'

I laughed, letting the first prickles of orgasm rise up inside me. My body was uncurling, atom by atom, turning into heat and reaction.

'I'm going to drown you,' I said, clamping my knees

around his waist.

'Well I'll keep you tied to me and we'll both go down together,'

'I'm going to come,' I said then, and although I was fixed and unable to move, I felt the spill and rush of the orgasm wash over me and carry me the length of the world and back. We sailed together then, for a few lost, dark minutes, cradled in each other's arms, no longer performing and no longer playing.

For a little while, we were both breathing underwater.

The Price Of Freedom
by Carmel Lockyer

Sylvia knew the moment she woke that something had changed. It was the sound of the streets outside – a sound she'd heard once before, when the war in Europe had ended. She opened the window, struggling with the heavy blackout curtain, and leaned out. A small boy stood on the pavement outside, a pile of news-sheets under his arm.

'Japan surrenders! VJ Day declared!' he yelled. 'Two days holiday for Britain's brave home front!'

Sylvia drew in her head and sat on the bed. Two days' holiday would mean a new show at the Blue Moon Club. She moved to the mirror and began the painstaking work of turning her long curls into a proper Veronica Lake, smoothing the hair down with the brilliantine one of the sailors at the Club had given her. She heard Dulcie stirring next door and ran to shout the news through the other girl's door.

'Dulce, the war's over! The Japs surrendered!' There was an answering groan and Sylvia skipped back to her mirror, dropping her nightdress from her shoulders so that it fell to her waist, cupping her breasts with her hands. Her feet began to move to silent music as she whirled around the tiny bedroom. She knew she was only a reasonable dancer, but she had a wonderful voice, and the men who flocked to the Blue Moon loved to hear her expressing the sentiments they hoped their own sweethearts would be feeling – although that didn't stop them picking up girls and taking them back to billets, hotel

134

rooms or even the alleyways around blacked-out Pimlico for unsentimental sex.

She stopped twirling. Her hands slipped down her body, unbuttoning the nightdress until it fell to the floor. She had creamy skin, with a faint dusting of freckles on her nose and shoulders, wide-set breasts with petal-pink nipples and a narrow thatch of brunette pubic hair which she trimmed every night with nail scissors. In all, she had a body to be proud of, a body that pleased others, and a job that allowed her to feel her pride and their pleasure on a daily, or nightly, basis.

She began to hum 'God save the King' as she bent over the basin and dipped her toothbrush in the tiny smear of toothpowder that was left in the tin, before pulling on her girdle and knickers and easing her utility dress up over her hips. There was no point dying her legs with gravy browning yet, as she had only to walk to the club, but she peeked into the tin to see how much was left – very little. Still, what did it matter? Now there would be toothpowder and stockings galore – it was 15 August 1945 and the War was over.

But as she got closer to the Blue Moon her happy gait slowed. She'd loved the burlesque club since her first accidental visit a year ago, but in the past few weeks her pleasure in what she did had been soured by one person: Lily Maltravers. She stopped outside the club and dug in her pocket for a cigarette, needing the solace of smoke in her lungs before she entered.

A year ago she hadn't even known what burlesque was. A year ago she'd been a Land Girl who'd contracted pneumonia and ended up in a nursing home in London to recover her strength. On a shopping trip she'd been caught in an air raid and, pressing against the nearest doorway, had found the door open. She'd crept down the stairs to find a cellar to hide in until the bombers had gone. Instead she'd found a fairyland.

There was a tiny stage in pink plush, with a tiny orchestra pit. In the pit was a pianist and on the stage was a lush redhead wearing top hat, tails and not much else. Sylvia had stood at the back of the club, staring, her eyes getting wider with every twirl and turn, every dip and bend of the redhead's body. She watched the other woman expose one breast, tipped with a silver star, then the other, then both, and then drop the tailcoat to the floor to stand resplendent with another, barely larger, silver star covering her most private parts. In that moment Sylvia knew what she'd been born for, even if she didn't know what it was called.

A voice came from the stalls. 'Again, lovey, with a bit more oomph when you take off the jacket – get them hot, then get them hotter.' It was the voice of an elderly woman, but the personage Sylvia eventually found was a man – a man with plucked eyebrows and rouge. Sylvia didn't care. She introduced herself as a potential performer. The rouged man pinched his nose. 'And what do you think you can do?'

'Whatever you want,' Sylvia had said. 'Whatever it takes.'

And now she was in the burlesque. She'd told her parents she was working as an ENSA entertainer, and it wasn't far from the truth – the men who came to the club wanted entertainment, that was for sure, and they loved beauty and charm. 'Ma' Bantling, as she'd learned to call the old queen who ran the place, had become a surrogate mother, and if Ma turned a blind eye to what some girls did, he didn't make the others do it if they didn't want to. It was live and let live at the Blue Moon, and Sylvia had been as happy as a cat in a dairy, until Lily arrived.

Ma had auditioned this Lily and said afterwards only, 'She's talented,' but this was Ma's highest praise and the other girls had waited with excitement to see what Lily could do. On her first night they'd found out. There was no green room chumminess with Lily: she sat in silence, applying her make-up. There was no friendly rivalry either – Lily wiped the floor with them all, and they knew it.

Lily opened her act sitting on top of the piano and elevating her legs into a scissor shape as stark and elegant as Bauhaus architecture, and from then on her performance was a dazzling display of style. She looked like a panther and moved like a Siamese cat. While she had only a reasonable voice, she was careful to pick songs that didn't strain it, so she sounded better than she was. The audience loved her and the other girls crowded around her in the wings at the end to congratulate her.

'Really,' she said, pulling her dressing gown back on over the red pasties and French knickers with which she'd finished her set, 'you are such a provincial gaggle. There's nothing to congratulate me on: the pianist is a tub thumper and the lighting was just awful. If I didn't need the money, you wouldn't see me here for dust.' And she'd swept off. Lily, to be blunt, was a bitch.

'Ma, I do the last turn every night or I'm leaving,' had been her first demand, and so what had been a rotating show, with each girl getting her chance to provide the finale, became the 'Lily Show'. But even worse were the poisonous comments she made. Last week Sylvia had heard them applied to herself during rehearsals.

'Sylvia!' Ma had called out. 'Your turn dear.' And she'd been heading for the stage when she'd heard Lily's voice from the stalls, as cold as iced lemonade.

'Which one is Sylvia?'

'Sylvia has the beautiful voice,' Ma had replied.

'Oh, you mean the one who looks like an ox?'

'Lily, that's not fair, or nice. Sylvia is very pretty and many men appreciate her wholesome appearance.'

'Sorry Ma,' Lily had said, sounding not at all sorry. 'I meant the one who looks like a heifer, of course – very wholesome. You could get a quart of milk from her anytime.'

In the wings, Sylvia had blushed and burned, and Dulcie had given her quick pat of sympathy. 'She's only jealous, Syl, because she doesn't have your cleavage.'

It had been sweet of Dulcie but Sylvia knew it wasn't true. Lily wasn't jealous; Lily didn't know the meaning of the word. She'd been heard to make similar comments about every member of the troupe and open rebellion was only held in check because none of the girls wanted to add to Ma's problems. And the problems were big: Ma provided what costuming was possible in the dark days of rationing and fought to keep the club open.

'We're not the Windmill Theatre,' he'd said to the girls. 'We have to be on our best behaviour at all times or we'll get closed down by the Lord Chancellor and, once we're closed, we'll never reopen. So please, lovelies, keep your private arrangements private.'

'Private arrangements' meant the things Dulcie did with a constant parade of lovelorn men. She hung a loofah on her door-handle when she had company and Sylvia put cotton wool in her ears so as not to hear the sighs and giggles. She could have had 'private arrangements' of her own, but somehow, she never did. It wasn't that she was a prude; she'd lost her virginity to Dai Lloyd-Williams before he'd gone off for airman training, but when he'd died in a bomber over Germany, something had switched off in her and it had never switched back on.

Now she stubbed out the cigarette and pulled back her shoulders. The war outside was over, but the war inside Blue Moon continued. She'd be brave and resolute and see if she couldn't strike a blow against the enemy.

Ma was handing out roles for the VJ Spectacular. Each girl would represent a country in burlesque style. Sylvia slipped into a seat and listened.

'Angela will be Norway, as she's the blondest. Claire will take India as she's the darkest. Dulcie shall be our heroic allies in Russia, if she ever gets out of bed …'

Sylvia made a note that her own winter hat might serve for a Russian Cossack.

'Sylvia can take on France, and Japan will be the finale. That role goes to Lily.'

Lily smiled like a cat. 'Thank you Ma, and that's an ideal running order. The audience will have a chance to refresh their drinks or stretch their legs during Sylvia's efforts so they are ready for me. I know where I can borrow a silk kimono, which will work perfectly for striptease. I just wish –' she frowned slightly. 'I wish I had some silk stockings, but they are *sooo* hard to get hold of these days.'

Sylvia wanted to spit. How dare she! The implication that her own act would be so bad that people would walk out was just vile.

'You've got twenty-four hours,' Ma said, frowning back at Lily. 'Please tell Maurice what you need as music so he can prepare. Give this performance everything: style, sentiment, topicality and oomph. The boys deserve it.'

The girls began to move, some heading for the pianist, others searching out costuming. Sylvia sat still, rigid with anger. She was going to give it oomph all right – she'd knock Lily into a cocked hat! And she was going to give it something else, too, something Lily couldn't deliver: silk stockings. She ran back to the boarding house and pulled the black fur hat from the top of her wardrobe, flinging it onto Dulcie's crumpled bed.

'You're Russia,' she said.

'What's the rush?' Dulcie yawned.

'Oh, I've got something to do. I'll see you later.'

Ten minutes later, outside Pimlico tube, she took a deep breath and checked her hair with her hands. The station was used as a shelter during air raids, but the man she was looking for had appropriated a tiny room at the end for his activities. His name was Teddy and they called him the Prince of Sales, because he could get you anything, for a price. He often sat in the Blue Moon with his cronies, drinking the black-market champagne he supplied to Ma, and watching the girls as they performed.

She knocked on the door.

'In.' Teddy's voice was lazy.

When she stood in front of him, she felt stupid. Why should he give her stockings? She had no money. It was simply that sometimes she'd thought he watched her a little more closely than the others.

'I want some silk stockings.' Her voice wobbled.

'Do you? You're Sylvia aren't you? You've got a lovely

139

set of pipes, but how are your pins? Are you worth silk stockings?' His voice hid laughter but it was friendly.

'I think so, although … I don't have any money.'

'Then you're a charity case, and a charity case has to be deserving, doesn't it? Show me your legs, Sylvia.'

Damn! She should have used the gravy browning and asked Dulcie to draw a line down the back of her legs with an eyebrow pencil to make a seam. Still, she must be brave. She imagined herself a spy about to be interrogated and removed her jacket, staring into Teddy's eyes. He was so good looking, just like the photos of the Prince of Wales, with his light eyes, his soft blond hair and the elegant suits he wore. He was distracting her. She lifted her fingers to her dress buttons, reminding herself that he wasn't seeing anything he hadn't seen before, although usually she was onstage. Now they were within inches of each other and she could have shivered at the way he smiled as she fumbled with her clothing. She felt hot and clumsy, although the heat in her belly and between her legs wasn't at all unpleasant. In fact it reminded her of her few and furtive moments with Dai.

Teddy moved behind her and lifted her dress, pinching the shoulder seams and drawing it down her arms. The movement reminded her of her morning dance, half-naked, and she felt her nipples stiffen as her flesh was exposed to the dank air. She began to roll her girdle down but Teddy stopped her.

'Allow me,' he said and his hands undressed her. She couldn't read the expression on his face because her eyes had closed and she had the impression she was swaying, leaning towards him …

She felt his fingers on the waistband of her underwear and gasped. Teddy chuckled but continued and she kept her eyes closed as she put her hand on his shoulder to steady herself as she stepped out of her knickers.

He moved around her, brushing his fingertips against her neck, her spine, her thighs. She heard him chuckle again and then felt his mouth press against her collarbone, making her gasp. It was as if his hands were magnets – wherever he moved, she felt her body lean towards him, drawn closer to his touch, his body. She half-hoped he'd ask her for sex, but all he did was slide his fingers into her pubic hair so that her legs parted involuntarily, then move away so that she almost fell.

'Lovely legs,' he said conversationally. 'Well worth a pair of nylons.'

She opened her eyes and saw him holding out a small brown-paper parcel sealed with string and wax.

'These are yours as a gift, Sylvia. If you like them, you can say thank you later.'

She nodded and, before she'd really understood, he'd left and she stood naked with the packet in her hands.

Once she was dressed there was much to do. She tracked down the window-cleaner and asked to borrow his bicycle and overalls; she burrowed through the prop boxes at the Blue Moon to find a beret and fake moustache; and she found that there was not a string of onions to be had in the area for love nor money. She ended up going to the allotments and persuading an old gent to give her a bag of onions for sixpence, which she tied together with string. She told Maurice, the pianist, to play *Daisy, Daisy* all the way through twice, then the *Marseillaise*, and to begin to play when he heard a bell ring. Despite his confusion, she refused to rehearse. If she was going to win this battle she mustn't show her hand. Then she headed back to the allotments with the bicycle and practised, humming under her breath. Nobody was going to know what Sylvia could do until Sylvia did it!

The next night, she stood in the wings, shaking with nerves. The bicycle was heavy and her hands were slippery with fear. She heard her name and then she was off, swinging her leg over the crossbar, cycling out, circling the stage and then coming to a stop, face on to the audience. There was laughter, then applause. She circled the stage again and came to a stop, side on this time, and rang the bicycle bell. Maurice was ready for her and as the first notes of the old song rang out, she

141

leaned back, pulling off the beret and allowing her long hair to spill out, touching the floor behind her. The audience cheered.

She began to cycle round the stage, putting the beret in the wicker basket on the front of the bike, following it with the moustache, then unbuttoning one side of the overall, and then the other, so that the audience could see she was wearing nothing underneath, although her strategically-placed onion garland concealed her breasts from view. The watching men were yelling their pleasure now. As she circled she saw Lily in the wings, stupefied with shock.

Now came the difficult bit. She had to lift each foot from its pedal and keep the bike coasting, while kicking off the overall and making sure it didn't tangle in the spokes or chain. It was an insanely complicated manoeuvre, but she managed it, shoving the garment on top of the beret. Now they could see she was wearing just silk stockings and a tiny pair of flesh-coloured knickers. She turned from the audience and brought the bike to a stop so that her legs were braced on either side of the frame. She kicked down the stand and lifted her legs, balancing her body on the handlebars so that she formed a single long line above the bicycle. There were wolf-whistles and stamping feet.

She arched her back, letting her hair spill down and lifted one hand into the air, waving at the audience before tugging the onions from her neck and dropping them in the basket.

'Turn round, turn round!' the men chanted. She had one more thing to do first though, and she lowered her hand into the basket, seeking out the moustache, before jumping from the bike and arranging her hair to cover her body.

When she turned she was hidden from shoulder to hip in her long curls. She walked forward slowly, timing it so that she would arrive at the front of the stage as Maurice played the final chorus of *Daisy, Daisy*. As he did, she parted her hair and revealed that her false moustache was now stuck to the front of her knickers. The crowd laughed and roared as she pulled off the moustache and stuck it on one breast, then the other, before bending down and applying it to the face of a man at the front table. Finally she stood before them in just her stockings and underwear and Maurice changed key, playing the stirring opening chords of the French national anthem. She filled her lungs and allowed her voice to flow through the room.

'Allons enfants de la patrie,
Le jour de gloire est arrivé ...'

She sang as she'd never sung before, resting her fingertips on the tops of her stockings, with her eyes locked on one man who sat at the front: Teddy.

He pointed to the stairs while the applause was still ringing out. Sylvia slipped through the wings, pulling on her summer coat as she ran up the back staircase. She set her back against the bricks and reached for a cigarette. A dark shape blocked the light and she smelt Teddy's cologne. She opened her coat, as good as naked, and his hands didn't hesitate, finding her hips and pulling her towards him, his mouth meeting hers with unexpected roughness, making her gasp. Suddenly, Sylvia wasn't indifferent any more. She liked the cool night air on her breast as Teddy teased her nipple, wanted to open her legs wider so that he could press into her. She wanted to unbutton him, to fuck him, right there in the alley, so she did. He slid into her with a naturalness that made her gasp again, and as he thrust hard, his mouth at her neck, she heard him say her name. And that is how Sylvia had her first ever orgasm.

Back in the dressing room, Ma Bantling waited. 'You didn't stay for the finale.'

Sylvia grinned. 'There was somebody I had to thank. Sorry to have missed it, but that's the price I had to pay.'

Ma smiled back, slowly. 'It wasn't very good anyway, loads of people got up and fetched themselves drinks while Lily was performing. You take the finale tomorrow – that's the price you pay for upstaging Lily!'

Hidden Treasure
by Sarah Berry

Sylvie fastened her fake pearl necklace with a sigh. The piece of jewellery had been a present from the boy who'd plucked her virginity away, two years previously, and it always served to make her feel romantic and whimsical. It had also inspired her stage name, Pearl Necklace. In her act she shimmied around the stage to the *Dance of the Cygnets*, pretending she was a naive nymphette discovering parts of her body for the first time.

But now both the act and the cheap necklace were getting tiresome. She looked in the mirror and brushed her long blonde hair. Usually this served to soothe her but tonight she couldn't shake the feeling that she had let her new lover down.

They'd met a few weeks before. He'd been coming to the club off and on for about a month, always sitting on his own in the corner, sipping his single malt and occasionally tapping his foot to the music. Dressed in a uniform of fedora and double-breasted suit, he was like a figure from another time. And, Sylvie noticed one night as she flitted past him, playing social butterfly, he was older, much older than her.

Increasingly she felt him picking her out of the crowd with his penetrating eyes. At first she felt awkward under his gaze, but she quickly began to look forward to his visits. When he was there she would arch her back a little further than usual, her hips would wiggle a little more and her nipples would stand a little more on end.

She thought he didn't know anyone. It was like he was some phantom that only she could see. But one evening she found him talking to Gary behind the bar. When he went outside for a cigarette she slinked over.

'Who is he?' she asked nonchalantly.

'Ah, so you like Nick, do you?' he smirked, a twinkle in his eye. 'Fucking legend. Or he used to be. An ex-music journo. I usually see him around with some hot totty on his arm. Wish I knew how the fuck he does it.'

'Hmm,' she murmured. Maybe it was time to meet her admirer. She reapplied her lipstick and slid out through the crowd after him.

'Hey you. Got a spare one of those?' she said, motioning at his cigarette. He was much taller than Sylvie, and she felt frail and delicate standing next to him. Decades of smoking, alcohol and God knew what else had not been kind to his skin. But nevertheless she felt a flutter between her legs as the image of herself standing naked in front of him crept into her mind. She took the cigarette he proffered and, as he bent down to light it, inhaled the smell of tobacco mixed with the musky scent of his aftershave. She took a deep drag from the fag and coughed.

'Are you enjoying the show?' she asked, trying to regain her composure.

He laughed. 'Always. You're a very captivating young lady.'

'You've been watching me,' she said coquettishly, raising an eyebrow. 'Like to get to know me better?'

Nick dropped his butt on the floor and chuckled to himself. 'Darling, I would love to. But I'm an old guy who really should be at home with a cat and slippers. Shit, I've got records older than you. Now make sure you don't catch cold, I want you to be here next week.'

He turned to go back into the club, but Sylvie grabbed his wrist and pulled his hand onto her chest. They stared at each other and she could see Nick's resolve beginning to melt. He bent forward and kissed her. He was gentle at first, then he pushed his tongue past her lips, forcing it into her mouth. At the same time his fingers trailed down her body to the hem of her dress, then up her thigh to her soaked knickers. Sylvie felt her legs turn to jelly as she panted, 'Take me home.'

Nick hailed a cab and the pair sat in silence in the back seat. Sylvie looked over at the man who she knew was soon to be inside her. She felt she had the upper hand. She was giving him a treat, she believed, by letting him touch her young, soft flesh. That was soon to change.

Nick's flat was like something out of a Woody Allen movie, full of sixties art and ageing designer furniture.

'Help yourself to a drink,' he said, motioning to a small glass bar as he sorted through his record collection. Sylvie drank a hefty shot a whisky and smiled as Leonard Cohen filled the air. And then he was behind her, his hands under her dress, squeezing her ass as he bit her neck. He ripped her knickers off and started teasing her clit with small, powerful strokes. His sizeable erection was pushing against her through his trousers and she turned around to release it. He lifted her bare ass onto the cold glass surface and plunged into her. As Sylvie's hips bucked against him she realised that she was in his power. It excited and unnerved her.

In her dressing room, Sylvie picked up some glitter and gave her collar bone a light dusting. That morning he had kissed her there so tenderly, sending rushes straight to her cunt. As he'd gone down on her he'd cupped her fleshy bottom, making her squirm against his mouth. And then he'd inserted a finger into her ass and she'd frozen. He'd looked up from his task with a glint in his eye.

'Does that feel bad, my sweet?' he'd asked.

'No, not bad. I just don't know …' She'd moved away from him. 'I'll be late,' she'd lied and gone to shower.

Why was so she bloody prudish? It hadn't hurt; it had just been … different. She was sure her ass was clean, but it still felt dirty. What next? A cock up there? Did she really want anal sex? Up until now he'd been such a gentleman, gallantly helping her realise her sexual potential. But what would she gain by opening her ass to him? Men had G-spots there. She had nothing. Right?

Tonight Nick would be in the audience again. Usually she loved performing for him, but now her nerves were taking over. She'd disappointed him. He would no longer find her sexy and her act would seem ridiculous.

As she was tying up her corset a knock came at the door. The stage manager delivered a small jewellery box. It was from him. All must be fine. But when she opened the lid she gasped. Inside was a set of pearls. But they weren't for her neck. They were a set of very expensive-looking anal beads. They glistened beautifully in the light. She ran them down her cheek, feeling their warmth against her skin.

The beads weren't his attempt to get a thrill. They were a beautiful present for her. She remembered the feeling of the finger that morning. No. It hadn't hurt. She smiled. Could she? Maybe just a little try before she went on. He would know. He'd be able to tell, she was sure of it. And she didn't want to disappoint him again.

Sylvie sat with her legs open in front of the mirror, caressing her breasts under the boned corset with one hand, pulling her silk French knickers aside with the other. She breathed in slowly, then, as she breathed out, inserted her finger inside her anus. It felt much the same as it had that morning. But this time she was able to relax her muscles. She fit in another finger. Again, it didn't hurt. It was warm there and tighter than her vagina. She felt a ripple of pleasure go through her as she moved her fingers backwards and forwards. Her pussy was throbbing and her nipples began to stand on end.

For her act she used lubricant on her lips to make them glisten, and now she slathered the beads with a hefty dollop. Then she moved her hand over her sodden cunt. The gloopy lubricant mixed with her vaginal juices and she let out a moan. There wasn't long until she was to go on so she didn't have time to fanny around. Quickly she transferred the lube to her puckered arsehole. Then she held the pearls by the entrance. took a deep breath, and popped in the first bead.

The feeling of her muscles contracting around the beads was certainly not unpleasant and in quick succession she stuffed in three more. She wriggled around in her seat, enjoying really feeling the inside of her anal passage for the first time. She pushed in the remaining four beads and marvelled at the ring sticking out of the bottom. She felt naughty, liberated and very, very horny.

'If he could see me now,' she thought proudly. Her knickers snapped back into position and she eyed herself in the mirror. 'No one would know,' she whispered to herself. She stood up and ground her arse. She felt full and as she bent over the beads pushed against her tender walls. It was a strange sensation. She started to finger her pussy and felt her arse relax even further. She made up her mind: the beads felt good.

Another knock. Shit, she was on. No time to remove the beads; she went on stage.

'That's what he wanted,' she thought with a naughty smile. The audience cheered as she began to perform. 'They must be able to tell' she thought, and felt an embarrassing shade of scarlet creep up her neck. But as she danced she began to relax – though she had to keep her bottom clenched to ensure the beads didn't slip out. No one knew but she and her lover. She searched the crowd for him, squinting against the lights. And there he was, just a couple of metres away in the small club. She smiled at him and he nodded, a knowing look on his face.

As she turned around and thrust her arse at the crowd she felt her sphincter spasming.

'I mustn't come on stage' she thought, trying to concentrate on the music.

Then she felt it. What the fuck was that?

There it was again. The pearls were buzzing.

Jesus Christ. she felt her heart speed up as she peered at her lover. As she shimmied she could see him operating a device in his hand. Another buzz. There must be a motor inside the beads.

Sylvie could smell her arousal and imagined that everyone else could. She reached down and stroked her pussy through the knickers. Rather than acting out a pantomime of surprise, a genuinely lascivious smile spread across her face and she licked her finger. The crowd wolf-whistled, and off came her corset. She rubbed her fingers over her nipples and could feel them straining to be released from under the pasties. She bit her lip to suppress a moan.

By now the beads were buzzing in time with the music and she wiggled her bottom, feeling her clit rub against the gusset of her soaked knickers. She kept her breathing even so as not to tilt over the edge. She just couldn't allow herself to lose control.

As the music stopped, the buzzing went up a notch and, after a quick bow, she hurried off stage. In the wings she had her orgasm, her ass buzzing as she fingered her now-dripping slit.

'Encore,' cried the audience and, relieved, Sylvie went on to take another bow.

When she got back to her dressing room, flying high from the successful show and her intense orgasm, he was waiting for her.

'You were amazing,' he said, embracing her.

'You bastard,' she said, 'I almost came!' Then she collapsed laughing into his arms.

'You know, the most fun about those pearls is taking them out,' he smiled. 'As one pops against your ass walls your whole body spasms. It's the most incredible feeling.'

She shuddered as she pulled down her knickers, which were partially stuck to her. She put her hands on the table and stuck her arse towards him. 'You pull them out.'

He gently fingered her clit and she felt warmth creep through her. Now she didn't have to bite her lip and she moaned loudly. A few buzzes of the control and she was on her way to another climax. He tugged out the first pearl and she felt herself lurch. Then the second, so slowly, millimetre by millimetre. Her sphincter opening and shutting. All too soon the beads were out and a spent Sylvie fell onto the chair quivering.

'Thank you' she said beckoning him forward to kiss her.

'I've got another surprise for you,' he said and handed her another box. Inside was another beautiful string of pearls – this time for her neck. It was clear that Pearl Necklace had come of age. No longer the innocent pixie, but a grown women sent to titillate her audience. And she knew that next time she'd be wearing both new sets of pearls.

All Eyes Upon Her
by Donna George Storey

'You haven't slept with him yet, and you've been going out for a month?' Nicole sank to the dressing room bench. 'I'm sorry, darling, I'm so stunned, I have to sit.'

'It's not a month, it's six weeks,' Cara corrected her.

Nicole brought her hand to her chest as if to calm palpitations. 'So is there something wrong with him?'

'Quite the contrary. Jack's great.' Cara reached for her dress, a silver sequined sheath with spaghetti straps.

'Then there's only one explanation. The real Cara's been abducted and the aliens have left behind a sexless android in her place.'

'Come on, I just thought I'd try waiting.' Cara wiggled a bit as she pulled the stretchy fabric over her hips. 'Maybe I'll get to know more about the person behind the cock before I bed him.'

Nicole laughed. 'Well, Ms Alien, I'm afraid you'd better learn more about fashions on Earth first.'

'Why, what's the matter?' Cara frowned at her reflection in the mirror, although she liked what she saw. The slinky dress hugged her body in all the right ways. She hoped that Jack wouldn't be able to tear his eyes away from her shimmering curves.

'You may be talking like a lady, but that thing makes you look like a stripper.'

Cara's lips lifted into a smile.

In fact, that was just what she had in mind.

Cara's hand trembled as she pushed her key into the front door lock. Jack was still lingering on the porch, watching her. She could feel the heat of his gaze boring through the back of her coat. She turned and gave him a quick wave, then slipped inside her house and turned the deadbolt behind her. At last she was safe.

Safe, that was, from her own urge to run back through the door, drag Jack inside and fuck his brains out. She headed for her bedroom, wobbling as she walked. Strange how a bit of necking in his car, a lingering goodbye kiss on the porch, could affect her so deeply. It was so … mid-twentieth century. And yet her panties were soaked and her skin was so hot it ached. Nicole was absolutely wrong in saying she'd become a sexless alien.

She switched on her bedroom lamp and paused at her full-length mirror, shrugging her coat from her shoulders. This new 'stripper' dress did do her justice, but she felt a pang of guilt, too. At the restaurant, Jack had stared at her across the table as if she were a decadent dessert he knew he wasn't allowed to eat. She'd told him she wanted to take it slow, but in a get-up like this, there was no doubt she was teasing – even taunting – him. And he didn't deserve it. He was a nice guy. Sexy, too. She'd felt that the minute he'd walked into her office, a young history teacher interested in volunteering to show people around the museum's new exhibit on 'Shady Ladies and the Second City'. She'd signed him up on the spot.

Nicole was certainly spot on, however, about her past record with men. Usually Cara would have bedded such a luscious specimen within the week, if not that very day. But with Jack, everything had been different from the start. She supposed she had the stripper Sally Rand to thank for that. Sally was one of the stars of the new exhibition, the brightest and sassiest of all the notorious *femmes fatales* of Chicago's colourful history. Her seductive fan dance had been the sensation of the Century of Progress Exposition of 1933 and

1934. She'd once been arrested four times in one day on obscenity charges, but she'd kept dancing, insisting on her freedom of expression. She'd also been a tireless supporter of the poor and hungry, a shady lady with a shining heart of gold.

The day they met, Cara explained all of this to Jack as they paused before Sally's display: a collage of photos, an original souvenir poster and a set of frothy feather fans. Then Cara switched on the film clip of Sally's dance, her pale form swooping like a swan, tantalisingly bare, but always cloaked behind a veil, a translucent Chinese screen, a flourish of fan. She watched Jack watching, his eyes fixed on the screen. When the performance was done, he turned those same enchanted eyes upon her.

'Strange, isn't it? It's not explicit. Yet it's very erotic.' He blushed at his confession.

'So you like a woman who makes you wait and might never deliver the goods at all?' Cara asked cheekily.

He grinned. 'In some ways the waiting is the best part. And I don't mean to sound arrogant, but when I really want something, I'll do whatever it takes to get it.' His words hung in the air between them like a promise. That's when Cara had what Nicole would call her 'alien abduction moment'. Suddenly, the twirling figure on the TV screen before her was not Sally Rand, but her own desire. Until now she'd been on fast-forward, peeling off her clothes and jumping into bed in the blink of an eye. If the men she fucked looked right through her the next morning, she told herself she didn't care. But maybe she did want a man's eyes fixed on her, entranced by her luminous beauty, breathlessly awaiting the next revelation of female mystery.

She had to admit this waiting game with Jack was definitely sexy, but there was a down side. After each date of smouldering glances and steamy innuendo, her evening always ended in the same way: undressing in her bedroom, aroused but alone. Cara squinted at her reflection. Behind her, the air seemed to thicken as shadowy figures moved into view. Maybe she wasn't alone tonight?

She closed her eyes.

It was then her company shifted into focus. Now a whole room of men in dinner jackets faced her, puffing cigars, clutching tumblers of whisky in their sturdy hands. They were men of business, pillars of the community, the welfare of the city always in their sights. Except for now, when they only had eyes for her, a lovely young woman standing on stage in a slinky silver dress.

She began to sway rhythmically to the sultry music in her head. The men stirred and leaned forward in their chairs. Cara danced and twirled, like the burlesque divas in the exhibit. At last, when she'd warmed them up nicely, she paused at centre stage, posing for them, cupping her breasts as if in offering, all the while swivelling her hips.

The room was alive with murmurings now. *Take it off, honey. Let me see your tits. Let me see how gorgeous you really are.* She only smiled and danced on. After all, the waiting was the best part.

But, suddenly, the room grew hotter, unbearably so. Her body was covered in a thin film of sweat. Was it from the dance or those hundreds of eyes searing into her flesh? She could feel her nipples standing taut against the fabric, begging for release.

She reached for one strap and slid it over her shoulder. The room heaved a collective sigh. She coaxed the other strap down so it dangled loose, like a girl with questionable morals.

Come on, sweetheart, show us what you've got. Leaning forward, Cara hooked her thumbs under the neckline of the dress and inched it lower. She paused on the brink of the reveal, then pulled it back up again with a prim tug. Several voices howled in disappointment.

She arched back and slid the dress lower again, her hands palming her nipples as she went. Her belly was on fire; her pussy pulsed in time with the beat of the music. The waiting was hard for her, too.

On impulse, she yanked the fabric all the way down to her waist.

Shouts of approval rumbled through the crowd.

In her haste, Cara had also freed one of her nipples from her black strapless bra. With a saucy shrug, she tucked the pink bonbon back inside and turned away from them to show her rear view. Then she started to shimmy, pushing the bunched up dress down over her hips to reveal matching panties of black satin.

'What do you say, boys? Have you seen enough or do you want more?'

More! More!

The ceiling bulged upward with the force of their cries.

Cara reached back, unsnapped her brassiere and tossed it over her head into the audience.

A tussle broke out as half a dozen men scurried to claim the prize, still warm and fragrant with her musky scent. Over her shoulder she glimpsed the victor, a grey-haired gentleman with a fine moustache, who brought it to his face and inhaled deeply.

Cara turned, her hands shielding her breasts modestly.

'Now here's the big question. Do you want me to take my hands away?'

Her audience was beyond words now. Some men stood, reaching toward her, licking the drool from their lips. Others were now lewdly masturbating in their chairs, their swollen members poking up from open flies.

She scanned the crowd in triumph. She'd brought them all completely under her spell.

Then her gaze settled on a younger gentleman she hadn't noticed before. He was handsome, with a crisply knotted bow tie and a faintly arrogant smile.

Their gazes locked.

Bring your hands to your sides so I can feast my eyes on those lovely breasts. Then push your soaking wet panties down to your knees and show me how you pleasure yourself when you're alone. Haven't you waited long enough, Cara? Do it now. For me.

Although his lips weren't moving, she could hear his words

155

clearly, words that touched her in a way the other men's shouts and pleas had not. Cara let out a soft groan. She'd waited long enough. She wanted it now. Under his spell, she lowered her hands. Every man in the room seemed to swallow at once, a wet, desperate sound. There was no longer any art to her stripping, she merely pushed her panties to her knees as the young gentleman had instructed. Trembling with shame and desire, she pressed her finger to her swollen cleft and began to strum. Suddenly the other male figures faded into nothingness. This show was for one man alone. Her finger moved faster. She licked the fingers of her other hand and began to twist her nipple. Her thighs trembled. Her hips moved, but not with the liquid grace of her dance. She was thrusting into her hand, fucking the air … No, she was fucking his gaze, which arched toward her, insistent, demanding. *Do it, Cara. Let me watch you come.*

It worked like magic. All it took was a few more flicks of her clit and she was coming, rocking and shuddering and crying out her pleasure until her throat was raw.

She opened her eyes.

The vision in the mirror before her was positively shameless: a woman, naked but for the panties pulled down to her thighs, one hand between her legs, the other at her breast.

If only Jack were there to see it.

The next time he would be.

Nicole picked up the DVD from Cara's coffee table and smirked at the photo of the busty blonde on the cover. '*Exotic Dance: A Pro's Tips for Bringing Your Man to His Knees*? Are you leaving the museum curator business to start a new career?'

Cara laughed and topped off Nicole's glass of sangria. 'It's more of an after-hours hobby. By the way, I have my first performance in front of a select audience tomorrow night.'

'With Jack? I thought you were playing nun with him.'

'Not exactly. But we've always spent time in public places, properly chaperoned. Tomorrow he's coming here for dinner

156

all alone.'

'What's the plan? To eat take-out food naked in bed?'

Cara shook her head. 'Wrong on both counts. I'm serving a very proper dinner. In fact, I asked him if he had a tux. When he said no, I told him to get one; rent or buy, I didn't care, but I wanted him on my doorstep in black tie. He agreed without a peep of protest.'

'So you've got a bit of dominatrix in you? You are full of surprises. In any case, I want to hear all about it.'

'Naturally. Telling you about it is always the best part.' Cara grinned, but she was surprised to feel a twinge of sadness, too. Describing her conquests to her friend had been more fun than anything that had ever really happened in bed. But Jack was different. With any luck, after they played her little Sally Rand game tomorrow night, that part of her life would be history.

Lobster bisque, chicken Provençale, a fresh peach tart – Jack had praised each course of Cara's dinner with gentlemanly grace. Now he was seated on her sofa, a glass of cognac in his hand, waiting for the surprise she'd promised him.

Cara switched on the music, a slow, jazzy tune, and glided to the centre of the room. She wore a floor-length red dress with a draped neckline, the classiest number she could find online at the stripper's supply store.

'Remember the first day we met?' She gave him a coy look. 'When you said the waiting is the best part?'

Jack smiled. 'Over the past few weeks, I've often regretted those words.'

'Still you have been the model of patience and you deserve a reward, but I have one final test for you tonight. I'm going to dance for you. Like Sally Rand. But there's no touching allowed. You can only watch.'

He let out a sigh and shifted his weight to adjust the hard-on that now tented his trousers.

'Cara, you know I'll do whatever it takes.'

It was the right answer. Smiling, she began to roll her hips to the music. The movement aroused her as it always did – and indeed she was already tingly from their flirtation over dinner – but immediately she realised this would not be like her fantasy at all. First of all, she was keenly aware of his eyes upon her. His gaze really did warm her flesh. More distracting still was the sound of his breath, the spicy male scent of him. She'd hardly begun, and she was already sweating, her secret muscles tight with lust.

But the show had to go on.

Cara threw back her shoulders and cupped her breasts. She'd practiced this move before, too, but tonight her nipples were already rock hard and so sensitive she winced as her palms brushed them. Jack noticed – he was staring so intently, how could he not? – and his tongue made a quick circle over his lips.

'Do you –' Her throat tickled and she swallowed. 'Do you want to see what I have on underneath?' Her voice definitely lacked the throaty confidence of her solo performances.

Jack narrowed his eyes. 'Please.'

Turning with the step-touch-step move she'd learned from the video, Cara brought her hand to the zipper. She eased it down slowly, then turned to face him. She meant to linger, expose her flesh to him one inch at a time, but in her nervousness she lost her grip on the slippery cloth. In an instant, the dress slithered to the carpet in a crimson pool at her feet.

Blushing, she cast a shy glance at him. 'I'm sorry. That part was supposed to take longer.'

His eyes glided over her nearly nude body, down and up again.

'I don't mind. Really.'

But the mood was broken. She was no longer Sally Rand reincarnated, a temptress schooled in the art of the tease. She was nothing but an ordinary woman in a strapless black bra and thong, standing much farther away from her boyfriend than she wanted to be.

'I feel silly now,' she admitted.

'No, you're lovely. I've wanted to see you this way since I first met you.' He gulped visibly. 'It's even better than I thought it would be.'

'Was it worth the wait?'

'Definitely.'

She stepped toward him, and he rose, taking her hand, pulling her to the sofa. He sank back on the cushion and it seemed only natural to straddle him. She had to smile to herself – it was just like a lap dance, her planned conclusion for the evening anyway.

Jack stretched his arms out across the back of the sofa, as if he suddenly remembered he'd broken the rules.

'I love the looking, but may I touch you now, too?'

Cara was interested in moving on to the next phase herself.

'Please do.'

Now his hands began to dance tentatively. He stroked her shoulders, traced her collarbone with his fingertip.

She shivered.

The finger travelled over the trim of her bra. She bit her lip and tried to steady her breathing. His hands circled around to unhook it. Her breasts fell free and he tossed the bra away, his eyes riveted to her chest.

'I'm going to take this next part very, very slowly,' he breathed.

His thumbs circled her nipples, his touch sending searing jolts through her body. Without thinking, she'd started grinding her hips against him. For an instant, she worried she might stain the trousers of the rented tux with her juices, but in the next moment she was too lost in the delicious friction to worry about cleaning bills.

'May I kiss your breasts?' he asked, his voice husky.

She nodded, suddenly unsure why she'd ever said no to him. He touched his lips to her skin, softly at first. She whimpered, thrusting her hips faster. He took her nipple in his mouth, flicking the stiff point with his tongue. She groaned with every breath now. He began to rub the other nipple between his fingers, and his other hand circled around to squeeze her arse, forcing her harder against the tantalising lump in his pants.

'I'm going to drive you crazy tonight,' he murmured. 'I'm going to tease you, like you teased me with those sexy dresses and those little moans you made when I kissed you in the car. And then, when you're good and ready, I'm going to make you come so hard you scream.'

Cara caught her breath. The dance hadn't gone quite as she'd planned, but this part was exactly like her fantasy – the deep, soothing voice, the naughty words, rolling down her spine, pooling in her belly. She bit back a moan as a new gush of wetness flooded her panties.

'Jack, I –' her voice caught in her throat. 'I mean, actually, you don't have much time.' He gave her a questioning look.

'If you keep doing what you're doing I'm going to come and I'd rather have your cock inside me.'

He let out a soft 'ah' but his reaction confused her, because he immediately frowned and fumbled around inside his jacket. When he produced the condom, they both smiled.

Jack's strip show was hasty and incomplete, but Cara didn't mind. He yanked his pants and briefs to his knees, then rolled on the condom. Panting, she pulled aside the string of her thong and pulled him inside her.

They moaned in unison.

Jack's eyes locked on hers and she wondered if he really did have her under a spell. No cock had ever felt so hard, so *there,* to her before. He nudged against the knot of desire in her belly. No matter how much she'd masturbated, that tight, pulsing need had never abated, but now it was unravelling, the heat radiating through her torso, down her thighs.

She began to buck and Jack let her set the pace. Now her dance was frantic, pounding, desperate. Each thrust went deeper, pushing her closer. His steady gaze, too, urged her on – *come for me, Cara*. And suddenly she was bursting into a thousand glittering sequins. Throwing her head back, she cried out, slamming her hips against him. His groan was quieter, but he clutched her hard, thrusting with that tell-tale rhythm of male release.

She slumped against him. He held her, stroking her hair.

'That was quick,' he murmured lazily. 'Given past history, I was expecting a more leisurely warm-up.'

'Six and a half weeks wasn't long enough for you?'

He laughed. 'I guess so, but I fancy an encore. I've some moves I think would be a good addition to a duet.'

'We could probably work in another rehearsal tonight – unless you'd like to wait?'

'I'm all for moving right ahead, but I'm afraid we might need many sessions to polish the performance.'

Cara sat up and looked into his eyes. In the sky-blue depths, a whole weekend of slow, sinuous sex glittered before her. The downside was that she wouldn't have time to call Nicole with her usual full report for days.

But when Nicole finally did hear the story, Cara hoped she'd understand. After all, the best things in life are worth waiting for.

The Rise And Fall Of The Burlesque Empire
by Maxim Jakubowski

It could be that in another life I sold my soul to the devil.

And what is happening to me now is just a form of punishment, a kind of torture inflicted on me in some indeterminate circle of hell where I must be stewing.

There is no other explanation.

I have the gift of time travel.

But I can't control it.

I am randomly taken to places and times. In a loop that is nothing less than infernal, things happen to me that claw into the sheer fabric of my heart and soul and diminish me with every journey, eating me away like a rat gnawing at my stomach. And on and on it goes and, somehow, something inside of me assures me it will never cease and the terrible pain will endure forever because I am not allow to die.

In my sleep, I was transported to Times Square.

I knew it wasn't a dream. I could smell the street, sense the vibrancy of Manhattan, touch people, eat, do things you cannot achieve in your sleep. The smell of the hamburger and hot dog stands, the blissfully soft touch of women's bare skin, the sensation of thin urban rain peppering my hair; oh no, I was certainly awake. More than awake, in fact.

It was the heyday of Times Square when New York was both decadent and joyous, a period I could only recognise from film clips and photographs, as my first actual visit to the city hadn't occurred until much later, when I was in my 30s. A newspaper headline on a corner stand confirmed to me it was the time of the Rosenbergs' trial. In real life, I had then just been a small boy in short trousers.

One moment I was tossing between my sheets, the next I was standing on the corner of Broadway and 45th Street, drinking in the sight of oversize limousines and sports cars racing south and passers-by gazing in wonder at the neon jungle surrounding us.

Somehow I took it in my stride; unlike the naked Schwarzenegger-cum-Terminator from the movies, I was fully clothed. My left hand searched for my inside jacket pocket and found a roll of green bills and coins. At least I would not have to beg.

I have never been much of a tourist, so after an hour or so of walking around, exploring this New York of memories, my mind was already wandering. I hadn't even travelled more than four blocks in any direction from my point of arrival, as if a curse of some sort would break out should I venture too far, and I was literally a prisoner of 42nd Street and its wonderful excesses.

A brightly-lit theatre marquee caught my attention advertising 'the Original Burlesque Extravaganza', featuring women whose exotic names I had at some time or another come across in books or articles: Lili St Cyr, Bettie Page, Tempest Storm, Blaze Starr. I doubted they were the real article, but my curiosity was piqued. I parted with a couple of dollar notes and walked in. There was even a two-sided programme sheet I was handed by a bored-looking commissionaire in a frayed uniform before I entered the auditorium. Which confirmed the show was a homage to Bettie Page, Blaze Starr and others and did not in fact feature the actual legends.

The spectacle was all I could have hoped for: blissfully over the top and boisterous, comic, colourful. True, the show had little in common with burlesque's origins, with a lack of fat comedians tossing out New Jersey jokes and warming up

163

the audience prior to the arrival of the dancers in their attires of feathers, divine lingerie and layers of flimsy fabric in every shade of the rainbow. But there was a Master of Ceremonies, a thin, nervous guy who looked like Lenny Bruce without the sweaty, drugged pallor. No doubt a stand-up, slumming here between gigs, perfecting his scorn like a precursor to his future counterpart in Bob Fosse's *Cabaret*. But the thin audience – the theatre could at most hold a hundred or so punters and was barely a third full – blanked him totally, visibly there just for the gals.

It was fun. Most of the dancers didn't take themselves seriously and even attained, in part, a level of performance art in their crafty disrobing and dancing acts, balancing props and knowing smiles, teasing the anorexic crowd with twinkles in their eyes or the occasional thrust just on the right side of vulgarity. There was a Carmen Miranda look-alike whose scratched record kept on jumping on the turntable behind the small stage so her juggling plastic bananas were always that little bit out of sync; and then there was the dark-haired would-be biker girl, whose labyrinth of zips kept on getting stuck as she manoeuvred herself out of her leather gear and showed off an unbelievable number of layers of black underwear under her tight trousers. Then there was the regal Claudia from Germany, as the MC introduced her, she of the thunder thighs and red hair like fire who shook her arse with the best of them, and winked at me as she turned her head halfway through her set. Or maybe it had been a speck of dust.

I counted five dancers in all. But, strangely, no blondes. Was it an early hint that the devil was playing games with me? Or just me hankering for forbidden fruit?

The men in the audience came and went. There was a five minute break, and the show began again. No one was asked to leave the auditorium. One could spend the whole day here without being disturbed, it appeared. At the time, I still thought this was a curious sort of dream, not totally unpleasant, and, having nothing better to do, I decided to stay put and see the women again and maybe check whether

Teutonic Claudia's signal had been deliberate or not. After all, she did have spectacular breasts, strong, high globes whose red pasties harmonised perfectly with her flaming hair.

But when her time came in the order of rotation, after a young pimply stagehand had cleared the previous dancer's scattered red, white and blue feathers from the stage (she had performed a faltering but broadly comic French Ooh La La act), the regal Claudia did not appear.

Instead, the MC sheepishly slithered on and, leering outrageously, said: 'And now a real treat for all you amateurs of sheer pulchritude. For the first time ever on a New York stage, for the first time ever on any stage, it's the virginal, the beautiful Anais …'

A young woman hesitantly came to the fore.

He had not been exaggerating: it was visibly her first time doing this. She didn't even have much of an outfit. Just ordinary summer street clothes with a few silk belts and scarves and a scarlet boa, no doubt borrowed from another of the girls backstage.

She had long, dark, untidy hair that trailed all the way to midway down her back. Her pale shoulders shone like beacons through the tresses draped across them. Her aquiline nose stood out proudly, punctuating the savage beauty of her features. Her ruby red-lipsticked mouth stood out like a lighthouse in a starless night.

Jesus, I thought. She is the one.

As she embarked on her slow, languorous dance, more sad seduction than ironic burlesque, my fevered imagination was already working, writing her whole life story to that point, all the burdens and adversities that had led her there, forced to dance for strangers for a few dollars.

She was visibly an amateur. The single spotlight held her in its grip as she tried to inject some feeling into her movements. It didn't work. It was evident it was not her choice to be there. A man to my right heckled. Two more in the row in front of me stood up and walked away. Even the music she had chosen or been allocated was wrong for her, some big band tune that could never blend adequately with her innate grace as she attempted to negotiate its rhythms with the staccato clockwork movements of her private dance.

I was captivated.

Even from where I was sitting, the dark pools of her eyes drew me like a whirlpool of emptiness.

She attempted a brave smile as she pulled her white cotton skirt away with a minor flourish and slid the thin silk scarves to and fro across her flat, taut stomach. I gulped. Her clumsiness almost made me want to cry.

There were more heckles from the sparse audience. On stage, Anais lowered her eyes, as if ashamed of her imperfections. I wanted to applaud, to counter the negativity of my fellow punters, but didn't. She was now, apart from the boa circling her neck like a slave collar, just in brassiere and knickers, both black and plain, the pallor of her tall, thin body isolated like a pool of light on the heart of the stage.

Finally, the management put her out of her misery and the music accompanying her semblance of a dance stopped and the spotlight on her was switched off. There was a moment of silence through which I could just about discern Anais in the penumbra picking up the pieces of clothing she had earlier shed and hurrying off to the stage's wing. Then the circle of light returned and the ersatz Carmen Miranda was back, balancing her plastic bananas with a broad grin on her lips.

I rose. I didn't know what to do. I couldn't rush the stage and chase Anais. Some heavy would stop me and beat me up, in all likelihood, if I attempted that.

I rushed to the exit. Quickly walked to the side of the small theatre, seeking the door the performers might use to depart the premises. There was one on 7th Avenue that seemed to fit the bill. I stationed myself outside.

Night came. I became drowsy from all the waiting.

Somehow, my eyes closed and I was no longer in New York and again the time was now.

I couldn't forget Anais. Something about her had moved me

166

deeply. I wanted to see her again. I wanted to listen to her story, to touch her, smell her.

Months later, I travelled in time again. It was three in the morning, my own personal witching hour when memories and regrets tore me apart with both glee and scientific precision and I felt despair like acid killing me with every added second.

I blinked and it was Manhattan.

A bit greyer than on the previous occasion, as if a thin layer of dust had settled on my memories. The noise around Times Square was louder. The flashing neon more gaudy. I realised I was wearing the same clothes as on my last visit. A similar amount of money was in my pocket. The theatre was still there, but it felt older, as if several years had elapsed. And they had. Some of the bulbs inside the marquee had died and not been replaced. It now just read 'The House of Burlesque' in flickering motion.

I paid the entrance fee and took my seat.

The floor was sticky, the curtains frayed and the interior of the theatre stank of dust and bad days. The other spectators also appeared shadier than previously, many like refugees from the weather outside, some in stained clothing, holding brown paper bags with bottles inside.

It was no longer a burlesque show, but a run-of-the-mill and particularly unimaginative striptease. The costumes the women wore at the onset of their numbers were minimal and plain, and the performers all exuded a strong sense of boredom and indifference as they shed their clothes with metronomic regularity until they stood, for the final third of whichever song they were dancing to, nipples and pubic thatches starkly exposed for all to feast on. There was no longer any tease involved, just unencumbered and artless nudity.

I sat in silence as the strippers followed each other on the small stage, waiting for I didn't know what. There was no longer a presenter, just a muffled voice on the PA system mouthing a vaguely exotic name prior to each dancer's appearance: Mitzi, Christina, Melissa … During the performances, I could sense some of the other men in the audience touching themselves or more in the darkness.

A squat Latina woman whose genital area was, time-wise, halfway between a total wax and a full jungle bush climaxed her set with a triumphant bend and flashed us all a furtive glimpse of her pink innards, and the shoulder movements of the guy sitting in front of me increased significantly. I was about to abandon my quest and leave the joint, when the next act took over the stage.

It was Anais.

Or Anna Maria, if I believed the announcer.

She had changed.

She was older and no longer as tentative, as if she had spent the months (the years?) since I had seen her last taking lessons from the other performers, or had maybe just acquired the talent to be more sensual through some form of osmosis.

Her wild gypsy hair was the same, her pale skin still a delicate shade of porcelain, her limbs long and spidery and her stomach just a touch rounder.

She danced, stripped to the Eurythmics' *Thorn in my Side*, her movements sexy and deliberate, swaying in unison with Annie Lennox's vocal swoops. This time there were no heckles.

When she shed her final garments I held my breath, hoping that what I had imagined in my crazy dreams of her would hold up to the reality of her body.

It did. The shade of her nipples veered wonderfully between brown and pink like a kaleidoscope of shifting desire, and her breasts stood firm, just the right side of both large and small; delicate, calling for my tongue, tantalising, real. My eyes moved down and, as if following my signal, she slowly moved her outstretched hand away from her cunt as the last measures of the song entered their fade out, revealing her thick curls. I caught my breath and the music stopped and the lights went out.

The silence was deafening before a a few of us applauded.

The silence returned until the disembodied voice on the PA was heard.

'And now, the parade. Gentlemen, be generous with your tips …'

The strippers, all naked, walked on to the stage and gradually moved down into the auditorium and began making their way along the rows where the male spectators were sitting. Invisible signals passed between the erstwhile dancers and some of the men in the audience and, after a few bank notes had changed hands, some of the girls would rub themselves against the generous customers. I caught a glimpse of hands caressing flesh, straying, moans, movement, whispers. I declined the untold offers of the first few dancers who reached me and waited for Anais. I tried to see where she was, which men she stopped to gratify, whether she was part of this unholy procession at all. She was. Two rows away from me, she had her back to one fat punter, his hands running across her bare skin, no doubt kneading, intruding. Her eyes and mine met across the chiaroscuro of the strip club.

I waited. Turning down all the other strippers.

Finally, she reached me.

I handed her the first note I found in my pocket. Neither of us checked its denomination. She pressed her breasts against me.

'I saw you when your name was Anais,' I whispered to her.

Her eyes came to life.

'That was a long time ago,' she answered.

'I know,' I sighed.

'You can touch me, you know,' she said. I thought I could detect a foreign accent.

My hands moved to her shoulders. I could feel her breath in my ear. Her softness was like a sting. I closed my eyes and abandoned myself to the blissful sensation. One of her hands brushed against the front of my trousers. I was hard.

'I've been thinking of you ever since that first time,' I said. 'You are beautiful.' All I could come up with was a damn cliché!

She indicated she had to move on. My time was up; there were other men further down the row.

169

I was about to say, 'No ...' when she whispered, 'I am available, you know.'

'OK,' I spat out.

Five seats further down the aisle I watched as a suited Japanese businessman dug his fingers into her cunt, having no doubt paid more than me for extra privileges. Finally, the parade ended and the women trouped back towards the stage.

I met Anais outside the theatre ten minutes later. She had changed into jeans and a black T-shirt.

We did not discuss money. We walked to the Iroquois on 44th Street, crossing the early evening traffic on Broadway. I bribed the clerk to let me have a room at short notice, even though neither of us had any luggage or reservation.

Anais and I fucked for hours. Definitely fucking and not making love. Few words were exchanged as if we now knew that our respective stories, the equally tortuous and complicated roads which had taken both of us to this room, were of no importance.

I mapped every square inch of her skin with the unbound folly of an explorer of unknown worlds. I drank the moistness that pearled from all her openings like the survivor of a terrible trek through unending deserts.

I felt quite delusional as I noted how my cock fitted her cunt, as if we had been built for each other in some strange factory by a glove maker who knew every secret of our bodies. I listened to her gasps as if they were songs. My tongue, like a blind man's hand, surveyed the textured territory of her teeth, her throat, the ridges of her perineum, the crevice of her anus, the satin of her white skin until my own throat ran dry. I gasped.

'Wait,' she said at one point and moved to the sink, where she cupped her hands under the open tap and filled her mouth before returning to the bed where I lay prone and emptied herself down my throat to relieve my thirst.

Tired, raw, sated, our bodies spooned, half of my cock still embedded softly inside her, killed by tenderness, we were like corpses on the hotel room bed. She dozed off. I resisted the attack of the night but could not hold on to consciousness much longer.

I fell asleep and arrived back in the 21st century.

The next time I travelled back in time, yet again thousands of days had elapsed. Times Square was going downhill fast. The theatre no longer existed and was now replaced by a seedy peepshow. I had to purchase ten metal chits to get in and found out that the only way of spending them was to walk in to one of the dozens of narrow private cabins and feed the box on the far wall. At which point, a metal blind would rise, revealing a thick glass rectangular window behind which a woman would be either stripping, already in the process of touching herself intimately or even stuffing a dildo into herself. Occasionally a customer in a nearby cabin would slide a note under the glass partition where a space had been created for this process and would be treated to an intimate close-up that bordered on gynaecology.

Burlesque felt like several centuries away. This was sex at its most vulgar and humiliating. I was on my last chit when a new performer made her way from a side passage onto the mini-stage that was surrounded by the exiguous cabins and their glass windows.

I recognised Anais.

She looked tired, warn, sadder than ever.

From behind the glass, I waved, hoping she would recognise me.

She did not. Or maybe the glass window only allowed vision one-way.

I waved again, mouthing, 'It's me ...'

She would not hear me.

Anais wiggled her bum against the mirror but when I slipped no note through the thin gap she swiftly moved on to the next adjacent window. A ten dollar bill was pushed through to her which she grabbed; she held her ear to the partition and listened to the customer's request, nodded, and leant back to the performing platform where she had left a large tote bag, from which she pulled an oversized sex toy in the shape of a bee-stung cock. As she brought the object down towards her opening, the metal window lowered. I was out of tokens.

I rushed back to the lone attendant on duty and changed another twenty dollars into tokens, but by the time I returned every single cabin was occupied. When there finally was a vacant one and I'd fed the damn mechanism, it was another girl behind the glass, a small titless blonde who looked as if she'd just come off the street on a school day. Her cunt was shaved and pierced and a rose tattoo peered at me just above the nipple of her left breast. I realised the cabin I was now in was the one which had housed the man who had previously slipped the ten dollar tip to Anais to pleasure herself for his gratification. I looked down. The floor beneath my loafers was still wet from his ejaculation.

I walked toward the Port Terminal bus station at the other end of 42nd Street and was sick.

Only three days later I was back on Times Square and everything had gone to seed. Drug dealers were on every corner, half the cinemas and shop fronts were boarded up, and the derelicts and panhandlers outnumbered the tourists.

The peep show that had once been the burlesque theatre had changed its name and appearance again and now advertised 'Live Sex'.

Somehow I knew what to expect, but still paid the entrance fee, hoping against hope that the inevitable would not occur.

There was a bed on a raised platform and a crowd of guys pressed up against the improvised stage. I managed to make my way nearer as some of the men gradually peeled back and left. On the bed a couple was fucking, the woman's legs raised high in the air, supported by the man's shoulders, and the stud was positioned so that all the spectators had a clear view of his cock moving in and out of the vaginal aperture.

The bed creaked but neither of the performers made a sound, mechanically going through the motions. It absurdly occurred to me to wonder how long they could actually go on screwing for the crowd, and how the guy could stay hard semi-permanently, when the man and the woman finally separated and, wordlessly, rose from the bed and walked away into a dark area. The crowd shuffled and I was able to move to the front. Evidently the couple, or another, were soon to return, as the men stayed there waiting.

And the next live sexers appeared.

The man was a monstrously tall black man, with a grey towel draped across his midriff. He stood himself at the front of the bed with his back to us voyeurs and pulled the towel away. He must have been particularly big in the trouser department as a few men at the sides where there was a better view whistled softly in approval.

An instant later, his partner made her way to the bed. Anais.

Now visibly at least a decade or so older than when I had first seen her, in what was now for me the Golden Age of Burlesque. Her skin was still terribly white, but no longer shone with that inner light that had so struck me before. She had no towel, and moved fully naked towards the bed, her shoulders slightly stooped. Indifferent to the crowd of men facing her she leaned back and lay down, then opened her legs wide. Her labia looked bruised, overused. The black guy moved closer to her, holding his massive erection in one hand, and positioned himself.

Just like all those centuries ago, her eyes caught mine. Those pools of darkness were flat and dead and there was no sign of recognition. I noticed puncture marks on her thin arms as the man entered her in one movement, and she closed her eyes. He began his mighty thrusts.

I tore myself away from the crowd of men. At least I owed her that. Not to watch.

I've been back to Times Square many times since, on my time travelling journeys. It's different now. Burlesque is but a jewelled memory, and the whole area has been gentrified,

Disneyfied, cleaned up. And however much I troop up and down the area, and dip into shiny new souvenir stores and wondrous theatres with shows for the whole family, I have never come across Anais again.

Time passes faster and faster between every visit, so I assume she is likely dead by now.

And I remain the same age.

And will do so forever.

But I cannot erase the memory of Anais and how we fitted together so well, how I was allowed for just a few hours to experience joy.

So, every new visit to 42nd Street just exacerbates the memory and makes me ache more. Like being caught in a loop of ever-increasing despair.

Damn, why can't I go home again to the home of burlesque?

Kiss Of The Spider Woman
by Elizabeth K Payne

It was a hot Sunday afternoon and Tyler and I were coming back from a walk when we passed the theatre where he worked.

'Let's stop for a glass of water,' he said, getting his keys out.

The theatre was deserted – there were no shows on Sundays – so I nosed around as he went to get the water.

'I want to see those costumes you were talking about!' I said. The theatre had been hosting a burlesque show and Tyler had been raving about the costumes.

'Hmm, I suppose we could have a quick look.'

I followed him through a corridor and down some steps.

'Ta-da, welcome backstage,' he said, opening a door, letting me into a large, messy room, full of mirrors, boxes of make-up and, of course, costumes. There were corsets and plumed hats, wigs and ostrich feathers, parasols and elaborate, glittery outfits.

'Oh, they're so pretty!' I said, trying on a large hat. 'Does it suit me?'

'No, it's too big for you,' he said, catching me and tickling me, taking the hat off my head and putting it away. 'You can look, but you can't touch.'

'Why not?' I said. 'I want to try the costumes on!'

'I'll get in trouble if they get damaged ... Lucy! What are you doing?'

I had let my skirt drop to the floor, kicking it away, and was now unbuttoning my blouse. I walked towards him, naked except for flimsy panties, and pressed my body against his.

'Come on,' I whispered. 'Let's have some fun.'

'Such a pest ...' he said, but I could feel the erection in his trousers and his hands slipping from my waist to my bottom and thighs, squeezing and caressing my flesh as we kissed.

'I'm going to get dressed up,' I said, walking away. 'And then I might treat you to a special performance.'

He lay down on a sofa, no longer protesting, and watched me put on a pair of fishnets.

'You like?' I said, turning around and sticking one leg out like a ballerina, my feet in *demi-pointe*.

'Be careful! We'll have to replace them if they tear ...'

'Oh, stop grumbling,' I said, climbing on top of him, snogging him to make him shut up.

Watch it, missy,' he said between kisses, slapping my bottom a couple of times.

'Help me chose a corset,' I said, dragging him up.

We picked a black, satiny one, which left my breasts exposed, and he helped me put it on.

'What else do I need?'

'Hmm, how about these?' he said, presenting me with a pair of tassels.

'How do you put them on?' I giggled.

'Sticky tape,' he said, rummaging in a box, while I slipped on a pair of silky gloves and tried on a selection of fascinators. I settled for a beaded one with a black rose and, to complete the look, we picked a petticoat. I admired myself in the mirror while Tyler grabbed me from behind, a hand finding its way inside my panties.

'So, did you say something about a performance?' he said.

'Back to the sofa,' I ordered.

I found a feather and ran it lightly over him, unbuttoning his shirt as I did so. He reached out to touch my face and kiss me, but I admonished him: 'Lie down. Be a good spectator.'

I ran my gloved fingers across his chest, then his legs and

crotch, feeling his erection. I stepped back and moved as if to slow music, touching my own body, first with the feather, then with my hands. I touched my clitoris, enjoying the sensation of the silk, playing with myself, getting quite wet and close to climaxing.

His hand reached for his cock.

'That's not allowed,' I said, tapping him with the feather.

I climbed on top of him, this time in a 69 position, my mouth close to his cock, and my pussy pressed against his face through the moist fabric of my panties.

'Lick me,' I said as I unzipped his fly and took his cock in my mouth, sucking gently, stroking his balls and the base of his cock with my gloved hands. 'Make me come.'

He moved my panties to the side and his tongue tickled my clitoris. He fingered me rhythmically until I had my first orgasm, moaning loudly, my body contracting.

'I think it's time I was in control,' he said after I'd come. 'Get up.'

I obeyed, looking at him quizzically. It wasn't like him to stop me when I had his cock in my mouth.

'There are a few things I need to find first ...' he said, walking towards a pile of boxes.

I waited by the sofa as he looked around for something.

'There they are,' he said, getting a pair of wings out of a box. 'Come here, butterfly.'

'Oh, these are so pretty!' I ran around in them, pretending to fly.

He fished three more items out of the box: a silk scarf and a pair of sturdy wrist restraints.

'And what are you planning to do with *those*?' I said, giggling.

'You'll see. Come with me,' he held my hand.

He walked me up some wooden steps, through a curtain ... We were on stage!

'What's that?' I said, running towards a large structure made with ropes.

'That's for the Spider Woman act. She catches a butterfly

177

in it.'

'I see,' I said, smiling as he walked towards me and kissed me, pressing me slightly against the giant web.

'Let's dim the lights … put on some music …'

He was a stage-hand, so he knew exactly what to do. A soft, golden light bathed the stage – it was like a sunset, with pink and orange tones – and then the music started, slow and seductive, reminiscent of past times.

'Now,' he said. 'This is to blindfold you …'

He lifted my hair and fixed the silk scarf around my eyes.

'And these are to make sure you don't fly anywhere.'

He secured the restraints to the web so my arms were raised at either side of my head. I tugged at them – indeed, there was no escaping.

'There you are,' he said. 'I've caught you in my web, Madame Butterfly. 'Where has that feather gone? Let me go and get it …'

He walked backstage again and then, just as he left, I heard the faint ringing of a phone and him grumbling something about being back in a second.

Seconds passed, then minutes. This was starting to get quite annoying.

Finally, I could hear steps.

'You took your time!' I said.

There was no answer, just a surprised intake of breath,

'Tyler?'

'My name isn't Tyler, I'm afraid.' It was a female voice.

I moved my wrists, trying to free myself, to no avail.

'Who are you?' I said.

'Who are *you*, more to the point?' she said. 'And why are you in my web? You aren't part of the troupe. You shouldn't be here, and you definitely shouldn't be dressed in outfits that don't belong to you, dirtying and crimping them.'

'I'm sorry. I was just playing around with my boyfriend. He works here. He's called Tyler. You might know him … He should be back any moment.'

She walked towards me.

'I suppose you want me to free you,' she said.

I did – and then I didn't. She had a velvety, seductive voice, the sort of voice you'd expect a Spider Woman to have.

'What's the alternative?' I said, my heart beating fast.

'The alternative is I play with my prey – and teach her a lesson.'

So play with me.'

'Very well. In that case, let me get my toys.'

Was everyone going to abandon me? But the Spider Woman wasn't gone for long and, on her return, I heard a swishing sound and instinctively tensed up. There was no blow, but then she was tracing the contours of my body using what was presumably the end of a crop. I could feel it delicately touching the tassels covering my nipples, each in turn, then the skin of my breasts, my waist, my left leg and thigh, finding its way up my skirt, resting on my crotch, then tapping gently against my labia and clitoris. I moved, trying to meet the crop in the spot that would maximise my pleasure. She started rubbing it against my clitoris and I moaned, encouraging her to give me more.

Instead she lifted the crop then brought it down again quickly, smacking my thigh. I let out a little cry. More whimpering – and quite a lot of wriggling – followed, as she whipped my legs and thighs. Some blows stung, some simply warmed me up, leaving me all tingly.

Eventually she stopped. I could feel and hear her kneeling in front of me and pulling my panties down. She touched the tip of her tongue to my clit. She just held it there for a few seconds, then started to lick, slowly.

'What?!' Tyler had walked in.

The Spider Woman continued to lick me.

Look what I've found in my web,' she said, still facing me.

I was desperate to see Tyler's expression – or indeed what the Spider Woman looked like – but the blindfold covered all of my visual field.

'I'm sorry, Magda, we were just –' Tyler started to explain.

'You thought yourselves burlesque performers?' she said.

'But you should know that actors need a director. Come close.'

I could hear Tyler's steps and then her getting up, turning to face him.

'Take over,' she said.

No noise from Tyler. I so wanted to see his face.

There was a pause, a shuffle, and then another tongue on my clitoris, licking me. His tongue was rougher and his movements quicker. He was used to me – he knew how to make me come, what rhythm did it best. The Spider Woman had followed a different approach. She hadn't even seemed interested in whether I'd come. She'd just licked me, slowly and deliberately – as if I'd been ice cream – turning me on terribly, but not bringing me close to orgasm. Now, though, I was almost there, my breathing had changed, I was 'in the zone', as I called it with Tyler.

'Stop,' said the Spider Woman.

To my great frustration and annoyance, he stopped.

'I want to see you fuck her,' she said. 'But first you too must take your punishment.'

Tyler was silent.

'Take your clothes off.'

I could hear clothes fall to the floor.

'All of them.'

Silence. Then some steps. I imagined her pacing in circles around him, examining him.

'Very nice,' she said.

Then a swish and the crack of the crop against Tyler's skin. He let out a small cry.

'Kiss her.'

He stepped closer to me, so I could feel his naked body and his erection pressing against me, and he kissed me hungrily on the mouth, his hands on the back of my head, pulling me close to him. She struck him once more – I'm not sure where, perhaps on his back – then again, and again, while he kissed me passionately, sometimes tensing slightly when struck, other times not even showing a reaction, even though it must have stung; I knew what that crop could inflict – I could still feel a gentle tingle where it had landed on my skin.

'I want to see you fuck her,' the Spider Woman said again.

I could hear Tyler fumbling in the pockets of his discarded trousers for a condom and then, finally, his cock filled me. I was so wet he slid inside in one smooth movement. I moaned gently in appreciation.

'Lift her up.'

He picked me up, my wrists still restrained, and I wrapped my legs against his back. He stayed still, shaking my body instead, keeping a strong hold on me. I came quickly, with a long, uninhibited moan.

'Place her back on the floor.'

He obeyed. I wondered what our spectator had been doing while we'd been fucking, if she'd been touching herself. I imagined she'd just watched us, getting increasingly excited, a powerful, feline expression on her face.

'Step away,' she ordered, and Tyler, once more, did as he'd been told.

She walked towards me, standing between me and him, and kissed my lips, then again with tongues, while her hands worked their way from my waist, to my back, to my breasts.

Then she walked away.

'Fuck her until you come. This isn't for her pleasure. Just focus on what *you* want.'

He fucked me hard, lifting my legs so they rested on his shoulders, his hands on my butt, pushing me forcefully towards him as he thrust and rode to his orgasm.

'Tidy yourself up. Get dressed,' she ordered Tyler once he'd recovered. 'Free her. Leave the blindfold on.'

He snapped the wrists restraints open. I shook my hands – they were going numb.

'Take three steps forward,' she ordered me.

I took three hesitant steps.

'Stop. Now take your wings off. Hand them to me.'

I removed them and extended my arm, holding the wings, unsure where the Spider Woman was. She took them from me.

I imagined her putting them away neatly.

'Now the corset. Tyler – help her with that.'

Slowly, item by item, the Spider Woman ordered me to undress. The petticoat, nipple tassels, fishnets, fascinator, gloves – they all came off until I was standing naked, blindfolded, in the middle of the room.

'I've put them in a bag. Tyler, I want them returned, dry-cleaned, tomorrow. Understood?'

'Yes,' he said. 'I'm sorry.'

The Spider Woman ignored his apology. She advanced towards me and kissed me.

There was a pause.

'Suck,' she said, brushing my lips with a finger. It was sticky with her juices. Unlike me, she had long nails, which I imagined to be perfectly manicured and covered in dark varnish.

'Help her get dressed again,' she said to Tyler. He fetched my clothes.

'Skirt first. Now the blouse. Button it up for her. Panties. Sandals.'

That done, we waited.

'All right then. I have things to do, so leave me to it. Tyler, guide her to the foyer, remove the blindfold once you're there, leave it by the red vase, and leave. Don't forget this,' she handed him the bag with the costumes to dry-clean. 'And never bring her here again.'

'Goodbye Spider Woman,' I said, as Tyler guided me away.

I could taste her in my mouth but still had no idea what she looked like. And I knew that I never would.

Mignon
by Siobhan Kelly

The agency rang at nine o'clock on a Friday night. I work as freelance executive PA in offices across London and I'd just done a hard, if lucrative, week with a demanding chief executive in Canary Wharf. I was winding down with a good Merlot and looking forward to a weekend with Jim, my boyfriend, when my mobile rang.

'Hi Carey,' said Karen, my contact at the agency. 'Got a new job for you, starting tomorrow, if you're up for it.'

'Tomorrow?' I whined. 'But it's Saturday. I never work on a Saturday.' I kicked off the shoes that had been constricting my feet all day and rolled down my stockings, leaving them in a little pile at the end of the sofa.

'It's not a corporate,' said Karen. I could hear her shuffling through papers on her desk. 'OK,' she said finally. 'You'll be working as a personal assistant to a Mignon Pigalle, a burlesque performer doing a charity show on Sunday evening.' She paused before asking, 'What is burlesque anyway?'

'Basically you want me to act as a gofer for a stripper,' I said. 'Come on, Karen. Haven't you got someone a bit more junior who can do this for you?'

'Pleeease,' she wheedled. 'You're my best PA. You'll be helping me out of a real pickle if you take this on. It's only a two-day job.'

'How much?' I asked. She quoted a figure that exceeded what I'd been paid for the last week's work. Sighing, I fished in my bag for my personal organiser and switched it on, mentally kissing my weekend goodbye. I'd have to make it up to Jim later.

I took a taxi to the address. The deeper into the unknown streets I rode, the more nervous I became. I was used to working in glossy chrome offices, not in streets lined with kebab shops and dive bars. The run-down building that my cab eventually pulled up outside was one I wouldn't usually have looked twice at. I arrived at the front door as instructed and met an attractive but harassed-looking with a clipboard.

'Carey Riley,' I said, shaking her hand. 'I'm here to look after Mignon Pigalle.'

'Oh, thank God you're here,' she said, crossing something off a list on her clipboard. 'I'm Alison. Mignon's waiting for you in her dressing room. This whole thing is a complete nightmare and I just haven't had the time to give Mignon the attention that someone of her celebrity deserves.'

She led me down a labyrinth of rich red corridors whose peeling paintwork only added to the air of sleazy, faded glamour that permeated the building, and told me that Mignon Pigalle was the finest burlesque performer in the world, and that getting her to headline the charity show had been a major coup.

The woman who opened the door was unlike any creature I had ever seen. She looked like one of the women you saw painted on the side of battleships in World War II. I don't just mean that she had the same hair and clothes and make-up, although she did: she was dressed in a red corset, a tiny pair of khaki shorts and a pair of red wedge heels. I mean she actually looked like a painting. Everything about her had an air of gloss and glamour, from the waxy sheen of her alabaster limbs to the brush strokes of her immaculately coiffed platinum hair. The narrowness of her waist, ankles and wrists was only eclipsed by the swell of her ass and tits. I'd never been nervous in a work situation before but I found myself getting as tongue-tied as a teenager on her first date.

'How do you do?' I said. 'I'm Carey, your personal assistant for the weekend.'

Then it was her turn to look me over.

'Well, darling, aren't you exquisite?' came the reply in a slow, Southern drawl that was straight from *Gone With The Wind*. 'I'm Mignon. Do come in.'

'Right, I'll leave you two to it,' said Alison, clearly relieved to have crossed one of her duties off her list. 'I'll see you at the dress rehearsal at one.'

Mignon was a small woman, but she filled the room with her perfume and her presence. I got the impression that she would fill, and silence, any room she walked into. When I got out my notebook to make a list of her demands, I noticed that my hands were shaking.

'OK,' I said. 'What would you like me to do for you?' I looked around the dressing room, wondering if there was anything I could do to make it more comfortable for her. It was a tawdry little space, the wallpaper hanging off in sheets and the furniture shabby.

'Do you know, darling,' said Mignon, crossing and uncrossing her legs. 'I don't really know what you can do for me. I'm not entirely sure why you're here.'

In all my years working as a PA that was the first time I'd heard that.

'My manager arranged you for me,' she explained. 'My regular PA couldn't travel from the States, and I guess he just felt that I needed someone to look after me. But I'll tell you what you could do. You could watch me practice my routine. I just got a new pair of ostriches today and I haven't broken them in yet.'

I looked around in alarm, wondering where she had concealed two leggy birds, and wondering what the hell kind of show involved live ostriches. Mignon sensed my confusion and laughed.

'These are my ostriches,' she said, reaching behind the mirror to pull out a pair of ivory-coloured feathered fans. They were almost as tall as her. With an expert hand she extended them so that they touched both sides of the room, and then folded them into her body so that so that only her feet and fingertips were visible.

'Wow,' I croaked.

'You ever hear of Sally Rand?' she asked as she curved the fans gracefully around her body. Their sweeping arcs carved breezes into the room and it wasn't until I felt a rush of cool air on my skin that I realised how hot I was getting. 'She was the original fan dancer in the 1920s and 30s. My whole act is a tribute to her. Her trick was to keep the fans moving at all times but never, ever to reveal anything that might get her into trouble. No tits, no ass.'

The call came over the tannoy calling all performers to the dress rehearsal, and Mignon began to change. I had never seen skin like it. It was as white as copy paper, not a freckle or blemish breaking the snowy surface. The only colour came from her nipples. They were such a pale shade of pink that I could barely see them.

'Hand me my wrap, would you darling?' she said. Both my nipples were rock hard and there was a damp patch forming in my panties. The whole room smelled of my arousal, a musk as strong as any floral bouquet. I wondered if she would notice, and shocked myself when I realised that I hoped she would.

We walked to the stage together, me carrying Mignon's fans. The crowd of performers parted like the Red Sea and excited voices dropped to a whisper when she rustled past. I was beginning to understand what had made her a world-class performer. There was something absolutely mesmerising about her. Even though I had only known her for an hour or so, I was proud to walk behind her.

The dress rehearsal was an eye-opener. As I watched the various performers run through their acts, I felt ashamed that I had ever dismissed burlesquers as a bunch of glorified strippers. There were entire swing bands, girl groups who sang wartime harmonies, acrobats and dancers. I soon realised that the amount of skin exposed was almost secondary to the skill and personality of the performers. The troupe was definitely a

21st century crowd – they were of all nationalities and colours, free and easy and open – but their acts harked back to a lost innocence, a time when a glimpse of stocking could fuel an erotic fantasy that lasted for weeks. I admired their professionalism and their enthusiasm: they all clapped and cheered at the end of every act and were quick to each other support.

But the buzz fell quiet when Mignon took to the stage and performed her routine to perfection. The crowd made up of her fellow performers gave her a standing ovation. But afterwards, as I helped her back into her robe, she seemed subdued.

'I'm not quite happy with these new fans yet,' she said. 'Can I ask you to stay and help me perfect the act when the others have gone home?' I looked at my watch. It was already midnight: I'd been so absorbed in the performances I hadn't noticed the time fly.

'I'll pay you overtime, of course,' she said.

I thought of Jim waiting up for me at home.

'It's not that,' I replied.

'Someone keeping the bed warm for you?' she asked, raising one barely-there eyebrow. I nodded. 'Well, he's a lucky guy ... or she's a lucky girl.'

What was it that stopped me answering? I don't know; some instinct, some sixth sense made me bite my lip. I think I knew what was going to happen even then.

The other performers filed out to toast each others' acts in a late-night bar around the corner and Mignon and I had the deserted auditorium to ourselves. Sitting on a chair at the front of the stage, I watched in admiration as she went over and over her routine, swirling those fans around her like they were an extension of her fingertips. Eventually she was satisfied that no glimpse of nipple or flesh was visible.

'If the audience isn't allowed to see what's behind the fans, what's the point of you being naked?' I asked.

'Well, it has to be fun for me, too, doesn't it?' she said. 'A girl's got to get her kicks.'

I picked her robe up from where it hung on the edge of the

chair and went to help her into it. But instead of doing so, I simply stood inches from her and looked into her eyes. Pale blue irises danced beneath heavily-lined and lidded lashes. Something like an invisible current passed between our bodies.

Even now, looking back, I can't say who made the first move. The next thing I felt was sweet hot breath on my lips and then her mouth closing in on mine. She tasted like honey, sweet and liquid. I kissed her back, the roar of blood that rushed around my body drowning the little voice in my head that told me what I was about to do was not quite what was expected of a professional executive PA. Intuitively, I slid my tongue ever so lightly in between Mignon's lips and she received it greedily, parted her lips wide, extended her own tongue to meet mine. Our bodies moved together. She was throbbing with the same heat and energy I felt. I placed one hand on Mignon's ass and pulled her hips towards mine. She pushed herself close. The fans in her hand closed around my back and tickled the nape of my neck and the bare backs of my knees. My mind was racing as well as my body: I was fluctuating between letting my body tell me what felt good and thinking, this is Mignon, this is my boss, what am I doing?

That was the last coherent thought I remember having. After that, all I was thinking about, all I was feeling, all I could picture, was Mignon. Our kisses grew more urgent, our tongues clashing, teeth, lips and tongues sucking and biting voraciously. My hand ran to Mignon's nipple, erect and proud, and my fingertip swirled small circles around the soft flesh surrounding it. Her kisses grew deeper in response, so I increased the pressure, my fingernail lightly scratching that most sensitive area. Mignon let out an involuntary moan of pleasure and, at that sound, I felt the first drops of moisture seep out of my pussy. I took a step backwards so that I could look at her in all her glory. She spread her arms wide, holding her huge feathered fans out on either side of her, exposing that delicate, milky body. She looked like an exquisite creature from another world, half goddess, half bird. Laughing with pleasure, she dropped the fans to the floor and held out her arms to me. Shaking with desire and anticipation, I stepped into the slender tangle of her embrace and allowed her to undress me.

She undid the bow that held my wrap dress together and made a murmur of appreciation as the soft jersey fabric fell away from my body. Sliding it over my shoulders, I stepped out of it so that I wore just my lingerie. Mignon unhooked my bra and I raised my hands, allowing her to remove it. She squeezed my breasts, letting the flesh to spill through her fingers.

'My, my,' she said. 'You really are something special.'

With those same soft, slender hands she rolled my panties over my hips, down my thighs and over my boots. I kicked them off and made to unlace my boots.

'Oh no,' she said. 'You can leave those on.'

We pressed our bodies against each other, and leant in for another kiss, bodies colliding, skin on skin at last. It was so much more raw and sexual than it had been when we had been clothed. Our bushes rubbed together, creating a crackle of static electricity, and my pussy lips swelled with an uncontrollable craving for her touch.

Then she bent down and put her lips to my nipple, sucking and swirling so softly that I couldn't believe I'd lived my whole life without ever feeling something so amazing and sensual. I caressed the sensitive skin on her neck, whispered into her ear,

'Mignon, this is bad, but it feels so good …' She fastened her teeth over my tit and bit down, gently, but enough to make me cry out.

'My turn now,' she said, offering me her left breast. The nipple remained a pale pearly pink but had swelled and stiffened, doubling in size: I wrapped my lips around it, sucking it softly at first, but getting greedy as I got carried away: I wanted to taste her whole tit in my mouth, and spread my lips as wide as they could go, cramming it in like a sweet, ripe peach. Her nipple tickled the back of my tongue. Then Mignon's fingers found my clitoris and began to rub it, softly and gently, making me moan into her breast. I pulled my head up from her tit and kissed her, a deep, probing kiss, then pulled away to look at her one more time: feasting my eyes on her between kisses re-ignited my desire for her.

Mignon's legs were apart and she was staggering, dizzy with lust, her back against the cold tiles of the wall. I didn't need to work on her clit: she was already dripping. The smell, a sweet nutty odour like the one I liked to sniff in my own panties when I was aroused, was a sweet perfume that filled the air and made my pulse pound harder and faster than it ever had before. I made my hand into a fist and thrust all five fingers inside her. When she whimpered I made my other hand into a fist and stuffed it into her mouth. She bit down hard, my hand muffling her moans of pleasure. I twisted my fingers around inside her cunt, feeling the little raised knob of flesh that was her G-spot, and used my knuckle to stimulate it, slowly moving up and down, up and down, until her moans became screams of ecstasy. Mignon was so caught up in what I was doing to her that her that she stopped stroking my clitoris. Desire made me greedy and selfish: I fisted Mignon harder and faster, willing her climax to come so that she could give me mine. When she eventually had an orgasm she bit down on one of my hands and the muscles of her pussy convulsed around the other.

I had never needed to come so badly in my whole life. I pulled my hand out of Mignon: it was glazed with her juices. I took that slippery hand and grabbed hers: she knew what she had to do. Her legs gave way beneath her and she slumped to the floor. I stood over her, my pussy at her eye level. She put two fingers inside me and then slowly drew them part-way out, then in again; she licked my pussy lips and then held the tip of her tongue against my clitoris, stiff, wet and slowly circling the bud. My clit began to thrum hard, my climax building inside my body. Mignon stopped licking abruptly and then sucked hard on my clit. With a little flick of her tongue, I came, knees shaking like never before, the tension releasing itself and robbing me of control over my own body. I

190

collapsed, sliding my pussy down the whole length of Mignon's body, until I was sitting opposite her. We had one more kiss: I tasted myself on her tongue.

We lay in each other's arms on the deserted stage, so satisfied and so high on pleasure that I half expected the empty auditorium to ring with applause.

'Why,' said Mignon, post-orgasm drowsiness making her voice even slower and more sensual, 'I do believe that I've never had quite so much fun on stage.'

On the Sunday night I brought Jim along to see the show. I stood in the wings, watching his face as much as the performances. I could tell that Mignon's fan dance was the highlight for him, as well as the rest of the audience. The applause at the end of the night nearly shook the dust from the chandelier above our heads.

After the other audience members had filed out, Jim came to meet us backstage. I had never seen him lost for words before but when he saw Mignon there, one breast almost escaping from her red silk robe and her arms cradled with lilies, he could only stammer his congratulations. Once I'd booked a car to take Mignon back to her hotel room I had no more duties to perform as her PA.

'Your young man is delicious,' said Mignon as she kissed my cheek goodbye. 'Next time, why don't we invite him to join us?' The thought of sharing her with Jim, who I knew had always wanted a threesome, made me so crazily hot that it was all I could do not to reach out and place my hands on her breasts, to pull her body against mine. But she slipped into the car, leaving only the ghost of her kiss, and I knew I would never see her again. Part of me was sad, but another part of me was pleased I could preserve the experience as a perfect memory – one that would have my hands wandering to my panties whenever I chose to recall it.

The phone rang first thing on Monday morning.

'Carey,' said Karen. 'How did it go?'

'It was OK, actually,' I said.

'It was brilliant, more like,' she replied. 'The client loved you. So much so that she's asked if you'll be her permanent PA in London. She comes over here four or five weekends a year. What do you say?'

I needed the silence to catch my breath.

'Sure,' I said. 'Why not?'

The Lion Tamer's Scars
by Kristina Lloyd

Roxy Roxoff wanted to run away and join an office. Sure, the circus was fun and the contortionist was cute, but getting naked every night took its toll on a girl. For three spangly years, Roxy had been stripping right down to her well-waxed pubes, and now those watching eyes were starting to bug. In fact, Roxy was so goddamn tired of being ogled she could no longer have sex with the light on.

'Honey, I won't look at you, swear to God,' said her husband, Dan Handy, but Roxy just wasn't for budging.

At night in their trailer, she'd slip into a pair of PJs and declare, 'Total dark or I'm a nun.'

'How can I tie you up when I can't see you?' cried Dan on day three of the blackout.

Roxy shrugged (unbeknown to Dan). 'Not a clue,' she said. 'You know anyone who could use some blindfolds? I guess we won't be needing them now.'

Dan had one of the handsomest cocks Roxy had ever clapped eyes on and his work-worn hands scoured like sandpaper on her skin. He was sinewy and strong with gypsy hair, a thin cigarette practically attached to his lower lip, his body a mess of mismatched tattoos. His lips were the colour of raspberries, soft, plump and oddly kittenish on a man whose masculinity was lithe, grimy and carelessly hard. He wore tatty jeans, a spanner jutting permanently from his faded back pocket, and no one knew whether he owned several white vests, all oil-smudged and torn, or just the one.

He was loyal and kind and he made Roxy laugh. In total, he was everything she could have wished for, save for one flaw: he didn't understand the stresses of showbiz. Just an ordinary guy, he liked to say, whose taste for bondage had gotten a little out of hand. One moment he's lashing his sweetheart to the bed, the next he's senior rigger for Psycho Daddy's Circus of Sin.

Keeping the flying people up in the air, alive and untangled, was Dan's ideal job and, given half a chance, he'd probably monkey about on the ropes till the cows came home. Roxy generally thought it healthy they had separate interests. But sometimes it pissed her off and she'd imagine slouching at a bar, slurring, 'My husband doesn't understand me,' to any passing strangers.

'You should put in for promotion,' said Dan. 'You've been stripping long enough and it's only grade three. Why not go for a grade four post?'

Roxy and Dan were sitting in a near-empty marquee watching Bruno the Brave rehearse his lion-taming act.

Roxy scoffed. 'I'm just a jaded stripper, Dan. What could I do that's grade four? Those jobs need experience. Qualifications. Class. Well, apart from knife thrower's assistant, but no way am I doing that, not after what happened to Lexi.'

'Yeah, I miss Lex,' said Dan, crossing himself.

The two fell into silence, gazing ahead at the circus ring fenced in with steel. Behind the bars, Bruno strolled among four big cats, a chair in one hand, a whip in the other, thighs bulging below his trademark skinny shorts. With his graceful blond curls and he-man physique, he was a veritable Greek god, albeit one who'd been horribly mauled. The beefy wedge of his torso was lacerated with scars, and the flesh of one shoulder blade was a distorted patch of pink, glassy skin.

He moved with fearless pride, muscles rippling. It was easy to picture him flinging his whip aside and using nothing but brute force to wrestle those beasts into submission.

The thought made Roxy a little damp in the gusset.

'Hey, you could go on a training course,' suggested Dan. 'They're running one on circus skills next month.'

Roxy sighed. 'Oh, I don't think so. Besides, it's such a crowded market.'

'Yeah,' agreed Dan and he gave Roxy a reassuring rub, his calloused hand grating pleasantly on her thigh.

'So maybe I should take up office work,' said Roxy. 'Do something my old man would be proud of. Filing. Answering the phone. Stapling.'

'Babes, you'd be wasted,' said Dan. 'Anyway, look around you. There's more petty bureaucracy in this screwed-up circus than in the entire the civil service. What do you want an office job for?'

Dan did have a point. Psycho Daddy, the Circus of Sin's owner and ringmaster (or CEO as he preferred), was an overweight, heavily-pierced pervert with some serious control issues. Behind the glittering façade of razzle-dazzle and anarchy was an organisation tighter than a vestal virgin's hoo-ha. Psycho Daddy, although he wore lots of leather and shaved his head (but never his beard), might as well have dressed in pinstripes and carried a briefcase.

It was at one of Psycho Daddy's full performance-staff meetings, held weekly to 'keep everyone in the loop' that Roxy broached the subject of promotion. All attendees were gathered in a ragged ring under the big top, sequins, feathers and greasepaint rubbing shoulders with performers still in day clothes.

Psycho Daddy folded his arms across the balloon of his belly, his leather waistcoat revealing flabby skin fuzzed with hair. After berating Roxy for raising an issue she ought to have first added to the agenda, he said, 'Furthermore, your salary is a private matter. Why don't you stop by my trailer later and we'll talk about it?'

'Because,' said Roxy, sitting straighter in her chair, 'you'll only make me suck your dick for an 0.3 percent pay increase. Just like you did at my last staff appraisal.'

The tightrope walker, dressed in a lime-green leotard, raised his biro. 'Shall I minute that?'

Psycho Daddy shot a warning look at him then returned to Roxy. 'You're a stripper, Rox. That's grade three. End of.'

'So what if I take a look at my job description and apply for a regrade?' said Roxy. 'I reckon a cabaret burlesque dancer would be on, oh, about grade four.'

'A cabaret what?' asked Psycho Daddy.

'A cabaret burlesque dancer.'

Again, the tightrope walker raised his biro. 'Could you spell that?'

'And could you tell us what it is?' chorused The Gemini Brothers.

'It's just a fancy name for stripper,' said the third aerial acrobat.

'No it's not,' said Roxy. 'Burlesque is classier. And it's ironic. You know, tongue in cheek. And sort of retro. And empowering to women.'

Belinda Bitchlips, the unicycling transvestite, gave a snort. 'Same shit, different frock.'

'Not true!' said Roxy.

'A spade's a spade,' said Belinda.

'They're not the same,' insisted Roxy, getting heated. 'For one thing, I don't take off all my clothes. The emphasis is on tease, not strip. I googled it.'

Psycho Daddy guffawed. His face was so full of metal it was rare to get an animated expression, but his guffaw came close. 'We get less tit, you get more dough? You got ideas above your station, Rox.'

'Silk purse, sow's ear,' drawled Belinda. 'You can't make a from a. Rearrange those words to form a sentence.' Bruno chuckled, casting Roxy a lecherous look. His eyes dropped brazenly to her cleavage, assessing her like a piece of meat. He looked so hot and dumb, his pre-show stubble prickling his jaw with golden glints. Roxy felt uncomfortably aroused by his attention. Funny, because the attention of several hundred did nothing for her now.

She pushed the thought aside, inhaling deeply. 'This circus is behind the times,' she declared, feeling bold.

'Go sister,' sneered Belinda Bitchlips.

'Stripping is cheap and sleazy,' continued Roxy. 'And it's for dirty old men. Whereas burlesque, well, that's fun for all the … Um, fun for everyone.'

'No fun if I got to pay you more,' said Psycho Daddy.

Roxy glared at him. 'No fun if … if, say, I phone in sick tonight.'

'The show must go on,' chanted everyone wearily, almost as they'd been trained.

Psycho Daddy narrowed his eyes at Roxy, his piercings winking in the sawdusty light. 'You feeling unwell?'

Roxy gave a grand toss of her head. 'Peaky.'

Psycho Daddy harrumphed. 'Then what say you take the night off?' he replied. 'Maybe spend some time re-acquainting yourself with the staff handbook. Section 16, clause 3.1 should be of interest: No one is irreplaceable. Not even you.'

After dark, when the heavens were glittering like ten million sequins, the Circus of Sin became a twisted, magical place, a pageant of passion and perversion, of delight and enchantment, where fireballs flamed higher than the stilt-walkers' ears, the ringmaster twirled his menacing moustache, tigers roared and the crowds oohed and aahed as sparkly trapeze artists soared like rockets among the wires and ropes in the canvas sky.

Roll up! Roll up! Come and see the contortionist who can autofellate! Watch the sexiest sword-swallower deep-throat her dildos! Be amazed at the acrobats making love in mid-air! See the king of the jungle submit to the whip!

Dotted around the big top were vans selling burgers, candy floss, doughnuts and hot dogs. The catch of sweetness and fried onions drifted on the summer breeze, mingling with the smell of diesel, disinfectant, lion shit and straw in the circus's park of brightly-painted trucks. Cables snaked across the muddied ground, a generator whirred and backstage labourers milled about in the white haze of halogen.

Unnoticed, Roxy moved among them, heading for the darker outskirts. If she had a proper job in an office there'd be none of this crap. Management would take you seriously if you were ill, unlike Daddy, who'd virtually threatened her with dismissal. On civvy street, she'd be able to turn up for work in her flats and people wouldn't wolf whistle when she clocked on. Beforehand she wouldn't need to pluck anything more than her eyebrows. And at Christmas, there'd be a party and she'd be able to fuck on top of a photocopier like normal people did. Oh, what joy! Roxy imagined herself bent over a photocopier, clothes around her boring shoes as some brute in a suit rammed her from behind. The brute had a peachily round arse, hugged by the contours of his clingy black shorts. His torso was broad and magnificent and, as Roxy slunk towards the performers' trailers, she mentally undressed him only to discover that the magnificent torso had been savaged by the claws and jaws of furious lions.

Bruno the Brave.

Works in accounts.

Cute guy. Oh, you'd know him if you saw him.

Half lost in daydreams, Roxy picked her way over uneven ground until a noise stilled her. 'Ahhhh God, yes …' A voice floating across the night. Weird, almost as if her fantasies had transformed themselves into audible reality. Maybe she *was* ill, hearing things, going gaga.

'Uh, uh.'

Or maybe someone was fucking. That was possible too.

Roxy sighed and walked on. She hadn't had sex for almost a fortnight. Well, not good, hard, filthy sex, not the sort where Dan cuffed her, smacked her and called her 'slut, bitch, whore.' Boy, how she adored that. Had it really been only a fortnight ago? Felt like years. For a while, they'd tried no-frills sex but the novelty of fucking like blind people had worn off fast when the two of them had bumped heads, leaving Roxy worried she might wind up with a black eye, not a good look on a showgirl.

'Jeez,' Dan had muttered. 'A shiner from vanilla. They'd never believe us.'

Since then, they hadn't really been up to much.

'Ohhhh!'

The cry was louder, closer. Those were noises of the night, without a doubt. Dirty, sexy noises. Secrets. Sin. The circus seemed so far away now, a gaudy spectacle of splendour and light where miracles happened. Here, the humdrum rows of caravan trailers and camper vans were in semi-darkness, as bland as a suburban estate after midnight, the main difference being that at that hour in suburbia, everyone was asleep. In these empty makeshift streets of the circus, everyone was out.

Well, almost everyone.

The sounds were coming from a modern boxy motor home. A small square window cast a fuzzy amber glow, thin orange curtains drooping on their wire and split at the centre with a stripe of clearer light. Roxy checked over her shoulder before creeping nearer, slipping into a short grassy alleyway bordered by two vehicles.

The grunts continued, long and low, the sound of a man being very slowly fucked. Hardly daring to breathe, Roxy stood a few feet in front of the window. It seemed a miniature stage, the gap in the curtains wide enough to show a world beyond. The set was cramped and domestic, its shrunken furniture and fittings too big for a doll's house, too small for reality. At its centre was a manliness so wonderful it made Roxy catch her breath.

His scars were fine seams of silvery pink, shimmering faintly as his muscles worked. The wound on his shoulder blade was a satiny pink patch, twisted, puckered and lumpy. His pale arse swelled from the dip of his lower back, cheeks like ripe fruits, and his slow thrusts were as controlled and deliberate as torture. Sprawled at an angle over the fixed formica table was a second man, knuckles turning white where he gripped the edge, biceps popping, tendons taut. He was the noise-maker, groaning over and over as Bruno the Brave, his buttocks rolling with a leisurely swing, drove deep into his pert little arse.

Roxy gawped, instantly hot. Bruno and who? She shifted on tiptoe, trying to see. Her knees felt weak and soft, her pussy too. An athletic build and shorn shiny head. Perhaps one of the support acts, the guy who juggled alongside Belinda Bitchlips. Or maybe one of the animal handlers. Someone who, like Bruno, had already performed that night and wasn't needed until the grand finale.

Hell, it hardly mattered. Together, the men were mesmerising. In the buttery low-watt light, sweat shone wetly on the slab of Bruno's back, and at the base of his spine, downy gold hair glinted like filaments as he eased his cock in and out. He had one hefty hand planted on his partner's back, and with his other he held the guy's arm in a loose twist, clamping his wrist by his skewered buttocks.

'Tell me you want it,' snarled Bruno under his breath, his accent faintly Teutonic. 'Tell me you want it hard in your ass.'

'Oh, man,' growled the second guy. 'I want it bad, so fucking bad.'

'How bad?' asked Bruno. He withdrew almost fully, holding himself at his furthest reach, his thick shaft oily with lube.

'Man, fuck me! Fuck me hard.'

Roxy echoed him in her head. Oh, if only she could be spread on that table, wide open and ready to receive. Bruno smiled a fraction, still as a statue. The other guy gasped, trying to push back and tilt his arse to engulf Bruno's mighty cock. But Bruno kept him pinned to the table, only relenting after several seconds of begging.

He drove in a couple of deep, measured lengths. 'This hard enough for your ass?'

No, thought Roxy. Do me harder. Pull my hair. Cuff me and clip me and fuck me till I cry! Almost as if he'd heard her, Bruno began ramming with increasing ferocity, face twisting in agonised pleasure, blond curls sticking damply to his skin.

Roxy couldn't tear herself away, arousal and fear making her pulses thud. All it would take was for Bruno to turn his head and she'd be spotted, a bug-eyed woman spying on him in the dark. But how could she not look? How could she not be enormously turned on by that mauled Adonis and his glorious muscular beauty?

Roxy was so captivated by the peep show that she didn't hear the approach of careful footfall, didn't see the long shadow slope across the grass or smell the faint note of cigarettes until it was all too late.

From behind, a hand slammed onto her mouth, muffling her cry.

'Scream and I'll kill you,' he whispered.

Roxy recognised the voice at once and fell silent save for frightened breaths huffing through her nostrils.

'Good girl,' he said softly, and his words tickled her ear.

He drew her backwards, an arm around her waist, then side-stepped so she was pressed against the van opposite Bruno's. He twisted his hand so her mouth was still covered and Roxy stared into a pair of crazy brown eyes.

'So,' he said, 'you want him to tame you, huh? You want to be his favourite tiger? Pretty girl in the cage doing the big man's bidding?'

Memo to self, thought Roxy: my husband is one hot, horny pervert.

'No?' mocked Dan, his voice a gravelly whisper. 'That doesn't push your buttons?'

Roxy shook her head, feigning innocence.

'Well, I'm not sure I believe that,' said Dan. 'Let's check that little pussy, shall we? See how wet it is.'

Roxy struggled, half ashamed, trying to bat away Dan's hand as it slid up her thigh. In the motor home, Bruno was still going strong, his wild grunts and his boyfriend's gasps masking any noise of theirs.

'What's the problem, cutie pie?' asked Dan. 'Scared I might get angry?'

Roxy protested, her cries dying in the humidity of Dan's palm. She wriggled and bleated as he grappled with scraps of lace, his calloused hand grazing her inner thighs. He pressed her harder against the side of the van, chest weighing heavily against her breasts, and yanked fabric aside between her legs.

Roxy tried to wail.

'Shut up,' said Dan through gritted teeth.

Roxy stared straight into his eyes as his fingertips stumbled over the folds of her pussy. When his big hands found her hole, his grin broadened and he shoved two fingers high and hard.

'Well, well, well,' he said. 'Soaked. Now there's a surprise.'

Roxy couldn't help but groan.

'You like that, huh?' asked Dan. He waggled his fingers, churning her juices, and making her groan again. 'Bet you wish you had a cock in there, don't you? Maybe a lion tamer's cock? That what you want?'

Dan ground his crotch, the lump of his hard-on rubbing against Roxy's thigh. Dizzy with wanting, Roxy glanced over Dan's shoulder, still able to glimpse Bruno through the sliver of open curtain, his slashed torso tipping back and forth. She felt sandwiched between two marked men, one scarred, the other inked. Dan curled his fingers inside her, thumb on her clit.

'You like that idea?' he asked. 'Getting pronged by Mr Lion?'

Roxy shook her head but it was a feeble denial.

''Cause I'm not one for gossip,' said Dan, 'but I've heard a rumour you're not putting out for your husband. Denying him his conjugals. That true?'

His fingers kept on moving, making Roxy so randy she was about ready to collapse.

Again she shook her head.

'Well, I think I should give you a little test run,' said Dan. 'Make sure everything's working down there. So I'm going to take my hand from your mouth and fuck you senseless.' He arched his brows. 'Okay?'

Roxy nodded.

'Scream, and I throw you to the lions,' he added.

Cautiously, Dan removed his hand, allowing Roxy to breathe more easily.

'Now get my cock out,' he said.

Roxy didn't stir.

'Now,' hissed Dan, and Roxy obeyed.

Dan's boner jerked out of his flies, warm and resilient in Roxy's fist. Hell, but he felt good, she thought, so sturdy and thick.

'See, I knew you wanted cock,' whispered Dan.

Quickly, he tugged down Roxy's G-string, forcing her legs wider as she stepped clear of her underwear.

'Which is good news,' said Dan. 'Because I want cunt.'

Roxy whimpered, releasing Dan's cock. She felt so open, the night air cool on her wetness, her insides aching with hunger. Dan's fat tip nudged at her lips, then moments later she was stuffed solid, biting back a cry as his length surged high, splitting and filling her with one deep meaty thrust.

'Ahhh, baby. It's been too long.'

'Oh God, yes,' said Roxy, and she hooked one leg about Dan's hips, holding him close.

The camper van shuddered as they fucked, Roxy's arse bumping against the metal. She tried to keep quiet but it was impossible when Dan's big hard cock was sliding inside her, pressing her open, his every lunge making sensation flare. Anyway, who cared? In the vehicle opposite, Bruno and his boyfriend were fucking like there was no tomorrow. And what better way to fuck, thought Roxy, and she raised her eyes to the twinkling night, breathless with ecstasy, shimmering on the brink of celestial freefall.

It didn't take long.

'Come on! Come, baby!' urged Dan, and Roxy did, her bliss syncing with Bruno's, who peaked with a groan so darkly delicious his throat might have been made of burnt sugar and scar tissue.

'Oh, man,' breathed Dan, and he hammered on, thighs powering his thrusts until he held still, cock at max, hips quivering as he shot his load.

'Wow,' he breathed, recovering.

'Yeah,' sighed Roxy, and they stood there a while, wrapped in each other's arms, juices mingling while, high above them, stars winked in the black velvet sky and somewhere, far off, a lion roared.

Roxy Roxoff didn't run away and join an office. She sewed extra sequins onto her costume, invested in a range of nipple tassels and became a burlesque dancer at grade four, albeit on the lowest spinal pay-point. Psycho Daddy, though he missed Roxy's tits, said she was too good to lose, especially after Lexi, and promised to increase her salary (by 0.3 per cent) when she got better at irony.

'Funny guy,' replied Roxy with disdain, earning herself a Christmas bonus.

Though she still wasn't keen on being stared at every night, Roxy figured all jobs had their down sides and it was best just to get on with it.

Dan and Roxy let the light back into their sex life, enabling them to get dark again with bondage, hurting and role play. Sometimes Dan would fasten a leash to Roxy's neck and play lion tamer to her big cat. 'Come here,' he'd say, and, 'Beg for it, bitch,' or, 'Suck my cock,' and other things you shouldn't say to a lion.

Occasionally, Roxy would sneak off after her burlesque routine and watch Bruno shagging his latest squeeze in the squeeze of his motor home. Dan didn't mind her watching if it made her hot and she suspected Bruno didn't mind either, although he never let on he knew.

And Roxy stopped dreaming of office work almost entirely. Just sometimes, late at night, with Dan snoring contentedly by her side, she'd fantasise about being Bruno the Brave's PA, about rubbing healing emollient into his silvery-pink scars then filing the bottle in a drawer marked L – for lotion, lion, love and lucky.

The Finest Legs To Grace The Boards
by Katie Crawley

Picture this …

The lights dim. A hush falls momentarily over the crowd and, as the lights die completely, the first 'woot' rings out, accompanied by a light smattering of hands clapping. The rest of the audience soon follows suit and the applause grows to a crescendo, the watchers whipping themselves into a frenzy that peaks just as the red velvet curtains are whipped back and the spot bursts into dazzling light, illuminating a radiant ruby smile and a sparkling brassiere … Gracie Garter, hands on hips, shakes her curls over her shoulders, posed to perfection, waiting for the music to begin …

Laura Simpson – aka Gracie Garter – throws her arms into the air and prances and dances around her bedroom. In front of the mirror she stops to sing at her reflection, face animated and glowing with joy.

'There's NO business like SHOW business like NO business I KNOOOOOOOOOOW!' And she's off again, spinning and jumping right up onto the bed where she bounces up and down, arms waving, legs kicking and caterwauling at the top of her lungs: 'There's NO dancer like Gracie Garter like NO dancer I knoooooooow! Everything about her is appealing, everybody wants to take her hoooooooooome!'

Ah, but I get carried away. I must apologise, dear reader; it is impossible not to imagine the joy that Gracie – Laura – felt the day she received the news that she would be headlining the showcase that was Saturday Night Strip Tease at the Lounge. Since she was a little girl, all Laura had wanted to do was dance. Back then it was all ballet shoes and tutus, of course. But the Gracie I knew was the sweetheart of striptease, a belladonna of burlesque, the lady with the most luscious legs in London. Oh yes, Gracie Garter knew exactly how to dress up ... and strip down.

Laura was working at the Lounge – a club in a grubby little back alley in the East End – for six months before she was given the prime spot. No, the Lounge isn't the most glamorous of venues. In fact, by many standards it's a dive. Once upon a time it was a stylish little playhouse, the talk of the town. Well, maybe not quite the talk of the town, but stylish nonetheless. These days, however, it's reduced to a lounge bar that is empty most nights, save for the few loyal gents who come in to sample a fine glass of whisky and escape the wife. Rumour has it that the owner uses the business as a front for his drugs operation but, knowing the owner as I do, I can assure you this is untrue.

By far the best thing about the Lounge – and the most successful night – is Saturday. Saturday Night Strip Tease, to be precise. It showcases the finest girls that London has to offer. The finest girls that haven't been snapped up by the bigger and fancier venues, anyway. In the time it's been running, Strip Tease has developed quite a reputation and even gained something of a cult following. Whereas in the early days it attracted only a thin smattering of leering men in overcoats ogling the girls as they shimmied about on stage, now the audience has grown to such an extent that there's regularly a queue at the door of attractive young women in high heels and corsets. Quite an achievement, for a venue such as the Lounge.

Of course, it's the girls who bring the punters in. Men come to lust after them, women come wanting to be them. But the true secret of the club's success is the regular turnover of performers, keeping the acts fresh. Every few months there's a brand new headliner, bringing a unique style and signature. There was Lily Luscious, with the most admirable arse, and Pretty Polly, with the sweetest smile; Tantalising Tanja, remembered for her incredible knockers; and let's not forget Fi-Fi, famous for her unorthodox act involving a violin. Oh, if you could have seen her finger work: mesmerising! Each of the girls was a great success and developed quite a following (though, admittedly, of drunken middle-aged men). But each of the girls disappeared from the circuit not long after taking the headlining spot. Not that anyone really thought twice about this — it wasn't as if any of the girls had been well known on the circuit before they started at Saturday Night Strip Tease. Paving the way for Gracie's success — and dropping from the limelight after only a month at the top spot — was Nicky, sporting lovely waist-length red curls and known to her avid fans as Cutie Pie. With so many girls moving on after such a short time in the prime position on the bill, the other girls were beginning to twitter backstage about the headline spot being jinxed — or, worse, cursed. None of them wanted to take it. But our little Laura didn't care. Nor did she care where Nicky had skulked off to. All it meant to Laura was that her dream was coming true. When Nicky failed to show up for the performance one night, Laura gallantly stepped in. The following week, it became official. Nicky would not be back. That coming Saturday, Gracie — Laura — would be the new headline act.

On that momentous night, Laura arrived hours early to perfect her costume and make-up, for the first time ever in her own dressing room (a poky, grubby room that was more like a broom cupboard with a mirror and a chair in it). When the hour came, she was transformed. Gracie Garter was ready to meet her audience.

The lights dimmed, the chatter hushed, the curtains whipped back to reveal the stage. For Gracie's act, a rather large bed had been dragged to centre stage. Gracie stumbled onto the boards to a smattering of applause. With a black satin

207

top hat perched at a jaunty angle on her perfectly-slicked bangs and an oversized suit jacket that came down past her knees, she tottered on impossibly high heels. One hand clutching a bottle of champagne, she waved to an invisible friend off stage somewhere (presumably the owner of the jacket) and turned her attention to the crowd, doing a wonderful job of miming drunk.

First it was off with the jacket, then off with the scanty dress beneath, to reveal a black and silver two piece – very stylish. Gracie was clearly putting everything into her performance, and succeeded in getting the crowd in a real frenzy. Of course, as the last act of the night she was helped along by the copious amounts of alcohol already imbibed … though there's no denying, she was on form!

Those that had watched her dance before could see an energy about Gracie that night, an enthusiasm that beamed out of her. She had truly come alive, and it was most arousing. But we must not forget that it was also amusing; yes, this was tongue-in-cheek burlesque at its best.

In the middle of her act she lay back on the bed and began to remove her silky stockings. This was a treat. Gracie Garter had such divine legs. She knew it, though; of course she knew it. And she knew how to make the most of them. Flat on her back, she raised one leg in the air elegantly, her knee bent so she could grasp her toes. She started to pull her stocking off as if it were a sock, straightening her leg as the fabric stretched in her hands. She must have sewn several pairs in a long tube, or some such trickery, because as she pulled and pulled the fabric just kept coming – like a conjurer's handkerchief, it got longer and longer until she had it in her teeth, twisted around her body as she rolled about on the bed. Finally, finally the black fabric began to creep down her leg, revealing the milky white curve beneath. And, of course, the real treat came when she repeated the process with the other leg …

The rest of the act passed in style. The champagne cork popped into the audience (nearly taking someone's eye out) and the bubbles poured over her writhing body. But nothing could top her spectacular stripping of her stockings. Oh yes, that trick made the show. There is no doubt that after that night Gracie Garter would be remembered by the Lounge faithfuls as having the finest legs ever to grace the boards.

None could have been more taken with the performance than a lone gentleman loitering by the stage. When Gracie had tottered onto the boards, the cigarette he had been raising to his lips had stopped midway. He had not moved – he had not blinked – throughout the show, and when the music had finished and Gracie had collapsed back upon the bed, he had clapped and cheered harder and louder than anyone in the house.

The gentleman certainly cut a suave figure, standing there gazing enraptured at the new starlet. A wide-brimmed hat cast his face in shadow and he wore a sharp suit with an expensive cut. Laura – Gracie – had certainly noticed him as she danced. Her eyes had kept flickering to the corner of the stage by which he stood, the smile on her lips getting brighter each time she did so, so that by the end of it he felt she had danced for him and him alone.

Laura might not have recognised him, but almost any of the regulars would have. He was often there, at the corner of the stage, watching. Always alone. Always in the same sharp suit, always a cigarette or even a cigar in his fingers. But he only ever appeared for the headliner.

Following the spectacular performance of Laura – or rather, Gracie – the club emptied. The girls all drifted off home and the staff began to filter out. The last to leave, Laura wound her way through the darkened Lounge, weaving between tables and chairs and jumping nearly a foot in the air when a silky voice piped up from beside the bar. The gentleman who had been enthralled by her performance sat alone, the dim lights behind the counter casting his face in deep shadow.

He identified himself as the owner, and his effervescent praise of the outstanding performance he had witnessed warmed Laura almost instantly. Of course, she would be delighted to join him for a drink or two. Or three or four … So

209

that soon Laura (though he called her Gracie) was giggling and stumbling up the stairs to the little flat that the gentleman occupied above the club.

The stripping of Laura's attire was somewhat less elegant than the performance she had given for her audience. Indeed, it was with a hunger that bordered on brute force that her gentleman friend ripped her clothes from her small frame. Her breasts were crushed in strong hands, her buttocks kneaded so hard that red finger marks remained long after they had been released, his head was buried in her neck, kissing so hungrily that to an onlooker he might have been mauling the delicate beauty. Finally, he lifted her clean from the floor and threw her onto his bed. Laura, giddy, giggling, squirming down into the covers, preened for him. He looked upon her, devouring her with his gaze, eyes raking over the pert breasts and flat stomach. But it was on her legs that his gaze lingered longest.

It was to kiss those legs that he finally lowered himself to his knees beside the bed, taking a foot delicately and reverently in his hands and raising it to his lips. Laura sighed, though she might have been surprised at the sudden gentleness that had washed over her lover. He planted a kiss upon each of her perfectly pedicured toes before he started to work his way up her shin to her knee and beyond, a hundred fluttering kisses all over her thigh. Back down he went, the kisses becoming wetter and wetter as his tongue darted out to taste the remnants of champagne still sticky on her milky flesh.

Laura writhed on the bed, hands behind her head and a smile on her lips. Her eyes were closed and she was simply drifting on the ecstasy that his expert ministrations sent flooding through her.

Worshipfully he worked his way up and down the other leg, and then quickly rolled her over to start kissing her calves. There the skin was smooth and taut. Over and over he praised her legs, telling her how wonderful, how perfect, how beautiful, they were. He traced the elegant curve of her calf muscle with his tongue, down to the curve of her heel, tickling the sole of her foot so that she giggled out loud and wriggled beneath him. But despite her obvious ticklishness, he didn't move away from her feet. No, upon these little treasures he lingered. Sucking each toe into his mouth in turn, he delved his tongue in between them, he nibbled on the little pads and blew on the wet patches his tongue had left. All the while, his fingers worked, massaging her soles, relieving the ache in her instep.

Laura moaned and groaned throughout. It would be fair to say that she had never received such attention before. This man – the owner of the club, no less – was worshiping her legs as if she were a goddess. Literally kissing her feet – practically swallowing them whole in his eagerness.

He was kneeling on the bed now and had started to work his way back up her legs. No kisses now, but licking and lapping at her flesh, biting her thighs and becoming ever more vicious as he went. His hands were on her buttocks again, kneading just as roughly as before, adding new little red pressure marks where the others had faded. He pulled her cheeks apart just as he reached that most sensitive skin at the top of her thighs and there was a pause while he inspected what he saw … but a short pause, for he dived back down, his tongue urgently pressing between her buttocks into her anus.

Laura cried out in delight, her body tense beneath him for a moment, but soon relaxing. Her weight shifted and she pushed up from her knees, lifting her arse to press against his face, urging him ever deeper into that tight recess. One hand on her cheek, holding her crack open, the other had slipped between her thighs, long fingers pressing into silky folds. She was wet, of course. So wet she swallowed those probing fingers easily, first one, and then another, and another. For a few minutes he worked, ramming his fingers in hard and fast, stretching her wider and wider until soon she had taken the whole hand. So hard it was she was convinced that with this next push she would swallow his arm whole, right up to the elbow.

Laura's hips bucked, she writhed upon his hand, thrusting up into his face, and her cries of ecstasy filled the room. They could have filled the street and she wouldn't have known; she was oblivious to all but the persistent pounding against her womb and the firm tongue prising open the puckered star of her anus. Oh, but she was enjoying it. That delicate little girl liked it rough. She liked it deep. And she liked it hard.

After what could have been a few short minutes, or an hour, he rose for breath. He withdrew his hand from that dripping cunt and wiped the thick juices on his trousers. His breathing was heavy, urgent, and Laura, who had crumpled onto the bed with a slightly disappointed groan that this had all stopped before her own enjoyment had peaked, might have thought it were a wild beast, rather than a man, kneeling over her.

One hand remained upon her arse – he was reluctant to let that prize go – but his other hand was busy with his belt buckle, with his fly, busy removing the restriction of his trousers. There was no time to strip completely; there was barely time to rip open a condom and sheaf that throbbing member. He had to have her right then.

He didn't waste too much time on pleasantries, his hands kneading her buttocks, pulling apart the flesh so he could clearly see that tight hole. He spat on the already-wet skin, worked the spit in with his thumb and then guided his cock towards the hole. He was quick; he was rough. But he was in. A grunt and a relieved groan issued from him, but it was lost in Laura's scream of agony as pain suddenly burst through her. It would seem that particular recess had not been violated before. He didn't stop, however, to comfort his prize. No. For such niceties there was no longer time.

With hands on her hips he started to thrust deep and hard, pulling her up to meet the thrusts so that his hips ground painfully into her arse. Laura's drawn out cries became broken, short, punctuating each thrust and mingling with his grunts. One of his hands slipped round to find her dripping cunt, his fingers roughly pushing inside. This was a bit much for Laura, who was becoming completely overwhelmed. Stuffed full of cock and fingers, her own fingers twisted into the bed-sheets, her teeth biting down on the pillow, light

212

exploding behind her tightly-shut eyes.

But whatever protest she might have begun with, she soon forgot. Her muscles began to relax. It wasn't long before she had stopped fighting and trying to pull away from each hard thrust, but instead was bucking up to meet them, inviting him deeper and deeper into her arse. The pain was pleasure. The thumb working over her clit was utter delight.

'Harder,' she begged, 'fuck me harder.'

Of course, he obliged. And with her supporting her own weight on her knees, writhing back onto his cock, his hands were free to wander. Well, the one that wasn't raking at the walls of her cunt was. He found her nipples, hard and erect, and he rolled them between thumb and forefinger; he gently tugged them and tightly pinched them. This might have been too much for poor little Laura, who was rapidly becoming distressed again as the pleasure she was experiencing continued to mount. It built and built and her cries became whimpers, her breath shortening, her voice climbing and her body tensing … until finally, finally the wave broke over her. The pleasure peaked and in a great crescendo it flooded her senses.

No longer able to hold herself up, she saw stars. Her body jerked, every muscle in spasm, bucking her wildly so that she floundered like a fish out of water. He leaned back on his knees, holding her hips once more, lifting her back to him and refusing to let her escape, deeper and deeper, with muscles tightening about his cock. And then, as quickly as he had started, he was throwing her off him, spinning her round so she was on her back. He pulled the rubber from his cock just as a thick spurt of semen fired out of it. To Laura's delight, that hot seed splashed across her cheek. Her back arched and a long groan leapt from her. She writhed in pleasure, eyes on his cock as ribbon after ribbon pumped onto her sweat-soaked body. He kneeled over her, holding his twitching cock tightly at the base and calling her all the bitches and whores under the sun as milky pearls splashed over her face, her breasts, her stomach and thighs, drenching her. She relished his words,

213

nodding enthusiastically, agreeing fervently, rubbing that fluid over any inch of her chest that it had missed.

When it was over, every last drop spent, he collapsed, folding into her embrace. Those hot, wet thighs wrapped tight around his back, and in this heaven he lingered for the longest while.

Now, dear reader, you may be wondering how I, your humble narrator, gained such superb seats to this after-hours performance. Or, perhaps the more astute of you have already realised that it is I who in fact owns the club, that I am the lucky gentleman who despoiled the lovely Laura – or, as I like to remember her, the glorious Gracie Garter.

And she was glorious! I left her squirming on the bed, breathing hard; flushed and elated. I went to the bathroom, rather elated myself, I might add. Yes, she was divine. It was a shame, really, that it was to be so short-lived. But needs must … and I was so close, the night I saw Gracie dance, to realising my ambition. So many months of hard work, soon to pay off. Yes, the moment I'd seen her I'd realised she was exactly what I was looking for. I need not wait any longer.

But I could not – would not – deny myself the warmth of those beautiful legs. Could not deny myself the feel of them wrapped tight about me.

I had to leave Gracie – forgive me, I should say Laura – alone on the bed, and visit my true love. I had to tell her it would not be long until she was ready, until it would be she who wrapped her thighs about my back.

I found my precious lying upon the table where I had left her, of course. Without her legs she would not be able to get far, after all. I realised as I ran my fingers lovingly through those spectacular red curls that I had been careless with my tools. A large knife lay beside those long musician's fingers. I picked it up, tracing a finger gently over a seam beneath the left breast (an early attempt and not very neat). I had to apologise to my precious for leaving such a dangerous object where she could so easily have hurt herself, and I bent to kiss

214

those pretty lips … pretty, pretty Polly, how I wish you would smile that sweet smile for me …

But as I straightened, a shadow crossed the room. As I made to turn, I caught sight of a startled Gracie reflected in the blade of that sharp, sharp knife.

Her eyes wide and horror-struck, I'm sure her last words were, 'That's not Nicky's face!'

Making Sweet Music
by Emily Dubberley and Alyson Fixter

'Dance for me,' he said.

I blushed and giggled. Dancing has never been my strong point. I can move to the rhythm but I knew, remembering his tales of the lapdancers and showgirls, strippers and burlesquers in his past that moving from side to side in time to the music wouldn't suffice.

'Dance for me,' he repeated, this time with a sexy undercurrent of threat to his voice. He knew how to dish out punishment if I didn't follow orders.

'I need music, at least,' I pleaded. He started to hum, a slow tango, and I closed my eyes, letting my hips grind to the music.

'Open your eyes. Look at me.' He resumed his darkly melodic tune.

I acquiesced, my pussy fluttering at his gaze. He didn't mask any of his desire, any of his cruelty. My hips instinctively moved in a figure-of-eight motion.

'Strip. And stop expecting orders. You know what I want. Do it. The next time the tune stops, you're in trouble.'

I knew he meant business and, despite my embarrassment, let myself get sucked into his music, my writhing matching his rhythm. Swaying and rolling my shoulders to make my breasts jiggle, I felt his gaze enter me. Gaining confidence, I ran a finger up my arm and let it flirt with my bra strap, as the DVD he'd given me had instructed. I slid it over my shoulder, slipped my arm out of its bondage and repeated the gesture with the other strap. Now all that protected my breasts from his probing eyes was a flick of the fastening. Turning my back, I snapped it between finger and thumb, fumbled the first attempt, succeeded in the second, and threw my bra over my shoulder at him before turning, covering myself with my hands.

The tango was faster now and I shimmied before him, knowing he wanted me, knowing he'd make me wait. He unzipped his trousers and started stroking himself.

Now it was my turn to gaze: his cock had entranced me from the first moment I saw it. His hand slid up and down his member, matching pace with my dance, making it darken and glisten. Emboldened, I slid my skirt over my hips and stepped out of it, kicking it towards him with a flip of my toe.

His breath caught as I stood clad only in hold-ups, heels and frilly knickers. I turned again, and bent over, trailing a finger down my leg to emphasise its beauty. I could feel my knickers stretching and knew the gusset would be revealing as much as it concealed. He'd be able to see my wetness. I could hear the 'thwack, thwack, thwack' wet noises of his masturbation, and smell his arousal in the air. I wanted him. But still he denied me, kept humming his ever-quickening tune.

I wiggled my arse, was rewarded with another gasp, then stood and turned to face him. Bringing my hands to my hips, I edged the knickers down, matching his tease with their gradual descent. Then in one quick move I pushed them to the floor. His gasps and grunts were louder now, a percussion to his song. I turned my back again, spread my legs and let his gaze plunge into my centre as I fingered myself, letting him see the string of arousal as I pulled the finger from my pulsing cunt.

Without him uttering a word, I felt the spray of cum over my legs and arse, trickling down me, marking me as his own.

The music stopped.

'I wanted a burlesque performance,' he said. 'That was striptease. Stay in that position. It's just right for your

217

punishment.'

I heard him leave the room and waited, exposed, my cunt still pulsing to the tune he'd fed into my head.

The door creaked open behind me and I heard footsteps: the clack of heels on the floor.

'This is Lucy,' he said. 'No. Don't turn your head.'

I was used to surprises by now, but this one hit me hard. I didn't turn, but my legs quivered with the effort it took to stay still. I didn't know who was now looking at my come-splattered legs and wide-open cunt, but I squirmed inwardly with humiliation. Some other girl. I heard a soft, light giggle.

'Lucy's going to show me how it's done,' he said, and there was cold amusement in his voice. 'But you're not going to see it. You don't deserve that. Stay there.'

I was still squirming as I heard the click of the CD deck, and slow jazz filled the room. 'I put a spell on you ...' said the song, 'because you're mine ...'

As the shuffle of heels began, along with the swish of what I assumed to be fans, I heard him say, 'Oh yeah, that's it,' and anger rose in my throat. In my mind I was turning round, swinging my fist at him, stamping on those fans, scratching my nails down this stranger's face. But the anger fought with another feeling: my chest and cheeks flushing hot, the squirming of shame giving way to the ache of arousal. And the need to be a good girl. He knew exactly how to play me.

The shuffle and click of heels grew faster, the swishing of the fans louder, and I could hear Lucy's breath, now close, now further away, as she spun around the room behind me. I knew he would be hard again, turned on by the performance. I could smell my own cunt and I thought I could smell hers too. I could feel spasms in my belly and the slow slide of my juices down my thighs. I hated him, and loved him, for doing this to me.

'Oh fuck, she's good,' he said, and the half-moan in his voice made my jealousy rise so that I didn't think I could take any more. It was too much. She giggled again, and I heard the fall of clothing to the floor. In my head I could see her; beautiful, white-skinned and curvaceous. Blonde, definitely – he'd always gone for blondes. Her skin would be hot and scented, her breasts would be large but perfectly-shaped. I realised I was panting, the smell of musk tingling in my nostrils. I let out a moan, and he laughed at me.

And then she was between my legs, kneeling on the floor behind me. I felt her nose push between my folds and her tongue lap at my clit, her warm breath inside me. She pushed hard, insinuating her face deep between my legs, and licked the entire length of my cunt hungrily. I moaned again, louder, and pushed myself down onto her, my hips making slow circles. I didn't dare look, still, but I couldn't stop my body moving just as it had moved in my failed dance. I was doing a bump 'n' grind right there on her face.

And then I came, gushing onto her, with a cry of combined humiliation and rage and joy, and I couldn't help it; my legs collapsed and I was in a heap on the floor, her body pressed up against mine.

I turned and looked at Lucy, who was panting, hot and sticky as I was, clothes scattered across the floor, heels lying on their sides, face flushed and joyful. He was wearing my stockings and suspenders, and his cock stood proud, darkly red and still glistening with come, in beautiful contrast to the delicate lace of the suspender belt. My best bright red lipstick was harshly-applied and had run and smeared across his face, along with the thick black eyeliner he obviously didn't know how to use, mixing with my juices. His lips glistened with them. He looked beautiful, and I was proud.

'I'd like to see Lucy's dance myself, sometime,' I said. 'It sounded pretty good.'

He smiled at me. 'If you want a job doing properly ...' I silenced him with a kiss.

The Intimate Diary Of Martha Rae
by Mark Farley

14th June 1862, San Francisco

'That's a fine piece of ass you got yourself there, Mamma …'

'She's one of the best girls in the city, sir. She'll treat you mighty fine too.'

'Uh-huh.'

'Why, yes, sir. You wanna see the goods first? Ah'm sure Miss Martha Rae would oblige the kind sir a peek for thirty cents and a share of three fingers of liquor and some tobacco with her …'

'Come and lie with me, Miss Martha Rae.'

19th June

I have taken upon writing a journal. If nuthin else, but to document what has happened to me in the last few weeks and what will evidently lie ahead of me to those who survive me.

I arrived in San Francisco, six months previous. Three weeks it took on the wagon trains from states afar. Word came to us of my grandmother's ailing health and an obliging sense of family duty fell upon me to tend to her needs and head to California. Funds were short as my grandfather hadn't left her much, so I went out to find work.

I write home on occasion and speak of my long hours at a bakery. I do not tell them of where I actually spend all my time. I do not tell her of the Dew Drop Inn, where I twist and shimmy for all the local men folk and often do more on a

220

private basis too.

But hey, it ain't no deadfall. It's a proper dance hall, upmarket an' all and I certainly wouldn't frequent what would be considered as a deadfall either. At least not like those places what you see on Pike Street or down by Pacific and Kearny. Bagnios haunted by ruffians and skanks and the abandoned that offer no entertainment, just sad relief for the desperate. And we sure ain't as abandoned as those whores down at the Bull Run either, who happily come and shout their mouths off and flash their handsomer wages at us on their nights off.

Despite the odd quarrel though, I do think the Dew Drop is one of the more agreeable venues. It is not one of those places that house the sort that would give themselves away for a mere fifty cents. We serve very much the well-heeled gent, along with a healthy mixture of Negroes and Mexicans too, mixing in amongst the thick clouds of cigar smoke. There are gamblers, pimps, sailors and miners. All rowdy and a foul-mouthed bunch they are and, sure, it can be a bawdy old place too. The upstairs has no room for discretion, or suitability for a gent with a nervous disposition, as the area is an unkempt array of beds and strewn mattresses, arranged in quite the most disorganised way and often there are up to ten of us entertaining at any one time. The girls that live here have their own rooms mind, higher up in the house, that they use, but for us visiting girls, we take whatever facilities are at hand.

But one thing you can guarantee with the Dew Drop is that we will look after ya and make sure ya leave happy now, not like other places that slip Spanish Fly into your whiskey and lift your wallet. Places like the Bull Run!

22nd June

The house is run by Mamma Carter. At any one time, there are thirty of us girls hanging around on a busy Friday night. We all take turns to do dances and make up skits, jokes like. Between the two of us, Mamma Carter is like another mother to me and I know she loves to hear it when I tell her so.

I love watching her get up and do a turn with Old Wayne on the upright. She once fancied herself as a touring singer and had desires on going all the way to New York, so she did. I often think it's a damn shame that she ain't gotta tune inside o' her. Not that I would ever tell her that. Hell no. She is not a woman to be crossed. She's a no-nonsense Mississippian lady, black as the dark night and as wide as the many schooners arriving in the bay. She takes absolutely no crap from nobody. She once punched a fellow straight in the face, just for questioning whether one of us was worth the dollar fifty she was asking of him to lie with us for a time.

'Ain't no motherfucker gonna cheapen my girls …' she'd always say.

Then there's Lydia, who's kinda responsible for all of this in the first place, looking back. I was in the General Store on Main Street, almost pleading like, with the manager to offer me some work. She struck up conversation with me while I was feeling up the cantaloupes and wondering whether I could be affording one. She's a few years older than me, is Lydia.

Firstly, I was overwhelmed at how she was dressed. She looked so elegant in her long ruffled shirt and her fancy hat. She looked like she was on her way to the President's inauguration or something. She smiled and pouted at me as I told her of my sick granny and that I was looking for work to get by. I immediately felt an urge to stroke her fabulous corset and she saw me looking at it.

'It's nice, isn't it?'

'It's beautiful. I'd love one just like it … you must live in a big house and be married to a lord or sumthin' …'

'Not exactly …'

She then proceeded to tell me about the Dew Drop and that I should come over and watch her dance some. I wasn't sure immediately. I'd heard that these places were dens of iniquity, full of sinners and ne'er-do-wells but she assured me it was a respectable place, the men behaved themselves and perhaps I could meet the house Mamma and talk about work.

'Well, I'd be happy to show you now. I'm about to perform

onstage …'

So on we went and right there, next to the display of fresh produce, my world changed.

23rd June

I visited the Dew Drop a couple of times over the next few days. That first trip over the street, with Lydia leading me by the hand, was as unforgettable as they come. She sat me by the bar and disappeared behind the curtain as the patrons all looked my way, curious like. I was kinda uncomfortable at first, but I needn't have been as their attentions were soon drawn to the stage, where my new acquaintance reappeared to a hearty din and hollering. She'd lost the long frock coat and the fancy hat and had hitched and tied the front of her skirt up to her belly and also the back to the top of her cheeks to reveal her garters and pants. I caught a gasp in my throat and put a hand to my mouth as I caught sight of that pale flesh pillowing out the tops of her stockings for the first time. I had no idea how soon I'd be so much closer to it.

The out-of-tune piano played in the corner at her requesting nod and she skipped around the stage, with elegant turns and bends to the jazzy beat. She shimmied and shook the lacy ruffles on her derriere and ran a finger lightly up her outstretched leg. Desire poured from that girl as she turned once and looked longingly out to the crowd and then another pirouette and a quiver of her blisters. She tossed her hair back and turned towards me, giving me the sorta look I'd never seen from anyone, let alone another woman. She took her breasts into her hands and squeezed them as she crouched down before everyone, grinding her hips and swinging them round.

I knew not what I was feeling inside but it had to be released. I slowly ran my hands up and down my thighs through my dress as I was still perched on that stool, just as a large black woman appeared (Mamma, I guessed) and caught me looking upon Lydia, with what I can only describe as a filth-ridden craving for her body.

223

The next day, I had to return to see Lydia. It was a lot quieter and Mamma Carter nodded my way and tapped a forlorn body slumped at the bar. It was Lydia, who turned and beamed my way in surprise. She skipped over to me and gave me a tight hug.

'Child, I was so worried about you … you didn't even bid me a farewell …'

I apologised profusely, made my polite excuse and fell In with her insistence that I visit her room at once and let her dress me. Looking back, I never thought to question the intimacy we had almost immediately, and how we quickly became in the habit of laying like lovers do. That girl touched me like no other man does – or ever had at that point either – and quenched a need I have, deep-rooted in my bones an' all. I told her this and she gasped at my inexperience. I blushed as she looked at me right in the eyes, deadly serious.

'I ain't ever been with no man before, Lydia. Help me. Teach me how to dance, show me how to make love.'

That night, Lydia granted my wish and made a woman out of me. She penetrated me with her fingers and broke my insides. I lay on my back and bucked wildly in pleasure on her flowery eiderdown. We lay after and I told her about the pain. She explained that I was like a bottle of wine that needed to be uncorked, in order to be savoured and then drunk.

The next day, I started in the bar alongside Lydia, waiting, eager to be drunk.

25th June

I guess it helped how pleasant my first gentleman was. We were dancing close with patrons and receiving gropes and intrusions in return for an evening's access to liquor and tobacco as normal. Mamma Carter gave me a light shirt to wear with fancy garters and black stockings. She always insisted we showed class and covered ourselves onstage and in the bar, but as far as anywhere else went, it was anything goes.

I peeled for two gents, subtly mind, and earned myself fifty cents. I had asked the second if he desired to retire behind one of the partitions with me to go further into the matter, but he declined. Not before he took liberties, mind, him snatching himself a taste of me from down below, regardless. We both knew he shouldn't, but I was new and eager and didn't know any better. He flicked his digit on my button for a few seconds as we both stood there and he dipped it into my bowl, before bringing the finger to his moustached lips for a smell. What made me do it, I don't know but I felt the need to sink to my knees. I took him in my mouth for the first time ever. I remembered the way Lydia had shown me the night before as she suckled on my finger and I wouldn't let him go until he was done, just like she'd told me.

An hour later, during an interval between dances, this fancy gent strides up. He had a high plug hat, curled hair and a crimson frock coat. He looked quite the felonious dandy, if I do say so. His white, ruffled shirt peeked from a fancy waistcoat, which I unbuttoned as I laid him down on one of the beds upstairs. I crawled on top and giggled as I took my time in revealing what he had to offer me. Lydia was two beds across being done over from behind by this Mexican fella. She winked at me and I felt reassured that my friend was close by. I stroked his moustache and ran my fingers through the hair on his chest as I sank onto his hardness.

After that, there was no stopping me. Even Mamma commented on my confidence. She had thought I was gonna 'run a mile, as soon as any fella reveals it to you', which kinda made me laugh. Lydia and I were like partners in crime and were soon becoming popular as we could offer something that most girls could not. Each other. We'd perform together as often as we could, if nuthin but for the fun of it. We'd just goof around like we do in private half the time, cavorting together onstage in nuthin but our basques and slippers, playing up to the coarse suggestions from the patrons in attendance. We'd tease them by unhooking one another's lacing before digging a knee into our partner's back and pulling tightly on the laces. They'd go mad, thinking we were gonna strip all the way for 'em. We are such teases.

26th June

Mamma Carter is sending me to the naval stores at the Presidio to dance for the officers this week. It will be the first time I've contributed to her long-standing arrangement with the soldiers. An arrangement that keeps the house protected and in favour. That, to me, is enough of a sacrifice. I can see the pain in Mamma's eyes when 'one of my childs go away' and always try to reassure her. Mamma sends a different girl each week and it has finally come down to me. I have tended to avoid this task thus far, on account of my popularity on the dance floor. But, secretly, I think it has to do with her favouring of me. Normally, just the one lass is taken over on the wagon, but when they have a fancy occasion two go over. Thankfully, it is so this night and I get to go with my Lydia.

30th June

As we waited in Mamma Carter's room twittering about the sudden departure of another girl, she waddled in and tossed at us a new herring-bone corset each.

'That's for you girls to keep a hold of. Look after them, mind.' We both cooed excitedly at her and effused gratitudes upon her mountainous frame.

'Now, don't let those fellas maul you, ya hear? Look after, yo'selves …' she said.

'Yes, Ma!' we both trilled.

'The cart's here … Go change, be gone with ya … Look respectful now. I gotta reputation to uphold here …'

A few hours later, the cart arrived at the Presidio. Despite the lurid descriptions I'd received about happenings at the garrison from the other girls, we were treated as respected ladies as we were escorted down from our vehicle by the hands on offer. We pulled up our long skirts; the heels that we were not used to wearing made a clacking sound on the much harder ground of the parade square.

Inside, Lydia took my hand and led me into the throng and towards the bar in the corner of the room. She greeted and introduced me to a lieutenant, who nodded respectfully towards me, to which I replied in curtsey. I tried to waft away some of the smoke from my face as Lydia took my hand and put a healthy glass of whiskey into it. It was easily four or five fingers and I found myself swaying on the spot, not long after I had been handed another. By this time, there were two hands behind me groping at my bits and folds. A number of times I remember Lydia smacking hands away from my behind, only to replace them with her own.

'She's mine!' she hollered at the men around her. She pulled up the back of my skirt and kneaded my cheek. I swayed still, but I was more than content with the attentions. She continued to rub my ass before we clasped our faces together, to the obvious glee and outrageous din of the many menfolk around us.

Before long, we felt a number of hands at our backs, pointing us toward a door to another room. In there was the large, polished table I had heard of. We were both pushed against its side and the hands and mouths instantly came upon us both.

'Gosh, this is a frisky bunch,' I thought. Lydia pulled herself up backwards onto the table and grabbed at my shoulders, pulling me away from my suitor. She dragged me onto the sheen of the table top and asked for hush whilst we performed. She grandstanded with a bravado I hadn't seen in her before.

'I can safely say that tonight will be all of your nights, gentlemen. So if you would all grant us the courtesy of doin' our turn, then you can all have your wicked way with us … in time. Just be patient.' Lydia took my hand once more and raised me to my stockinged feet. 'And for those who are extra patient, you will get to see myself interact with my friend here in the act of physical lovemaking. So do, gentlemen … be ever patient …'

I tried to compose myself through the dance as the whiskey flowed through my bloodstream to my brain. We continued with our lewd posturing and Lydia brought me off with her fingers as we stood side by side and leered at the soldiers below us. I'm sure I peeled too quickly, as something sent the throng of men in our vicinity into a lustful rage and they all came upon us. Lydia pleaded and insisted that we finish our turn, to which she turned her attentions upon myself. She laid me on my back and straddled herself over me, covering my face with her desire and playing to the baying crowd, requesting what she should do to me. Jackets adorned with badges and signs of bravery and daring escapades of which I had little knowledge were tossed to one side, leaving tunics and ties askew. She rubbed her crotch over my face as she called for a nearby stud to join us on the table.

'Fuck her right here!' she ordered.

'Yes, ma'am ...' I heard him over the din.

Before long, Lydia and I took on the throng of flesh before us. Soon, I found a searching hand which first kneaded my breast but settled on clasping my hand tight. It was my Lydia, in a similar overwhelmed state to me. I squeezed her hand in response as my below was filled with soldier and the weapons of other men hung before me invitingly. I took each of them into my mouth one by one and every one in turn also pounded my crotch until they were completely spent and were happy to put their swords back into their sheaths, drained of their passion.

The garrison took us to count on all charges, giving us a thorough search before leaving us on the battlefield, spent and defeated. They chuckled amongst one another, returning to their flowing supply of whiskey pillaged from the smugglers, captured in the bay waters every week. They laughed and bellowed inconsiderately in the background about how they had duly conquered us.

4th July

The sky crackles and lights up in multi-coloured sparkles. We are celebrating our independence from the British. I stand outside the Dew Drop with Mamma Carter. The hustle and bustle of life goes on around us. Some celebrate, some need not care. Some are looking for their next taste of opium and some just the next taste of someone like me. They look in wonder and curiosity, these figures who have lain with me in the more recent past. I can see them wondering about the etiquette of approaching me outside the safe confines of the inn. Mamma Carter puts a big fat arm around me and hollers the first few bars of an out-of-tune blues number.

'You ain't got no hold over me, ma sugar ...'

The Stage Is Her Slave
by Wanda Von Mittens

Devora, my mistress, my employer, slayer of my stolen heart, was the kind of woman people would follow to the ends of the earth. She was a woman of precision who knew to keep her followers at the right distance behind her – until she let them take flight.

This is the story of how Devora found me and helped me finally unleash myself on the world. She scooped me up and introduced me to the stars and comets of the Burly-Q universe. You'll know, I'm sure, its greatest starlet, the luscious, lascivious Miss Lydia Lynx. Of her fine flanks they murmur day and night, and the sway of her nips and hips causes grown men to sob.

But enough of the glamour and sparkle for now; we start in the dull, cavernous streets of *Les Vieux Jeux* – the theatre district – one early Summer evening. Devora appeared flawlessly dressed in green velvet, her red hair a flaming beacon beside her pale rose complexion. It always rained in Les Vieux Jeux; the theatre patrons would dash from doorway to doorway to make their way to the shows, shaking off their coats in the opulent foyers of the district's four theatres. But on the night Devora arrived there was no rain, only a brilliant ray of rare sunlight which she brought with her.

I worked the streets of Les Vieux Jeux, shining shoes. At dusk you couldn't see me. I was the same grey as the streets and it was only the glint of my metal polish tins that drew my customers to me.

First I saw only the tip of her boot as it peeped from beneath the heavy green velvet of her skirts. Then, with a swish, she gracefully seated herself at my workstation and lifted the skirts to her calves. I trembled. Not just because I knew this was the flawless vision who had lit the streets only moments before, but also because it was simply not done for a lone woman to walk the streets unescorted – no matter how wealthy or entitled – nor was it correct for her to have her boots cleaned by a street urchin, in such flagrant public view.

I was transfixed by her footwear and the tease of her shapely ankles and calves. Her boots were made of the softest cream-coloured leather. They had small, round, leather-covered buttons up the insides which had been carefully pushed through perfectly-stitched buttonholes. I caught a glimpse of her thick silk stockings, the exact same colour as the leather of the boots I was working so religiously on, as though in the presence of an angel who could decide the future of my soul.

Indeed, she did have intervention in mind where I was concerned and, as I finished her boots (resisting the temptation to lick the soles clean with my tongue), she slowly rose and looked down at me, on my knees at her feet. She stooped, bending smoothly at the hips so she could bring her head comfortably close to mine.

'My name is Devora,' she said, 'but you shall call me Mistress. You shall work for me.'

Her voice had the predatory purr of a tiger before it pounces. 'I expect you at *L'Opera* at six tomorrow evening.' I didn't answer her, and she didn't wait for my reply. By the time I opened my eyes, she was gone. I listened for the click of her heels on the cobbles and even after the sound had faded I willed myself to hear it still.

If that first night when she arrived in Les Vieux Jeux became a matter of fevered gossip, it was nothing compared to what was to come. It transpired she was the new owner of L'Opera, the house that, of the four theatres in the district, was the one that had fallen on the hardest times. It was the epitome of faded grandeur, its façade was crumbling and its productions had overindulged themselves to the point of obscurity. L'Opera had remained pompous at a time when austerity seemed arrogant and inappropriate. Audiences were screaming out for frivolity and laughter, not worthy drama told po-faced, with rounded vowels. L'Opera was poised for her divine intervention.

I moved in as instructed with my one bag of meagre belongings. In my new quarters I tried to familiarise myself with bathing and, after mournfully splashing some water about my body and pouring a pail of the same freezing sink water over my hair, I turned my attention to my clothes which, like me, hadn't seen water, other than Les Vieux Jeux's perpetual rain, for some time. Knowing in my head and heart that nothing I owned was acceptable, never mind fit for association with my divine new mistress, I slumped into a pile of cushions propped against the far wall of my room, curled up naked and buried my head between my knees.

She didn't knock, but entered with a flourish of brisk purpose. I jumped, but dared not jump too far for fear of revealing my pathetic skinny grey body. To say I was embarrassed was an understatement. I was ashamed; utterly ashamed. To be gazed upon by the strong green eyes of my mistress in this state felt like having a fire swell up around me and scorch every inch of my skin. And how I wished a real fire would swallow me up and burn me to cinders for the wind to blow away.

'Don't be silly,' she said, her voice firm but accompanied by a tender giggle. She found me amusing! Better that than to have her appalled at the sight of me. I still trembled. 'I've chosen a suit for you from the dusty costumes of this stuffy coffin they call a theatre. There's lots to be done. But we'll have this place ablaze like the phoenix when we're through.'

'Mistress ...' I spluttered, my voice squeaking like a rodent's. 'May I ask, what are my duties?'

She laughed. Such a beautiful laugh. It made my heart soar and I wondered if this I was feeling ... was it happiness? Could it be that it made me happy to hear her laugh, even at my own expense?

'Darling ...' she began – that word made her voice like a song to me – '...your duties are to watch and to learn, to follow me, to stay close but always three steps behind. You'll learn ... and then, when you're ready, you'll know ...'

As the door closed behind her I realised I was in love.

For the next few weeks the theatre was full of people, day-in, day-out. Workmen knocked down and rebuilt, took down and re-adorned. It took several weeks but eventually a new kind of theatre was born.

There were rumours. Many wicked and vicious rumours. The most distasteful was that Devora had built a whorehouse. The gaggled masses had nicknamed the theatre *La Chabanais*, after the famous Parisian brothel. The gossip about Devora and where she came from was just as salacious. They said she was a prostitute-turned-courtesan who'd had the means to buy the theatre given to her by a wealthy client. No one knew the truth, least of all me. But as the posters went up advertising auditions for 'men and women of vigour, poise and modern values for chorus and other roles' the mystery remained fervently unresolved and the rumours continued unabated.

'Sit with me for the auditions, beloved,' she said to me as the day dawned. She had many pet names for me, but 'beloved' was my favourite. She only showed affection with words.

Devora had already employed stage hands, runners and a pianist, and that morning a friend of hers (she called him Hugo, but pronounced it *Huge-o*), had arrived to act as a choreographer. He was a funny-looking man, a man most certainly – but one who had modified his gentleman's attire with feminine touches; a pair of high heels, a string of pearls and matching earrings. I was most aghast at the smear of rouge at his cheeks and the brush of paint on his lips.

Hugo blustered about the stage, taking charge of furniture and props, moving things around with a great flurry of effort and perspiration.

'Always a performer ...' whispered Devora as he paused to mop his brow with an oversized white handkerchief, using oversized movements.

'Your eminence! Divine Devora!' Hugo wailed in a shrill pitch, peering out from the stage but unable to place my mistress. 'Are you ready to slaughter the little lambs?'

One day of auditions wasn't enough; they took up the rest of the week. A constant train of hopefuls chugged onto the stage and then off again, some of them dancing with glee at being chosen, others flouncing in disgust once they came to fully understand the kind of modern theatre Devora was creating. A fair few considered it beneath them and denounced what Devora was doing to the grand institution of L'Opera, to which she quietly replied so only I could hear, 'L'Opera is dead. Long live Devora!'

The production was called 'Venus' and was about a statue of the Goddess of Love that comes to life. The quickened statue sets out to experience the joy, beauty and pleasure of love, only to find humans miserable when consumed by that mysterious passion and equally miserable without it. In despair, she returns herself to stone. The role of Venus was to be played by someone Hugo had practically fainted at the sight of. Even Devora's restrained exterior had betrayed a faint glow. Not some strong voluptuous woman who looked as though she'd been hewn from marble, but a meek, skinny boy aged all of 16.

The topsy-turvy world of Devora's production of 'Venus' didn't end with a pubescent boy cast as the Goddess of Love. She reversed the roles so that all the women were played by men and all the men played by women. The chorus line in particular totally bemused me. A hotch-potch of men of all shapes and physiques, chosen not for their ability to dance or sing, but for the size of their cocks. All had to be a minimum of ten inches, and this fact became a source of great masculine pride to them, as though they felt they must compensate for their newly-feminised states. Hugo nicknamed them 'the bovines'. They were told that they were to wear flesh-coloured hosiery and nothing else.

After a week of auditions came three weeks of rehearsals and, full of illustrious creativity, the theatre took on a new air, a new personality. Devora had changed, too; she no longer hid enigmatically in the shadows but made her presence very clearly felt. No one doubted that she was in charge, though she never once raised her voice. If she disapproved, all it took was a look, and everyone knew at once and would work harder to please her, while her laughter became the sweetest reward for a job well done.

It was now commonplace for me to be called to her rooms to share a nightcap with her. Each night I seemed to be permitted to sit a little closer. Though she never discussed herself, she wanted to know everything there was to know about me. In the beginning I protested that there was nothing to know, but she persisted, asking a constant stream of questions that slowly had me realise that there was more to me than I had ever imagined. The amazing outcome of her ruthless inquisitiveness was to restore my faith in myself and my future. And in return I so desperately wanted to give her something. But what? What could I possibly offer the divine Devora?

One night I asked her.

'You've already given it to me,' she replied, reclining on her chaise longue in satin cigar pants and a matching knee-length wrap that fell open to reveal her décolletage – more than I'd ever seen of her before. I couldn't imagine what she meant and she could tell I was confused by my furrowed brow.

'You love me, don't you?'

'But of course,' I replied without hesitation.

'Then I have what I want for now. I'll have the rest when I'm ready to take it.'

I didn't sleep a wink.

As opening night approached, the bustle of the theatre

intensified to a deafening clamour. No one seemed to stand still for a second and sweat dripped from every pore of every dishevelled stagehand, dancer, actor and singer. Devora, of course, remained immaculate, gliding serenely through the theatre's bustle.

On occasion she was forced to intervene. The bovines had been causing trouble, not fully understanding that being ungainly and ridiculous was their purpose. They had expected more classical training from Hugo, who had merely encouraged them to make big oafs of themselves. Now they flounced like prima donnas demanding more attention and tutoring.

Devora burst into their final rehearsal demanding that they strip naked immediately. Hugo giggled insanely and, for once, took a back seat, while I blushed incandescent. She proceeded to first tease, then humiliate them. She set about arousing them by fluttering a purple ostrich feather across their bellies, nipples and cocks and, when this light touch had no effect on some of the sullen bovines, she took the remaining limp penises in her leather-gloved hands and pulled them to attention, wearing a devious smile on her lips. That smile alone was enough to arouse me.

With their cocks hard she told them to perform their opening number, telling them that if their members did not remain proud that she would dock their pay. She also announced that the dancer who could keep himself hard while maintaining the most vigorous performance would receive double his usual wage. It was all the incentive the competitive cows needed.

Of course they all looked ridiculous, and none of them could imagine that they could ever look more ridiculous, jumping about naked with hard cocks bouncing about, slapping on their bellies and thighs, slap, slap. Their final warning was that if they complained one more time they would do all their performances naked. No one heard a peep from the bovine boys again.

On the morning of opening night Devora stood outside the

theatre, surveying the installation of the new name signs. *Le Phoenix* was born, ready to catch the streets of Les Vieux Jeux on fire.

Opening night was a roaring success. A full house hushed the gossiping dissidents who'd willed L'Opera to expire under Devora's leadership. In fact, the foundered institution was laid completely to waste and in its place stood Devora's magnum opus, the theatre reborn in a blaze of nouveaux glory.

But this is not the story of Le Phoenix, the hugely successful burlesque theatre you know so well, with its striking starlet Miss Lydia Lynx performing to packed crowds baying for a glimpse of her shimmy and shake. No it's not the story of that most successful of music halls; it's my story.

With Le Phoenix finally silent and in darkness after the riot of opening night, I found myself alone with Devora in her suite. After weeks of such intense hard work and constant anticipation, I'd expected to be exhausted, but the opposite was true. Devora and I were both buzzing with the thrill of outrageous success. I giggled and skipped and twirled about the room, with Devora laughing loudly and luxuriantly, a rare sense of abandon about her. Not the tranquil abandon I'd encountered when she'd reclined on her chaise longue and let her wrap fall slightly open, but an air of more careless, more dangerous release.

I stopped my dance and fell exhausted to the floor at her feet, my favourite position. She placed her hand to my cheek and smiled warmly down at me while I fought to retrieve my breath.

'Are you ready?' she asked.

I nodded and felt a warm glow all through my body, a fire starting in my toes that was fed by my adoration of Devora. I'd been a slave to her in this theatre for two months and my devotion and adulation for her had only grown, not waned. I didn't know what she had in mind but at that moment I was ready for anything; I would have done anything for her – even died for her.

'Undress for me, beloved.'

Momentarily the spell was broken and panic quenched my fire, but one reassuring smile from Devora and a barely detectable nod of her head restored my surrender. Now at last it would be total, now at last I would give all of myself and all of my secrets to my Devora.

I undid my shirt first, shyly, still sitting on the floor at her feet. With the shirt removed, she saw the bandages that, for as long as I could remember, I had bound around my chest to deny my sex. This had allowed me to live the fantasy that I was male – so I could pass as an unseen child of the street. The colour drained from my cheeks as I looked up at Devora, for the first time as a woman.

But her expression told me that this was no shock to her.

'You knew?' I gasped.

'Of course. From the first touch of your polish on my boot, I knew what you were.'

'You knew I was a woman?'

'You're not a woman yet … finish undressing.' Her voice was harder now. I hurried off the rest of my clothes and stood up to step out of my baggy trousers, finally, naked and pale, the merest stretch from Devora.

'I'm going to show you what it really is to be a woman.' She took me by the hand and led me through to her bedroom, a room I'd never seen before and had never expected to be led into.

Devora had me lie on the bed while she went behind a large ornate screen to change. I heard the pop of buttons and stays and the crumple of heavy skirts. Yet even when I deduced, picturing it all in my mind, that she certainly must have removed all of her clothes, she did not emerge.

Instead I heard new sounds; drawers opening, wardrobe doors creaking, the barely-audible sound of fabric pulled across skin. I couldn't imagine … how could I? I had never in my life seen or heard of anything close to what I was about to witness.

Devora came out from behind the screen. She was a

startling vision, one that dazzled 100 times brighter and more formidably than even that first night I had seen her. She wore cream leather opera-length gloves that were trimmed in red, and she had let loose her blazing mane of red hair so that it tumbled about her shoulders. Her breasts were as naked as mine, though they were infinitely larger and perkier from being worn so proudly, rather than crushed under a sheath of bandages. She'd kept on her stockings – the same cream-coloured silk that I'd peeked at that first night – but those stockings were held up, not by the usual garters low on the leg, but by six ribbons high on her thighs, each of which was in turn attached to a cream leather belt around her waist. And it was the thing I saw attached to this belt that truly took my breath away.

From two straps of leather that ran from her waist belt down over her belly and between her legs there stood a thick, hard, red cock. Her bedroom was dimly-lit, but it was unmistakable. Very clearly, my mistress was a woman, but a woman who had equipped herself as a man. I was aghast, afraid, in awe anew.

She glided over to me and lay next to me on the bed on her side, propped on her elbow, so that she could survey my body. She put her gloved hand to my knee and ran it along the length of my thigh, over my flat stomach and up to my breasts, which she began to pay particular attention to. I felt tense and firm, finding it difficult to let my guard down. I had never been gazed upon, never mind touched, by anyone. Gently kneading my breasts, she tweaked my nipples so that they took shape and stood more proudly, helping to redefine my female form. Then without warning she swooped her face towards me, whispered, 'relax', before tenderly placing her lips to mine, parting her wet mouth and letting her tongue tease my lips apart. I'd never kissed mouth to mouth before but I was lost instantly to her lips' embrace. The warmth in my toes spread like wildfire, coursing up between my thighs towards my most unknown, most undiscovered part.

Devora positioned herself on all fours over me and I began

to feel her red cock pushing against me as she moved above me in an evocative rhythm. Though I was obviously a virgin, unkissed and untouched, I found the rhythm within me too; it beat in time to the pulse of the fire that I felt between my legs and I began to push my body up off the bed to be closer to Devora. Her red cock resting on my thigh, I then felt her body shift as she began to probe me with her beautifully-fake strap-on penis. Just as she had parted my lips with her tongue she began to part me below with her cock and I felt myself open up for her and urge her inside me.

She didn't push forcefully or too soon. She kissed me, tenderly; stroked my face, my hair, kissed my breasts and my tummy, she kissed me all over, with her cock all the while gently nudging at my opening as I began to burn with ever-growing impatience. Then, just at the point where I felt I would have to force her into me, she did it; she thrust inside my body, between my quivering legs.

I squealed a little. It hurt, but wasn't unpleasant. There was a part of me that had longed for Devora to hurt me, but I could never have known that the pain she would inflict would bring with it so much pleasure. She pulled out and I felt myself restored, then I yielded again to another thrust. I panted and moaned and this encouraged Devora to thrust into me harder and with more frequency, until she was pounding me with an eager, decisive rhythm that I prayed would never stop.

But it did stop. It had to. She made me die *le petit mort*. Devora took my virginity and made me climax too. I'd never wanted to be a woman until this point, so I had never touched myself and never known the pleasure of this sensation. It was a mutiny of pounding heart beats, jumping flesh and tingling skin; it felt like an arrest of my body, a malfunction; it took me away into space but safely returned me to earth, a trembling but deeply contented mess.

My benign, omnipotent Devora, custodian of my stolen heart, showed me how to be a woman. Not just how a woman can take a cock, but how a woman can be as magnificent as she – the giver, not just the receiver. How could I fail to be spectacular with such a superb teacher?

And that is my story. From the grey of the streets to the glory of the stage, tutored by the divine goddess Devora who took my virginity, made me a woman, and had me reborn on the stage of Le Phoenix ... as Miss Lydia Lynx.

If The Slipper Fits
by Mat Fraser

I was new in town when I first walked into the Slipper Room Burlesque Bar in Manhattan's Lower East Side. Uptown yuppy couples excitedly slummed it with their digital camcorders, recording every second to prove where they'd been; City boys took it in turns to stumble from their groups and put dollar bills in the tiny knickers of the go-go dancer, her left thumb doing the hitch hike, the right obligingly lifting the strap ever so slightly, enough for each man (I use the term loosely) to slip the bills between her ample hips, a sequinned stars and stripes triangle covering her inner gyrations.

I took off my coat, ordered a beer and began to watch the show from the bar, but was almost immediately distracted by the DJ. She looked about 28; olive-skinned, wide lips and black hair, taut naked midriff undulating between a stretched white T-shirt and faded hipster jeans. She was cool, gum-chewing, and exuded a sexiness that hooked me more than the sexpots on stage. Her lowered eyelids clung to her eyeballs like the cotton T-shirt clung to her small nipples, which jutted out from a flat chest as she cued in the next track. Her neck crooked on to the one headphone against her shoulder, making her hair fall nonchalantly over her face while the MC introduced the next burlesque dancer.

I found myself staring at her, wondering what she would look like unclothed, when suddenly her gaze bored into my face, taking me in as I had her, and she broke her New York look of disdain and smiled. My stomach spasmed. I felt spot-lit and looked away quickly, unable to return her smile. I studiously watched the girl onstage, now bending over, skirt riding high enough for us to see her fleshy buttocks strain and bulge against the red mini shorts that were fast disappearing into her crevice. She looked at us over her shoulder and slapped her arse hard, making it wobble and ripple. Then, with one quick reveal of her nipple tassels, she was gone. I could still feel the DJ looking at me and turned away, going downstairs to the toilets.

As I opened the door to the gents I heard voices coming from one of the cubicles. I listened, trying to make sense of the New York conversation as I peed.

'Apparently she was annoyed because when they found the body, there was vomit in a bucket next to it, and she was like, "What, he had time to vomit but he couldn't make a call?" and then she just got shitfaced on Jack.'

'Oh. My. God,' said the other one, and I thought how excellently NYC this all was. I concentrated on not dripping as I did myself up, then suddenly heard, 'Hey, you guys, you wanna come here and help with something?'

I turned to see the DJ standing in the doorway, looking straight at me. The cubicle door opened and two bikini-clad girls came out, waving away the smoke that trailed in their slipstream. It was the big-arsed one with curly hair and the one in the stars and stripes bikini from earlier. They both smiled, not at me, but through me, and all three women approached. My heart rate increased and I realised I was growing hard. □

'This here is Camille, and she likes you. You ain't goin' nowhere until you make her come. You are tonight's Camille-come. Congratulations,' said stars and stripes.

The two women stood either side of me as Camille approached me, grabbed me round the back of the neck, pulled my face towards hers and kissed me full with those lips. It was an instant turn-on, and I felt my body surge with lust at the New Yorkness of it; the toilets, the singled-out randomness. Now the other two were fondling me. One knelt down and I felt my button and zip being undone; the other flicked her tongue in my ear and nuzzled her lips against my neck as my now fully-erect cock was greeted by a wet mouth, which took in at least half of my sizeable length.

Camille took a step back and began to undo her low-riding belt buckle, while the neck nuzzler began chewing on my earlobe. All the time Camille's eyes bored into mine, like she had hunted me down and was now going in for the kill. She roughly pushed down her jeans and knickers and faced me, jeans below her knees. She began to pull her nipples under her T-shirt, watching the others kiss, lick, fondle and suck me. Her right hand went down and she began to finger her hairless clit, frowning slightly.☐

'OK, now bring him here,' commanded Camille, and she turned around, both hands up on the wall as if ready to be frisked. The two 'fluffers', for I guess that's what they were, grabbed me and pulled me towards her. I was made to stand behind the slightly spread arse cheeks that faced me, and guided in to her. As my rock hard cock sank into her tight wet cunt, we both gasped with lust.☐

'Oh fuck, yes, fuck me you piece of shit, and you better not come before me.'☐

I did my best to smoothly ride in and out, up to the hilt each time but not too hard, trying to hold back my orgasm. I could hear the muffled strains of Sonny Lester and his band as another gyrating, gum-chewing act got into full flow above us, but it was difficult to stay cool; my cock-sucking friend had positioned herself under my crack and was sucking my balls and licking my perineum, while the other one was leaning back against the wall, watching and wanking herself from behind. This was some fucking night out!

My thrusts began to increase in intensity as Camille moaned and growled with angry pleasure. I was going to explode in a few seconds and my thoughts raced: 'No, please! Don't! Think of something; broccoli, blackboards, peach skin, pus, shit, anything …'☐

'Oh, fuck, come on, yeah, nggg, fuck me you asshole,

come on you fucker, give it to me. Yes! Yes!'

Camille was certainly a woman who knew what she wanted. With her left hand spread out on the wall to steady herself and her right hand frantically rubbing her mound, I began to pound her with all my might, all four of us caught up in this climactic moment; dirty low-down New York toilet sex in the seedy basement of a burlesque club, the crouching fluffer squatting and wanking, the other girl going crazy with her fingers in her mouth and other hand pulling her nipples, and my new DJ friend growling like a dog about to attack.

The music upstairs was drowned out by cheering of some sort and, as Camille came, she froze, cunt muscles clamped onto my engorged tool, then shuddered. I finally let go and rabbit-fucked her as I began to come, but the crouching tigress whipped my now-bucking, pumping cock out, and sucked me hard until I exploded into her mouth, intensely spasming spunk as all four of us peaked and began to slow.

'That's better. Now get rid of him and get back on fuckin' stage,' said Camille. She hitched up her jeans, swept her hair off her face, and walked out, not even bothering to look me in the face. What a woman.

'Who the fuck was that?' I asked my two remaining companions

'That was Camille, honey, our boss. Welcome to New York City.'

The Princess And The Prophet
or
The Comedy Of Salome
by Claire Wordley

The Princess sighed wearily and rolled over, staring at the ceiling. She lowered her kohl-heavy lids, her sumptuous lashes casting charcoal shadows onto her high cheekbones. She sighed again. Today was the day. The day she'd be brought forth, like a bejewelled snake from an embroidered bag, to dance for him – a serpent with its mouth sewn cruelly shut, swaying but unable to strike. He would leer as she spun her pretty body, not knowing, not caring that she was only trying to shake herself free from his dank and clammy gaze. The thought sickened her.

She made ready to sigh once more, but was interrupted by the giggling entrance of her seven personal maids. Distracted, she smiled and rose, her bangles tinkling, and asked what was so amusing. Her maids giggled harder as they vied not to be the one to explain. Tears rolled from the scrunched-up eyes of Talitha; Vashti gasped for air and clutched her bare stomach, rippling with laughter below her skimpy top (the Princess preferred her maids with as much humour and as few clothes as possible. It whiled away the hours). Syene was pushed forward by the others, blackberry eyes sparkling with mischief and mirth.

'I – I – I pinched – they dared me – I pinched – the Prophet's bum!'

The girl collapsed on the floor, shrieking and convulsing like a delicious tan rabbit in a snare of vermilion silk. The Princess stared at her in horror, outrage and disgust. Then she burst into hoots of laughter. You wouldn't have expected such an elegant-looking creature to laugh like that, whooping and jiggling, smudging her frescoed eyes as she wiped away big, hearty tears. She panted out a response.

'Why –dear God – why would –? What did he do –? What did he say -? You minx!'

History paints the Princess in heavy make-up: a necrophiliac Jezebel, a whirling harlot, a spoilt, shimmying, vindictive brat. But seeing her thus with her maids, history must blush crimson at its barbed analysis. We see here no petulant adolescent, but a woman able to laugh at life even on the eve of humiliation. True, she lived a life of opulent splendour, her clothes set with gems, her chamber adorned with sumptuous silks; but she didn't have what she yearned for above all else: her liberty. She couldn't leave her gilded cage except to walk in the sacred cedar groves with her maids as chaperones. And she had to endure the constant, cancerous presence of her mother's uncle, her legal stepfather: Herod Antipas, Tetrarch of Galilee and Perea.

She lived though her maids. They were her eyes and ears. They acted as she could not, running barefoot though the streets with loose hair, stealing sticky treats from the palace kitchens, and, best of all in the Princess's mind, bestowing frequent sticky treats upon the local males. For in this respect, salacious and damning history actually has a point. The Princess could, by uncharitable onlookers, be described as a devious hussy. More sympathetic spectators may have explained her sexual preoccupations as normal for a vivacious young woman with great lust for life, locked away from most forms of human contact. However you choose to interpret her predilections, though, one thing was clear: she loved to fuck. Rarely could her seven scintillating servants get a man past the heavily-guarded door of their mistress's bedchamber. But this did not deter our lascivious heroine. The flesh of her entourage was just as tempting to her as that of any man.

Well, almost any man. For two weeks, the Princess had been uncharacteristically lethargic, despondent and even downright dull. When pressed, she had eventually revealed her secret. She was in love with the Prophet.

Her companions were genuinely shocked.

'The Prophet your stepfather is holding in irons within the castle walls for treachery most vile?'

'The Prophet who calls your mother a wily temptress and an incestuous whore with a womb of venom?'

'The Prophet who called you a painted and idolatrous viper born of the blackest bitch ever to degrade these shores with her unsaintly presence?'

'The one with the beard?'

Yes.

Yes, the teenage tummy-twirler was in love with the ragged, dignified Prophet. She worshipped his angular cheekbones, his clear grey eyes, his wise mouth and kind smile. She adored the way his bare chest lifted softly as he shifted in his chains (she had to admit that she rather enjoyed the sight of a bound man). She cherished his gravitas, his calm and measured manner. And it turned her pussy pink and wet when he lost it and raged pugilistically against her family. She fucked herself senseless when he called her stepfather a depraved and corrupted maggot feeding on the rotting corpse of his country. She gushed on the spot when he spat copiously on her mother's favourite purple gown. He said what she wanted to say, did what she wanted to do. Although manacled to the wall, he was free.

She soon realised that his hatred for the royals extended to her. Weirdly, it turned her on even more, hearing him abuse her glittered visage, her adorned person, her ancestry, lifestyle and morals … Yes, it turned her on most when he abused her morals. She still blushed a little, recalling how violently she had pleasured herself the day he had called her a degenerate slut with a wanton and insatiable cunt who'd suck all the men in Phoenicia dry for a handful of coins. She'd had to push him pretty hard to get that, but it had been worth it. Her own hand hadn't been sufficient to satisfy her lust, and she'd had to rely on her tireless maids to lick and finger her hungry pussy into exhaustion.

The news that Syene had tweaked her love's sacred derrière, had, much to her surprise, rather titillated her. When she had finished laughing, she drew herself up royally, brushed her hair from her face and imperiously commanded Syene to step forward. She circled the maid like a hungry lioness eyeing up a baby antelope, her pointed slippers padding silently over the floor.

'We've been a bit naughty, haven't we? We touched our Mistress's property, didn't we? So we need to be punished, don't we?'

Syene blushed and squirmed a little. The corner of her mouth twitched slightly upwards, and she cocked an eyebrow knowingly at the Princess.

'Yes, Mistress. I've been bad. I do need to be punished.'

'Girls, bring her to me.'

The Princess sat down on one of her sumptuously-upholstered chairs. The maids lay the not-unwilling Syene over their mistress's lap, her loose ebony waves brushing the rich rose coloured rug. Still giggling deliciously, they bound her pretty golden-brown feet and hands together with scarves pulled from their hair.

'My, what a delectable morsel!' chuckled the Princess.

She softly trailed her elegant fingers over Syene's soft, rippling hair, then wound the maid's tresses tight around her wrist and pulled her head back, forcing her spine to arch sensuously. Still tugging hard on her hair, the Princess bent and kissed the girl softly on the mouth. She slipped her tongue between Syene's ripe pomegranate lips, teasing her exquisitely, then pulled away, leaving the maid panting with lust.

'You enjoyed that, didn't you, you little slut?'

Syene moaned lustfully in response.

The Princess pulled up her maid's skirts to reveal the

voluptuous globes of her bare behind. She slid her hand delicately over the girl's bare cleft, then brought her hand down hard on one inviting cheek, making Syene buck and squirm in surprise. She spanked the maid slowly, calculating; watching as the girl pushed her appetising buttocks up to the Princess's punishing palms.

'Answer! Tell me you enjoyed that, my pretty whore, my fuckable little slave. You loved it, didn't you?'

'Yes, please – please –' she gasped brokenly.

'Oh yes, you love being touched by a woman, and you love the pain – don't you? But if you keep advertising your pleasure with such immoderate noises it will attract attention.' The Princess pulled a silver dagger from an ivory scabbard and cut the girl free of her undergarments, which were moist with juices.

'Bela, put these in Syene's mouth. We can't have her alerting the guards to our game.'

Syene felt her pussy swell and blush as her underclothing was forced into her mouth, fragrant, sweet and slightly metallic. Her midnight-black pupils dilated and her eyes glazed as she savoured her own secret taste, her hot bare pussy exposed both to the cool air and the heated gaze of the onlookers. It was so humiliating; bound and exposed, she could almost feel her body being violated by the hungry looks of her audience. She grew a little hotter at their imagined touch.

The Princess pulled her up again by the hair, causing her scalp to throb with pain, and her clit with longing.

'You touched something that I wanted, defiled something I adored. Now you'll pay.'

As she saw the dominance in her Mistress's glittering eyes, Syene felt scared for the first time. She knew that the Princess needed to be in control, needed to be obeyed, because she only had true power over the maids. As her head fell down between her bound hands, she felt the adrenaline course dizzyingly though her body. The sensation of being really, physically afraid and totally aroused at the same time made her hips twitch and press against the Princess's silk-clad thigh, and a muffled moan escaped her gagged mouth.

The Princess grinned with delight. This afternoon was proving to be a lot more fun than she'd anticipated. She felt her own silky folds moisten as her maid's succulent hips pushed against her, dampening her peachy gown. She slid a finger between the girl's swollen pleats and into her tight passage, feeling her contract snugly as the Princess manipulated her aching clit with her thumb. Then she drew her hand away, smiling silently as Syene writhed sinuously in frustration. She made her voice stern.

'Did you pinch him like this, my wayward little strumpet? Or like this, or this?'

She grabbed the girl's rump, forcing her fingers deep into the generous olive flesh to thrill her servant's nerves. Leaving Syene's bottom flushed with finger marks, she held her waist securely with one hand and moved the other to the maid's firm, ample breasts, pinching the supple skin, working her way to the girl's bronzed areolas. No kindly caress was this – her Mistress twisted and yanked her sensitive rosy buds until tears sprang to her eyes, but her guttural gasps were still those of pleasure, and hot pearly emissions tricked down her thighs. She almost sobbed with relief when her Mistress began to slide the handle of her dagger into her drenched and frustrated cunt, so buttock-clenchingly slowly that she instantly tried to thrust her whole body back onto it, desperate to be filled – but she was thwarted by the Princess holding her still.

'Now, now, patience, my pretty slut. You've got it all coming to you … and more.'

The Princess beckoned over a strikingly beautiful girl that her stepfather had brought her from Arabia the previous year. The Princess had soon discovered Zebida's special talents – her tongue was loquacious, her fingers virtuoso and her mind filthy. Her carved silver necklaces bounced against her breasts, the colour of milky coffee, as she bent to hear the Princess's whispered command. The maidservant's mischievous smile widened as she listened, and she knelt behind the prone Syene, swiftly untying the helpless girl's legs and binding them, spread, to the legs of the chair on which the Princess sat. She leaned in, relishing the musky, metallic tang of Syene's scent, and began to softly tongue the satiny ruffles of her throbbing sex.

The Princess pushed Zebida's face hard against Syene's cunt, groaning in a kind of displaced ecstasy. Breathing heavily, Zebida lapped eloquently at her friend's warm lips, then rubbed her tongue roughly over Syene's sensitive clit. She began to caress the hidden, raised, fleshy spot, just inside the girl's hole, with first one finger, then two. Syene was rapidly approaching climax, the sodden cloth in her mouth barely repressing her screams of pleasure. The feeling of being restrained and helpless was new to her; it was unbelievably arousing to be at entirely someone else's mercy. Particularly someone as gorgeous and talented as Zebida. The Princess took Zebida's finger and carefully wet it in her warm mouth. Then she placed the maid's fingertip on the tight, virginal bud of Syene's arse. Smiling with delight, Zebida teasingly pushed her finger against her victim's snug aperture, not quite hard enough to slip inside but enough to elicit a squirming spasm from Syene. She nudged it a little further, sliding just into her friend's tense passage, then out again.

Syene was sweating hard, struggling, her breasts pressed painfully against her Mistress's lap and her legs splayed around Zebida's face. She began to feel an intense need to be filled as Zebida began to finger her arse in earnest; this dark uncomfortable pleasure was thrilling her every nerve, resonating with something dangerous and delicious inside her. She felt a deep and primal stirring, intoxicating, lustful and aggressive. She yowled like a wildcat, her nervous friends filling her mouth with more underwear to prevent the guards from hearing.

Zebida furiously tongued Syene's gorgeous clit as Syene pushed back hard onto the other girl's finger, unable to get enough of this new and tormenting delight. She came in a rush of dark satisfaction, her cunt pulsing, as a treacherous red lava

252

singed her veins.

The Princess dipped her hand down to her own sweet folds, which were slick with arousal. She was deliberating as to which of the maids she would choose to tend to the needs of her own pussy when there came a sharp rap at the door. She had forgotten that it was so late – she had to get ready to dance. Her lust fell away and she resumed her burden, cold and heavy as a block of granite, as she donned her dancing clothes.

After the feasting, it came. Herod called her up before him, and asked for his birthday present – his chance to have a sanctioned drool over the nubile body of his stepdaughter. His wife watched with narrowed eyes and pursed lips as he bade her daughter to dance, on this occasion powerless to intervene.

Head held high, Salomé turned away from the Tetrarch to face the Prophet; still chained to the wall, he had been forgotten amidst the night's festivities. Over the distance between them, she locked him into her feline gaze. Made sure he knew that she was talking to him, dancing for him.

'Tonight I dance the dance of Ishtar and Tammuz. So great was the moon goddess's love for the sun god that upon his death she followed him to the underworld, shedding earthly encumbrances along the way to open her body and mind to the divine knowledge she needed – one garment at each gate of hell. Esteemed guests, witness the Dance of the Seven Veils.'

All eyes were upon her as, tambourine shaking, Salomé began to dance. She moved slowly, sinuously, her hands and feet as elegant as a ballerina's. Poised and in control, her muscular pelvis started to undulate suggestively. Her silver nose-stud glittered through her veil, her hair was intricately coiffed and decorated with white peonies, invoking the ancient gods of healing. The Princess's lips were vermilion, half-hidden below a translucent mask of silk; her eyes, black as the void. Silently, the crowd watched her graceful steps.

She danced to her own rhythms, growing more rapid as she progressed. Pearls of perspiration gathered like dew on her glowing skin. Her bare feet slapped the boards faster and faster as she whirled, twisting and contorting until, before the audience knew what was happening, a magenta veil dropped, floating softly towards the floor.

As she revealed her curling, coiling abdomen to the sweaty crowds, to her stepfather's voracious glare, to the Prophet's cool, dispassionate eyes, she smiled. She was shimmying out of her skins, like a snake, to emerge afresh. She was teasing her way out of her worldly trappings, tap-dancing out of the identity that constrained her, shaking off her bindings to follow her lover into the beyond. Another diaphanous serpent of cloth wove its lazy way to the floor to settle beside the first, revealing her strong, slender arms. She turned to face Herod, jaw set with defiance, and rolled her pelvis. Her navel, inviting as the opening of a tiny sea-shell, stretched and contracted as she moved; her stepfather was transfixed. He reminded Salomé of a hideous black beetle pinned to a board, unable to free himself from the impaling nail of her magic and carnality. She stepped closer as she danced, her breasts bouncing a little under her veils. Herod twitched as though skewered through his black heart, and Salomé contemptuously turned away.

No longer need she obey this man; she controlled him. She wondered how she had failed to see it for so long – that his mouth could loll helplessly as well as sneer cruelly, that his eyes need not be harsh and stern but could glaze over, helpless with lust, at the sight of her navel – merely her navel!

Surprising herself, she began to enjoy the dance.

Baring her brown legs, she pounded the ground in a frenzy of spiralling and stamping. Her jasmine perfume gave way to feral civet as tiny beads of sweat spun from her torso, which gyrated to her personal and primal beat. She flung back her head and swayed, her hair tumbling freely down her back. The Prophet watched intently; he recognised something of his own religious trances in her glazed and rapt expression. Whirling like a dervish, she tore away the veil that had clothed her breasts, revealing their delectable roundness, their tantalising pertness and the cheeky plum-coloured nipples that peeked through her tousled tresses. The Prophet felt an unaccustomed heat in his loins as he thought how each breast was a perfect handful; his normally pure mind wondered how soft and light and warm they would feel to touch, how those jutting peaks would stiffen as he encompassed them in his mouth …

He found himself growing hot and hard as he contemplated which veil she would remove next. The one covering her mouth? Or the one concealing her even more tantalising lips? Temptress that she was, Salomé toyed with the cloth around her waist before exposing her painted pout, mouth open to reveal her pink tongue as she heaved deep breaths. She undulated the curves of her waist, struck her hips forward forcefully, repeatedly, the music racing to a frantic climax as she teased away the final veil:

For a fleeting moment the Prophet saw her, stock-still and gasping for breath, naked but for the few flowers left clinging in her hair. The sight of the dark hair covering her sex captivated him; he caught himself straining forward as he glimpsed a flash of silky, rose-coloured flesh.

Then the torches were extinguished and girls were running forward to wrap the Princess in cotton robes. He slumped down in his chains, ashamed of the erection that strained against his clothes like an eager puppy against its lead. God, to be so utterly aroused by a primitive idol-worshipping girl as he stood chained and helpless – it was a bit of a turn-on … he wondered if she danced like that in the temple for her golden calf, or whatever it was that she called upon to answer her petty prayers. He wondered if the golden calf enjoyed it.

Salomé, now demurely covered, shook the Prophet from his reverie. She was speaking to the Tetrarch.

'You said – I could have anything that I – I desired in exchange for the … dance …'she panted, sides still heaving from her exertions.

'I did.' came the muted response – perhaps the mighty ruler feared for his kingdom.

'I demand head – head of the Prophet,' giggled the Princess.

Relieved, Herod stood up.

'Certainly, my cherub,' he boomed. 'On a silver charger? Garnished with rosemary? I'll throw in another traitor's head for free if you like.'

'No. I want his head between my thighs. I want it to give me satisfaction,' said Salomé. 'While still attached to his shoulders,' she added hastily.

Herod was dumbstruck. He couldn't enjoy his stepdaughter – his wife would skin him alive – but he had hoped to prevent any other man from doing so. But he had given his regal word, and there was no way out of it now. He glowered as he signalled to his guards to release the captive.

Salomé smiled like a veritable Cheshire cat as the Prophet settled his grave face against her sweet pussy. As he began to lave her with his masterly tongue, you could almost hear her purr. She writhed slowly as he licked the full length of her delicious crevasse, teasing every inch of her warm wetness.

And that, dear readers, is where we shall leave them, curled up snugly in Salomé's boudoir – with the Prophet's tongue nestled firmly inside the Princess's cheek …

About the Authors

All the authors in this book donated their stories free of charge to help *Burlesque Against Breast Cancer* raise money for cancer charities.

Alcamia was an award-winning child essayist who started writing seriously in her teens within a number of genres. Over the past 10 years she has been devoted to her favourite genre, erotica. She has written copious short stories and novellas and is working on two cross-genre novels that marry erotica with psychology, the paranormal and supernatural.

Carmen Ali is a freelance writer and performs burlesque under the name 'Miss Aurelia Dare'. Carmen writes poetry, stories and articles and has been published by *Leaf Books* and *Scarlet*.

Richard Bardsley's first collection of short stories, *Body Parts: The Anatomy of Love*, was recently published by Salt and longlisted for the 2008 Frank O'Connor International Short Story Award. Richard's next project is a satirical novel, currently entitled *This Is How I Will Destroy You*, mainly because he likes how it sounds.

Sarah Berry is staff writer for *Penthouse Forum* and *Desire* magazines and makes the occasional appearance in *Scarlet*. She's also a reluctant burlesque dancer: after training at the London School of Striptease, she now dons a habit and whip to save the souls of her audiences.

Daphne Bing is the pseudonym of a writer whose erotic fiction has until now only been available on the internet, although under other names she is a published author and occasional journalist. In her spare time she has run multi-million pound projects and dated inappropriate men.

Elizabeth Black's erotic fiction has been published by *Excessica*, *Scarlet*, *Tit-Elation*, *For The Girls* and *Xodtica*. She also writes for sex toy companies and works for a website devoted to former porn star Traci Lords. She lives with her husband and five cats a few blocks from the Atlantic Ocean.

Katie Crawley takes her name from a beloved family pet who also spent most of her time on her back. She has been published in *Scarlet* and works in politics, hence the pseudonym.

Portia Da Costa is author of more than 20 novels and almost 100 shorter fiction items. Her recent titles include *Gothic Heat*, *In Too Deep* and a paranormal novella, *Ill Met By Moonlight*. Discover more about Portia's books at www.portiadacosta.com and more about her at http://wendyportia.blogspot.com.

Olivia Darling is the author of *Vintage*, a racy novel set in the world of winemaking, featuring lust, murder and lots of champagne. She is closely related to Chris Manby.

Aimee DeLong's writing has appeared in such places as Hotel St George Press, *Cherry Bleeds* and *Lit Chaos*. Check out her website at www.aimeedelong.com.

Emily Dubberley founded www.cliterati.co.uk and was founding editor of *Scarlet* magazine. She script-writes for the *Lovers' Guide*, writes for magazines including *Look*, *More*, *Elle* and *Glamour*, and has been syndicated worldwide. She's written 17 books, and created Burlesque Against Breast Cancer with her partner Sam Eddison and a team of incredible volunteers to whom she is eternally grateful.

Jeremy Edwards' greatest goal in life is to be sexy and witty at the same moment – ideally in lighting that flatters his profile. Drop in on him unannounced (and thereby catch him in his underwear) at http://jerotic.blogspot.com .

Mark Farley spends far too much time obsessing about the book trade and celebrities. He has contributed to *Scarlet* magazine, *The Idler* and other books from *Xcite*. He has a cat and a girlfriend and lives in London.

Katie Fforde lives in Gloucestershire with her husband and some of her three children. She is the author of fourteen novels and is working on her fifteenth which will probably be called Book Fifteen as she can't think of a title for it. It took her a long time to become published as she foolishly thought writing for Mills and Boon would be easier than for the mainstream market. However, she learnt so much about her craft through trying she doesn't consider those years as a waste of time. And nor is playing Spider Patience on the computer ...

Alyson Fixter is a freelance journalist and writer. She has been editing *Cliterature*, *Scarlet*'s free erotic fiction magazine, for two years, but still can't get over the fact she gets paid to read porn all day. She was approached to be co-editor of *Ultimate Burlesque* and used her contacts to help collect some of the world's best erotica writers together in one anthology.

Mat Fraser is a disabled actor, writer and cabaret performer, who is known for his irreverent disability comedy. Having just finished his third play, his contribution to this book was inspired by an unforgettable night in New York's infamous Slipper Room burlesque bar.

Maxim Jakubowski has written or edited over 100 books (novels, story collections and anthologies). He is best known for the *Mammoth Erotica* series. His last novel was *Confessions of a Romantic Pornographer* and the next one, if the gods of Eros permit, will be *I Was Waiting For You*. He lives in London.

Siobhan Kelly is a journalist and author who's written four short story collections, two novellas for Ann Summers' erotic fiction imprint and six non-fiction guides to sex and relationships. Currently suffering from RSI, she dictated most of her contribution to *Ultimate Burlesque* using voice recognition software, much to the delight of the builders working on her neighbour's loft conversion.

Kristina Lloyd is the author of three best-selling erotic novels, including the controversial *Asking for Trouble*, a dark psychosexual thriller set in Brighton, where she lives. She has been described as a 'fresh literary talent' who 'writes sex with a formidable force'.

Carmel Lockyer writes and edits erotic fiction. She used to be a model and spent three years as an agony aunt for nudists.

Nikki Magennis is a Scottish author of erotica and erotic romance who writes for Cleis Press, Virgin Black Lace and others. Find out more at http://nikkimagennis.blogspot.com.

Chris Manby is the author of thirteen bestselling romantic comedy novels including *Running Away From Richard* and *Spa Wars*. She lives in London.

MonMouth is a part-time blogger and full-time pervert. His blog can be found at http://monmouth.blogspot.com. He welcomes email at mouth.mail@gmail.com.

Elizabeth K Payne is an erotica writer based in London. Her short stories have appeared in the award-winning Agent Provocateur anthology *Secrets: A Collection of Erotic Fiction* and in *Dark Desires: A Collection of Erotic Short Stories*.

Marcelle Perks is a journalist and the author of *Incredible Orgasms*, *The User's Guide to the Rabbit* and *Secrets of Porn Star Sex*. Her fiction covers all the most important aspects of life: love, sex and death.

Jo Rees had her first novel, *It Could Be You,* published in 1997 under her other pen name, Josie Lloyd. She then met Emlyn Rees, and together they wrote seven internationally-acclaimed books. Recently Jo has started writing contemporary racy bonkbusters. *Platinum* was published in hardback in May 2008 by Bantam Press and will be published in paperback in May 2009.

Christiana Spens is the author of the novel *The Wrecking Ball* (published May 2008) and her second book, *The Socialite Manifesto*, will be published in February 2009. She has written for *Studio International*, *Rockfeedback*, *Notion* and *Scarlet* and is at Cambridge University. She's 21 and loves dancing, men and music.

Donna George Storey's erotic fiction has appeared in more than 80 journals and anthologies. Her first novel, *Amorous Woman*, a semi-autobiographical tale of an American's steamy love affair with Japan, was published by Orion/Neon. Read more of her work at www.donnageorgestorey.com.

Alison Tyler's short stories have appeared in more than 80 anthologies including *Rubber Sex*, *Dirty Girls*, and *Sex for America*. She is the author of more than 25 erotic novels, most recently *Melt With You*, and the editor of more than 45 explicit anthologies, including *J Is for Jealousy*, *Naughty Fairy Tales from A to Z*, and *Naked Erotica*. Visit www.alisontyler.com for more information or www.myspace.com/alisontyler if you want to be her friend.

Wanda Von Mittens was born several decades later than intended, but makes up for it by being first at all the best parties. Convinced of the superiority of the female sex she spends her time trying to convince other women of the same. She takes her pen to paper to write shopping lists, schemes for female world domination and the odd short story. For more information see www.wandavonmittens.com

Lauren Wissot is a gay boy born into female form. Currently working as a critic and columnist, Lauren is also an award-winning filmmaker bent on bringing an S&M flavour to the big screen. *Under My Master's Wings*, a sexual memoir about her time spent as the slave to a gay-for-pay stripper, is available from Nexus Books. For more information see www.laurenwissot.com.

Claire Wordley started erotic fiction writing when at university after a night earning drinks by telling raunchy stories, and has had several stories in Scarlet magazine so far. She is currently studying for her Masters in Zoology.

For full author biographies see www.ultimateburlesque.com

Win a Year's Supply of Orgasms

By purchasing this book you're helping the Burlesque Against Breast Cancer organisation raise money for Macmillan. As a thank-you, Xcite Books and Burlesque Against Breast Cancer are offering you a chance to win a year's supply of orgasms – in the form of sex toys and sensual treats – in association with www.onjoy.com. The prize is worth over £250 and consists of the following toys and sex accessories:

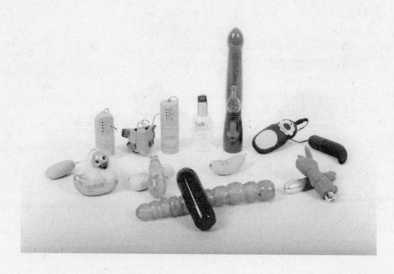

Ramsay Rabbit vibrator
Lelo Lily
Travel Size 'I Rub My Duckie' Paris version
Hot Pink Personal Lubricant
Rechargeable O-gasmic Orbiter
Ring a Rabbit Mobile Phone Powered Vibrator
Candy Girl Stimulator
My First G-Spot kit
Sensual Bender

Pure Butterfly
City Vibe
Inner Desire Waterproof Controller and Egg

For your chance to win:
email competitions@burlesqueabc.com with your name and address, answering this question: What is the date of the Burlesque Against Breast Cancer Ball? For a clue, visit www.burlesqueabc.com. Normal terms and conditions apply.